A.S. McMillen

The Seventh World

SEARCH FOR THE LOST KEEPER

– BOOK ONE –

Publishing Services provided by Paper Raven Books

Printed in the United States of America

First Printing, 2020

Paperback ISBN= 978-1-7355932-0-3

Hardback ISBN= 978-1-7355932-1-0

Dedication

◆•————————•————————•◆

To my best friend and loving husband. Thank you for all the support and your belief in my dreams and imagination. I would not be who I am without you. (P.S. Thank you for the big words!)

To my grandparents Tom and Claudine (my David and Ruby), who always thought I was special and loved my imagination and weirdness.

To Hulk and Luna, my loves and my Aphrodite and Apollo.

And to Sammi (aka Bella), my love and best companion, *don't worry sweet dog, I'm okay and will find you soon!*

Acknowledgements

I would like to give a big shout-out to all my professional teams that helped me get here.

Thank you to Kevin Anderson & Associates and my fantastic editing team!

Thank you to my Paper Raven team for all your hard work and helping me bring my book into the world!

And a big shout-out to all those who still dream and chase those dreams…never give up!

Table of Contents

Prologue
Marina and Magnus

The room was dark and cold; the only light came from a few candles scattered throughout the massive space, flickering with such a faint glow that the shadows around the room looked like they were undertaking an eerie and sacred dance of death. The large windows were slightly cracked open, a dim rumbling of thunder grew louder in the distance, and the smell of petrichor filled the air as the rain continued to fall heavily in the darkness of the night. Marina Ó Cuinn sat in an overstuffed chair, which swallowed her small frame, located in the farthest corner of her father's bedchambers. She was glad for the chair's location and size, as it

1

seemed to keep her hidden (for now) from the others in the room. She watched in troubled silence from her temporary safe spot as her older brothers, her mother, and her father's manservant bustled around the room with worried faces and hushed voices. Her father, Magnus, was dying.

As Marina watched the others in the room help her father and have their last-minute conversations with him, she found herself absorbed in her thoughts as she pondered over why she felt so anxious and tense about her father dying. As she searched her scattered memories of her father, she sadly came to realize that she wasn't exactly sure why she felt this way. For the sixteen years she has been alive—living in the gigantic, ancient, and miserably cold castle—she barely had any interaction with her father, and what little interaction she did have with him was mostly confusing, mysterious, and filled with secretive intrigue.

No one had noticed her yet, so Marina thought back some more on her past as she waited patiently for her turn to speak with her father. She came to the realization that she wasn't bewildered by just one thing, but by several aspects of her father. The first thing she thought—and always made her question her father—was, *why is my father so much older than my mother?* Marina never understood why her young and beautiful mother would marry such an old man. She asked her mother this question and was given the reply, "Some marriages are necessary."

That was the only answer she was ever given, no matter how many times she asked. Then, to make things more curious, Magnus also had claimed that he was a man of great universal power; and adding more to this confusing and mysterious claim, Magnus always explained he had this great power because he wasn't from Earth. He also had told her many times that their name wasn't Ó Cuinn but Deae; this was the name he took from someone he called "the mother"—one of the creators of the universe. However, Marina never believed these claims nor that he was powerful, since all she had ever seen him do was lock himself in his great tower room, poring over his old books and scrolls. Marina also thought his declaration of having unearthly powers was absolutely crazy and made her think her father might have lost his mind in his old age; but still, some things Magnus would say or do always made her speculate about whether his claims might be real—though she never asked him further about her curiosities—making her more confused about her father's true past.

Marina shifted in her seat as she drifted in the odd feelings and unanswered questions she had about her father, and began to remember the few rare loving memories. Her fondest memories of her father were when they would walk through the large garden on the castle property while he explained the purposes of all the plants and flowers. On these garden walks, Magnus would tell Marina several other fascinating and remarkable stories. Many of them, he would say, were from his own past, but they too seemed farfetched. Again, she never let her father know these thoughts because she was worried that he would stop their rare garden walks.

Marina also remembered he always seemed more peaceful and patient when he was teaching her or telling her these stories, and sometimes, she felt as though he was guiding her, or rather, leaving little hints about something much more important or much greater than the garden or his magnificent stories. Still, she never asked him for more explanations about what he taught her—she was just glad she got to spend some time with him. As she looked across the room once more, she thought, *If I have to go over and talk to him, I will just ask about the garden again.*

Marina was still not summoned by anyone to come talk to Magnus, so she began to think about her relationships with her other family members. Although she knew she had a distant relationship with her father, her relationships with her mother, Seraphina, and her older twin brothers, Joseph and James, were even more detached. Marina had even fewer interactions with her mother and brothers, and the few times she tried to ask them about her father's claims, they would either ignore her or chuckle under their breath and change the subject, leaving Marina more flustered and confused. Marina even tried to prod her father's manservant, Abrax Aswad (a tall, dark, and skinny Egyptian man), into telling her more about her father's past, but each time she asked, he would always say, "All will be known in time, my dear" before walking away.

Before Marina could think any further about her mysterious father or her other family relationships, her mother interrupted her thoughts. "Marina, please come here child, your father is calling for you."

Marina scowled, as only a teenage girl could, and then felt a cold chill throughout her body. Not only did she not want to talk to her father, she also didn't want to see him dying. She realized she couldn't stay away forever. So, she slowly got up, leaving the safety of her chair, made her way across the cold hard floor, and approached her father's bedside. Magnus's eyes were closed and she thought of turning around when, suddenly, she saw them flutter open and lock onto her. She lingered in silence for a moment longer until she saw his mouth start to move. Marina couldn't hear him, so she leaned over a little closer to make out what he was saying. She then clearly heard him say, "My heart is broken, my love…this is why I am dying. I am sorry I could not do right by you or all the others who needed me." His whole body then shivered as he took a deep sigh.

Marina pulled back a little. She was shocked to hear her father say these things to her. She quickly looked around the room and wondered if he had told this to anyone else. However, her thoughts were quickly interrupted when she heard him mumble again. "Remember there is always love to be found, my child. Remember your dreams…remember *aoratis anoxis*."

Marina pulled back, even more perplexed and shocked this time. She had no idea what his words meant. She knew that she always had vivid dreams and she often thought her dreams had some meaning. However, she never told anyone about her dreams, especially not her father. Once again, before she could ask Magnus for an explanation, his eyes fluttered and shut. He coughed and sputtered as his body violently shook. Marina then watched Magnus release his final breath.

Despite the estranged relationship she had with her father, Marina suddenly felt more lost and alone than she ever had in her entire life.

Part One

◄——————●——————►

EVIE

Chapter 1
A New Life

As Evie sat up on the edge of her bed, rubbing the heavy sleepiness from her eyes, the world around her began to come into focus and she found herself safe in her own bedroom. She looked across the room to see her roommate, Lauren, giving her a deep glare of disgust. "You were screaming again," Lauren said. "I'm sick of always waking up to you screaming."

Lauren gave her another look of disgust and left the room, slamming the door behind her. Evie shook her head and rubbed her eyes once more, as if she was trying to get rid of the remnants of the awful nightmare that had consumed her sleep that night.

She remained on the edge of her bed trying to collect herself and began to think about the dream that woke her up in a screaming panic. She remembered in the dream she wasn't herself but a large man she didn't know. Evie then thought about how she was usually not herself in her dreams and felt like she wasn't really dreaming, but living someone else's memories. She always thought it was a crazy idea that she was dreaming someone else's memories, but she could never seem to shake this belief.

Evie continued to sit a while longer on her bed, still trying to gain enough strength to face the day after her dreadful nightmare, and started piecing together the fragments still running through her head. She remembered that in the nightmare, the dream man was escaping an awful massacre. The dream started with a group of seemingly peaceful (and very bizarre) people meditating around this large man, when suddenly a group of warriors wearing strange armor and carrying large fiery swords came in and started attacking everyone. Evie, as the dream man, woke from the meditative state and tried screaming for the people to wake, but they wouldn't rouse from their trance-like state, and many were immediately killed by these warriors—mostly by decapitation. A few people finally did awaken and instantly began to discharge weird bolts of light from their hands, attempting to fight back. However, the light they had released from their hands deflected off the attacking warriors and came back at them, turning them to stone or setting them on fire. Evie (or the man she was in the dream) tried desperately to help, but couldn't. There was an overwhelming weakness that consumed the body and mind of this dream man, and Evie could feel his struggles like they were her own. Then, in a blurry haze, the dream man grabbed several things from a nearby table and ran. Evie remembered that when she turned her head back around in the dream, all the people left in the room were either stone replicas of themselves, burning alive, or dying in some other horrific way. It seemed that no one was able to escape these warriors. In the last moments, as the dream man was escaping the chaos, Evie heard heart-clutching screams echoing all around her. Then she heard through the madness the name "Magnus!" yelled out before she woke up screaming herself.

Evie shuddered again and shook her head one last time to rid herself of the awful dream still swirling in her head and began to think about all her other dreams and nightmares. For as long as she could remember, Evie always had vivid dreams. Many of her dreams turned into awful nightmares, even worse than the one she had that night, and Evie could only feel pain, suffering, and sadness all around her. These dreams always made her feel as though things were creeping and crawling in the dark shadows just out of her reach or understanding. In many of the awful dreams, these shadows seemed to get deep inside her head and tell her horrific things she wouldn't usually believe, and they didn't entirely leave her when she was awake either—making it hard for her not to believe these shadowy nightmares. No matter how hard she tried, Evie could never wake herself from her night terrors and found herself (most of the time) being woken up by someone else as she screamed and shook with fear.

However, not all of Evie's dreams were nightmares. She also had beautiful and wonderful dreams that were full of love and happiness. When she would wake from these amazing dreams, Evie would try to hold on to the love and happiness she felt as long as she could. The good dreams were sometimes all she had to remind her of love.

Evie didn't know when her dreams first started, so as she sat on the edge of her bed for a while longer, she thought back to her earliest memories, trying to figure out when she had her first dream. She decided to take as much time as she could; besides, she thought, *I'm in no hurry to leave my room to face Barbara, that terrible woman in charge of this awful home.* So, she took her time and thought back to her early life and began to fill in the details to determine when her dreams started.

Evie knew she was the only child of Collin and Maria MacDunleavy, and they had named her Evangelina, or Evie for short. She knew that her father came from Ireland, while her mother's maiden name was Borbón, reflecting her Spanish descent.

However, her parents left their places of birth—why they left was unknown to Evie—and moved to the United States to live in the beautiful city of Denver, Colorado, where Evie was born.

She remembered her father was a large, muscular man, with thick red hair and a bushy red beard to match. He never took much care of his fiery red hair and wild beard, so Evie often thought he looked a little frazzled and crazy. Evie also remembered his dazzling green eyes and his contagious laugh. Like Evie, he was funny and had a keen wit. He also, at times, could have a quick temper. Evie remembered laughing as he stomped around cursing in his thick Irish accent about whatever had angered him.

Evie remembered her mother was quite the opposite of her father. Maria was a beautiful woman who was tall and thin, with features so delicate she almost looked like she could break. She remembered her mother had long dark wavy hair and deep brown eyes, and was very patient, kind, and compassionate. Although her mother's Spanish accent wasn't thick like her father's Irish accent—and Maria spoke much more quietly—Evie loved how she spoke and particularly how certain words rolled beautifully off her tongue. As Evie thought of her mother's gentle features, she looked down at her own hair that was lying just below her shoulders and sighed, wishing she looked more like her mother. Evie seemed to get most of her father's traits. She analyzed her own pale skin, deep red, curly, long and tangled hair, as well as the millions of freckles across her cheeks, nose, and the tops of her shoulders. She also had sparkling, vibrant, green eyes like her father, which she was happy about. The one thing she did share with her mother was her petite and skinny build, although she was somewhat lanky and awkward too.

Evie remembered her first six years of life were wonderful. Her father was an English professor at a local university in Colorado, and her mother was an artist and worked for a local nonprofit art museum. They lived a quiet, simple, and happy life. As she thought more about her early life, she could remember her mother's beautiful garden and her teaching Evie how to be patient and kind to help the plants and flowers grow. Her mother also taught her many things about the arts and helped Evie take time with her own creations, while her father taught her many things about literature, history, and opening her mind to different possibilities. Evie remembered she would sit on his lap often as he told her about staying open-minded about what was written or what she read. He also told her to seek the truth and constantly look for answers that may not have been written.

As her mind wandered through her past, she remembered that she was trying to think of the time her dreams first started. She began to focus on that instead since she couldn't remember much else about her parents. As she thought about her dreams, she realized she couldn't pinpoint exactly when they started. However, she did remember she would often wake up at night when she was little, terrified of her dreams, and her father would come in and console her. To help her ease her mind, he would tell her ancient stories of how good conquered evil to remind her that whenever there is evil, there is always good to be found. Evie remembered he would always say, "You must find a way to defeat this evil whenever you have a bad dream by searching for the good as well, my love."

Thinking of her father's words brought a wave of sadness over Evie as she thought about how desperately she missed her parents. Evie wiped a tear from her eye as she thought back to the horrific night that took them from her life forever.

She had been starring in a school play, at six years old, and remembered trying to search for their faces in the crowd when she was up on stage, but couldn't find them. After the play ended, she was ready to go search for her parents when her teacher pulled her to the side and took her to a room where a couple of police officers were waiting for her. One of the police officers bent down to one knee so he was eye level with Evie and with a somber tone said, "Your parents were on their way to your school play," he paused and took a deep breath. "But they were in a horrible car accident."

He then teared up and said, "The doctors did everything they could, but they couldn't save them. I'm so sorry."

Evie remembered, after hearing of her parent's fate, that the whole room began to spin and everything around her became muffled, as if at a far distance from her. Evie only remembered that the next few days were a complete blur, full of worried faces and quiet conversations. She also remembered that the day after her parents' funeral, a woman came to Evie and told her that they couldn't find any relatives. Evie was to become a ward of the state.

The woman took Evie to her first foster home, which ended up being a less-than-ideal situation for her, since the foster parents she was placed with were neglectful and sometimes verbally abusive towards her. She was removed from that home, and for the next couple years, Evie bounced around among several different homes. All the homes she was placed in were equally awful, until she finally landed in her current situation—a residential children's home where many wayward and unwanted children ended up. Evie shuddered as she thought about how much she had been through, just to arrive here, but before she could think about her past or her dreams any longer, she heard a loud pounding on her door followed by a booming angry voice. "Get up, you lazy brat."

Evie cringed as she thought about Barbara, the angry woman outside her door. Although Barbara wasn't as neglectful or abusive as some of the past foster parents and homes she had been in, Barbara was no peach either. Barbara was a large dumpy woman who huffed and puffed all the livelong day about order and cleanliness. Sometimes Evie thought she was just an overworked or harried guardian, but Barbara seemed to be mean just for the fun of it. Evie thought Barbara missed her calling and should've been an army general or dictator the way she commanded the children around like small army forces. Barbara also had a large round face to match her large round body, and bright red cheeks with dark beady eyes. Evie didn't know if Barbara's cheeks were naturally that red or if it was just because she was always angry and upset about something. Evie then realized she was still sitting down thinking, so she slowly raised herself from her bed and got dressed. She knew that if Barbara had to come back a second time, that just meant more chores as a punishment for her laziness.

Evie was now thirteen years old, and the home she was in was for girls all ranging from ages twelve to eighteen. As she left her room and walked into the hall, she followed a group of girls slowly making their way down to the "mess hall," as Barbara called it. Each girl had a task assigned for that day written on a chart hanging on the wall next to the entrance of the mess hall. They would stop and look at what their duties were for the day before entering to eat the morning meal. The meals were awful and usually unrecognizable as food. As the girls read their assignments for the day, they would mumble and grunt their dissatisfaction over what they had to do. No one ever let out too loud of a grunt because if Barbara heard them complain, that just meant more chores.

As Evie looked up at her duty for the day, she saw that she was in charge of weeding and tending to the small garden and felt a bit of happiness flow through her. She liked working in the garden since it was on the far side of the property and was usually quite peaceful since Barbara didn't like to walk that far out. The girl behind Evie leaned in close to her. "Lucky," she whispered.

Most of the girls felt the same way as Evie about working in the garden because it was far from Barbara's fury. Evie was also excited to see that her partner for the day was Jessie Garcia, a girl close to Evie's age whom she considered to be her closet friend in this miserable dump.

The girls quickly found their assigned spots around the large dining tables and ate in silence for the most part. Barbara didn't like them talking except if the girls had to ask that something on the table be passed or to answer her demanding questions. At 7:30 A.M. sharp, Barbara made a sound like a barking noise and announced that breakfast was over and it was time to start their morning chores. It didn't matter to her if the girls weren't finished eating their slop. Barbara ran a tight ship and everything had to be completed on the dot or further punishment was given—always.

Evie quickly made her way out to the garden shed to get her supplies for the day when she heard someone running up behind her, huffing for breath as she finally reached Evie's side. "I'm so glad we get to work together today!" Jessie said, smiling from ear to ear.

Evie turned to smile at Jessie. Jessie was much taller than Evie and had beautiful dark hair and skin to match. She was much more voluptuous than Evie and already had a womanly body, which Evie sometimes envied. She also liked Jessie because, like herself, Jessie always managed to look at the positive side of things. Although Evie considered Jessie to be her closest friend, their friendship was not a normal one since Barbara didn't let the girls have much free time or interaction outside of chores and school. Usually, the girls only got Sunday afternoons for a couple hours to have free time. Since it was now summertime and school was out, Barbara also allowed them a couple hours on Tuesday afternoons for what she called "physical training"; however, most of the girls just played basketball or soccer on the disheveled and unkempt fields and courts.

As Evie and Jessie were working in the garden, they talked quietly. Although they were well out of earshot of their foul ruler, they still didn't want to talk too loudly—just in case. As the two girls made their way to the far side of the garden, where a group of sunflowers stood, Jessie motioned with her hand for Evie to follow her. Evie followed Jessie behind the tall stalks, which kept them mostly out of view from any eyes that might be looking. As Evie reached Jessie's side, Jessie pulled out a small package wrapped in paper with a hairband tied around it. Jessie looked at Evie with eager eyes. "I got you a present for your birthday next week. I would've waited until your actual birthday, but I didn't know when we'd get a chance alone next."

Evie smiled at her friend and gently took the small gift. She knew that if Barbara caught Jessie with what Barbara called "contraband," Jessie would've been punished with more than just extra chores. Contraband was strictly forbidden. As Evie unwrapped the gift, she saw that there were four pieces of chocolate and a small note that said, "just for you." Evie's smile widened and a tear even began to fill the corner of her eye. She knew how hard it was for Jessie to get this and it had been such a long time since she had anything so sweet tasting. Barbara didn't think too highly of sweets either. Evie looked up at Jessie earnestly. "Thank you very much. It means so much to me," she said, with watery eyes.

Jessie flashed her beautiful smile back at Evie. "You should eat them now so you don't get caught with them."

Evie shook her head in agreement remembering the last time she got caught with contraband and had to spend three days in the basement trying to catch spiders and rats while also attempting to clean the dust that never went away. Evie quickly popped the treat in her mouth and handed a piece to Jessie. Jessie held up her hand to refuse, but Evie interjected. "You went through so much trouble to get these. Please share them with me."

Jessie then quickly put a chocolate in her mouth, and both girls bit into the chocolate gooiness and hummed with delight. The first chocolate went by fast, so when they ate the second piece, both girls sucked on the chocolate for as long as they could before it slowly melted in their mouths. After they finished, they giggled a little at their reactions to such a simple treat, and then quickly got back to work.

As the sun reached over their heads and the heat began to increase, they heard the bell ring for lunchtime and went running across the field to get to the mess hall in time. Tardiness was also something Barbara didn't tolerate.

Lunchtime was just as quiet as breakfast, but then Barbara broke the silences and stood up, making a loud grunt. She then turned her head and looked directly at Evie with her intense black beetle-like eyes. "You, girl." She pointed her stubby finger at Evie before saying, "After your chores are done, come to my office."

Evie cringed at the thought of not only being singled out by Barbara, but also having to go to her stuffy office and be alone with her. Evie's mind then raced as she thought of what she might've done to get called to Barbara's office and wondered if she had been caught with the chocolate gift that Jessie had given her. She quickly pushed that thought aside because she realized that Barbara didn't call out Jessie. Evie took a deep sigh of relief because she realized her friend was safe, but then her mind began thinking of other possible reasons that Barbara would summons her.

Evie spent the rest of the afternoon in the garden thinking of anything that might be the cause for her dreadful situation. Jessie tried a few times to prod Evie into a conversation, but Evie was trapped in her mind. Evie tried to think of all the reasons for her impending doom, but she was never the type of person to wallow in self-pity, so she began to escape into her imagination. Evie had a vivid imagination, which was very useful when she found herself in awful situations and needed to escape to somewhere better. She would often imagine that she was a brave warrior at sea in the ancient days, like characters in her father's many stories of past sea voyages and battles. Other times, she would pretend she was an archeologist like Indiana Jones, movies she loved, and that she was discovering new and sacred artifacts that could help stop evil in the world. Sometimes she would imagine herself in outer space, where once again she was a fighter against an overwhelming evil, bent on destruction. As Evie escaped further into her imagination, she laughed and thought, *I always imagine I'm a brave warrior fighting some kind of evil, but I can barely keep my real-life evils at bay*. She shrugged it off and once again imagined herself in a galaxy far, far away, like her other favorite movie series, Star Wars.

Sometimes, after a dream or a particularly vivid imaginary escape, Evie would feel that her dreams or imaginings were more real than she thought, as if there was something just out of reach of her understanding. However, she could never figure out why she thought her dreams might have a real meaning behind them.

When Evie first came to the children's home, Barbara would scold her often because Evie would have a hard time separating herself from her dreams and fantasies. At times, the dreams and wonderful imaginings would bleed into her reality, so she couldn't tell the difference between her escaped thoughts and her real world. When she first arrived at the home, she would also tell the other girls of these great trips and adventures she had been on in her dream worlds. She did this not as a way to lie, but as a way to ease the pain she and the other girls felt, hoping that they all would dream of something greater. This really upset Barbara, and Evie was often punished in her early days at the home for her elaborate stories. Evie also remembered that once when she was cleaning the dishes and got caught up in her imagination again, she dropped a stack of plates on the ground. Before Evie could even clean up her mess, Barbara came storming in, ranting and raving about order and the cost of things. She made Evie work her fingers to the bone to pay of her debts for several days after. Barbara then told Evie, "You will never be trusted again with delicate tasks."

After that, Evie spent most of her days doing more dirty work than the other girls. She quickly learned to keep her dreams and imaginings to herself and tried her hardest not to get too lost in her thoughts.

Evie's thoughts were soon interrupted as she saw that the sun was beginning to dip down in the western sky and the air began to feel a little cooler. Evie looked Jessie in the eye as she slowly made her way across the garden. "Wish me luck," Evie said anxiously as she began to walk away.

Jessie gave Evie a weak smile. "You'll need more than that."

Evie managed to summons an unconvincing smile as she made her way to Barbara's office. Once Evie reached the door, before she could even raise her fist to knock, it flew open. Barbara's large body almost completely filled the doorframe as she grunted, "Come with me, girl." She then pushed her way past Evie and began to storm across the main entryway.

Evie reluctantly followed Barbara out of the main building and across the property to the small

31

school building that was part of the residential home. As they crossed the field, Evie began to wonder if Barbara had some awful chore that needed to be done at the schoolhouse. Once again, Evie's mind began to spin as she wondered what gross or disgusting task Barbara might have in store.

When they finally reached the front door, Barbara pivoted her large body around in a jiggly flurry and bent her fat head down so it was directly in Evie's face. Evie could smell her weird fishy breath and felt hot air blowing out of her nostrils. Barbara then said, "Be on your best behavior." She paused for a moment as a malicious smile stretched across her face before she finished saying, "I doubt that would matter anyway. Nobody would want a lazy brat like you."

Evie stepped back for a minute to get out of Barbara's hot stink and deep glare as she thought about what Barbara said. Before she could think any further on it, Barbara grabbed Evie's upper arm with her sweaty, meaty grip and pulled Evie through the front door. Barbara released her grip as they made their way around the corner, where Evie saw another woman standing in the hallway.

Evie immediately recognized the woman as her social worker, Beth Anderson, whom she had been paired with for the last couple years. She liked Beth because she always listened to Evie and tried to do her best to help whenever Evie needed it. Although Evie also knew that there were times Beth couldn't do much to help her, Beth certainly tried her best anyway.

Beth looked at Barbara with a courteous smile and nodded. "Thank you, Barbara. That will be all."

"Just be sure she is back in time for dinner," Barbara huffed, shaking her fat head.

Evie knew Barbara didn't care if she got dinner or not. What Barbara really meant was, *make sure Evie is back in time for evening chores.* Evie watched as Barbara stomped around the corner and waited until she heard the front door slam shut before she turned back to Beth. "I'm so glad you're here. I can't stand that woman or this place anymore," Evie admitted.

Beth looked at Evie with her deep beautiful blue eyes when Evie saw a smile widen across her face. Evie had never really seen Beth smile. This was probably because most of the time when Evie saw Beth, she was removing her from an awful place and was saddened to hear about what Evie had gone through. As Evie admired Beth's smile, Beth reached out and lightly placed her hand on Evie's arm. "Well then, I think you'll like what I have in store for you." Beth then looped her arm into Evie's and guided her down another hallway before entering a classroom door.

As Evie entered the room, she saw an older couple sitting at one of the round tables used for group activities, both smiling broadly at Evie as she and Beth approached. Though the man was seated, Evie could tell he wasn't much taller than herself. He had silvery gray hair with only a few black streaks showing through. His eyes were deep green, and they sparkled, which reminded Evie of her father's eyes. He had a few wrinkles, but they were mostly around his eyes, which she could tell were worn in from years of smiling and laughing. The older woman was shorter than her husband; even seated, she was about a head shorter than him. She was plump and had beautiful blond hair that was cut short and curled the way women wore their hair back in the early 1950s. She wore a modest amount of makeup, which highlighted her rosy cheeks and bright blue eyes. Like her husband, she also had smile and laugh wrinkles around her eyes. Evie took a seat across from the couple. "Evie, meet David and Ruby Jones," Beth nodded at the couple.

David extended his hand out and Evie realized he wanted to shake her hand. She extended her hand to his. He clasped his other hand over the top of hers and shook it gently. "I'm so happy to meet you, Evie!"

Ruby then reached her hand out to Evie, but changed her mind and instead got up from her seat, walked over to Evie's side, and wrapped her arms around Evie's shoulders. Ruby gave Evie a quick squeeze before pulling back and looked Evie in the eyes. "I'm just so very happy to meet you, too." A beautiful smile then brightened across her face. "We both are just delighted!"

It had been a long time since Evie was touched in a kind way, so when Ruby first touched her, she thought of pulling back, but instead she immediately felt the kindness and love in Ruby's touch. Evie was surprised to find herself leaning into Ruby's arms ever so slightly. As Ruby made her way back to her seat, Beth cleared her throat. "Evie, David, and Ruby would like to know how you would feel about living with them."

Evie sat there stunned for a minute. She knew that it was hard to find a home for any child her age; most people wanted younger children, and by the time you got into your teen years, finding a home was really next to impossible. Evie shook her head for a minute thinking she might be dreaming or imagining this meeting. After a few more moments of stunned silence, an odd feeling of joy began to fill her body and she felt tears begin to fill her eyes. She shook herself once again and sat up straighter in her chair. Evie wiped away a tear that was now falling down her cheek. She cleared her throat, brushed another tear away, and sniffed, recovering herself. "I'd absolutely love that."

David clapped his hands together and rubbed them back and forth vigorously. "That's fantastic!"

Evie then saw tears began to fall down Ruby's cheeks when once again, she got up and wrapped her plump arms around Evie, squeezed her in a tighter embrace, and kissed the top of Evie's head.

The rest of the meeting was like a blur, similar to the time when she heard the news about her parents' death. She could see Beth's, David's, and Ruby's mouths moving as they discussed what would happen next, but again, everything seemed muffled and at a distance. Evie caught a few words here and there, words like "trial period" and "make sure it's a good fit." However, the rest of the meeting, Evie was just spinning in her mind, thinking that this was the best dream to ever come true. As the meeting wrapped up, Beth escorted Evie to the front of the school and told her to gather her belongings and come back. "You'll leave with David and Ruby tonight, if that's okay with you."

Evie teared up again and grabbed Beth around the waist. "Yes, yes, yes. Oh, thank you so much, Beth!" she said through her sobbing.

Evie pulled away and saw a huge smile on Beth's face before she dashed across the field to get her belongings. When Evie reached the front door of the home, Barbara was there waiting for her. "I told you they wouldn't want you, little witch."

Evie gave Barbara a spiteful stare. "Move, you fat lard," she answered. "They do want me and I'm leaving now."

Evie thought she might regret those words later if David and Ruby didn't want her after the trial period and she ended back up here again, but she decided she would deal with that later if she did have to come back. She pushed her way past Barbara, ran up to her room, and gathered her very few belongings.

Before she dashed back down the stairs, she saw Jessie in the hallway. Evie made her way over to Jessie and told her the news. Although Evie felt guilty having to leave her friend behind, Jessie, being the kind, positive person she was, happily said, "You deserve this, Evie. Just don't forget me."

"I promise. I could never forget you!" Evie replied, tears filling her eyes again.

Evie wiped away the tears, hugged her friend, and ran as fast as she could down the stairs. Barbara was once again waiting at the doorway, trying to block Evie's path. Evie thought, *Will this woman ever cease?* Before Barbara could say or do anything, Evie heard Beth's voice from outside saying, "Come on, Evie. Your new life begins."

Barbara gave Evie one final black stare before moving out of the way, and once again, Evie made a mad dash out of the home. She ran as fast as she could to a red car, where David was waiting, holding the door open for her.

Chapter 2
A NEW HOME

The drive to Evie's new home was full of excited conversation. David and Ruby told Evie about her new home and asked Evie many questions about herself. It had been a long time since anyone had asked Evie anything about herself or the things she liked to do, so there were a few times she really had to think hard about the answers. David and Ruby were very patient and kind, and allowed Evie time to answer their questions. Ruby asked Evie if she liked to paint or draw, which brought Evie back to thoughts of her mother's many art lessons. Ruby's head was turned around over the passenger car seat as she looked lovingly at Evie. Evie felt a sudden pang of sadness. "My mother taught me how to paint and draw when I was younger," she said with a small smile.

Evie then noticed a hint of something behind Ruby's eyes, but she couldn't determine if it was sadness due to Evie mentioning her dead mother or something else, like some kind of distant memory the older woman was thinking of. Ruby slowly nodded. "She sounds like she was a very beautiful and wonderful woman. I hope we can help you find a way to keep her memory alive through your artwork."

Evie smiled and began to tear up, not only because she was thinking of her mother, but also because someone was showing kindness to her and she was finally with people who would allow her to remember her parents. Ruby returned Evie's smile and gave her a quick wink as the threesome finished talking about more of Evie's interests in school, arts, reading, and her favorite movies.

After an hour of driving, they pulled into a beautiful neighborhood in what Evie thought was an older part of Denver, Colorado. Many of the houses had a Victorian look to them with covered and pillared front porches, tall bay windows, and mature trees and plants growing in beautiful front yards. They finally pulled into a driveway as Evie admired the exterior of her new home. She then thought, *this is my home*! Evie gasped at the realization that she finally had a home and told herself she would do anything she could to make sure she stayed here.

The house was similar to all the other houses on the block. There was a large wraparound covered porch with beautiful white pillars covered in vines with small purple flowers creeping up the pillars. There were two rocking chairs on the front porch with a small table between them that had a fragrant bouquet of roses, which Evie could smell from where she was standing. David and Ruby led her into the entryway, where a long staircase angled steeply up. There was a small room to the left that looked like a library or office. Evie felt a wave of excitement sweep over her seeing all the books. It looked like her father's study, and Evie was eager to dive in and read again. It had been a long time since she had found a cozy corner and got lost in a new world that could only be found in a book and her imagination. David saw her looking at the books. "You can help yourself to whatever you want to read," he whispered.

Evie turned and smiled at him as he winked and took her bag up the stairs. As Evie went to follow him, she looked at the room to the right of the stairs and saw a small living room with a few comfy-looking chairs and loveseats, and several random throw pillows and blankets about. Evie thought, *I will definitely curl up with a book in that room*!

Ruby was behind Evie as they went up the stairs, and as the rooms below fell out of sight, Evie saw the walls around the stairs were filled with a multitude of pictures. She could see David and Ruby in several of them, smiling in each beautiful frame, and there were several other people and children smiling just as broadly in the pictures as well.

"These are all of our many children," Ruby said as she waved her hand over one of the walls. She then smiled and went on, "We'll have to get some photos of you soon and put you up here with our family… your family."

Evie felt another wave of joy overcome her as tears began to roll down her cheeks when she thought again, *home...family. I finally have both again!* Evie then felt Ruby's hand gently touch her and begin rubbing back and forth over the tops of Evie's shoulders. Ruby then told her, "You belong here with us, Evie."

Evie, feeling every emotion all at once, just dropped on the stair where she was and began to sob uncontrollably. This was all too much; she finally had what she always wanted. Ruby sat on the steps next to her, gently wrapped her arms around Evie, began to rock her back and forth as she hummed a beautiful song, and then kissed the top of Evie's head. After Evie pulled herself together, she stood up and turned to head back up the stairs. She saw David patiently waiting for her at the top and could see that he had a look in his eyes similar to the look Ruby had given her in the car when Evie mentioned her mother. David's face then changed into a smile as he motioned for her to follow. "Come see your room. I think you'll really like it."

Evie followed David down the hall and into a small but beautiful room. There was a bed with a white iron bed frame against the far wall and a lovely yellow quilt with delicate daisies stitched into it. Ruby then pointed at the quilt. "Beth told us you like yellow, so I made this for you."

Evie turned, smiled, and began to tear up again, but before she could even say thank you, David waved his hand. "Come to the window. We picked this room for you because we think you'll like this."

Evie made her way to the window, looked out, and saw a large, sprawling garden down below. It was magnificent. There were flowers of every kind and huge trees of several varieties around the edges. Evie could see a small pond in the center, and in the far corner, she could see a well-cultivated vegetable bed. Evie gasped again because it reminded her of her mother's garden. Evie thought, *it's almost exactly the same layout of my mother's garden, like my mother and Ruby both had some master plan that they had been working from*. Although Ruby's garden was longer than her mother's, everything seemed to be in the spots where Maria had planted her delicate plants and flowers. Evie again turned around to look at David and Ruby. They were now standing next to each other, holding hands, looking at Evie with gentle smiles and watery eyes. Evie walked over to the pair and she wrapped her arms around them, saying, "Thank you. I love it so much."

She pulled back and realized that all three of them were now tearing up when David wiped a tear away from his cheek and finished showing her the room. They showed her where the bathroom was, a dresser, a small desk, and the closet. There were already a few items in the closet when Ruby said, "They were our daughters' clothes when they were younger. I think they'll fit you and you can wear them for now until I can take you shopping for more."

Evie returned a grateful smile and thanked Ruby once again. David then said, "We'll give you a few minutes to settle in and you can meet us downstairs when you're ready. Ruby has made us a wonderful dinner." He winked at Evie as they left the room, leaving Evie by herself to unpack her meager belongings and settle in.

As Evie unpacked, she placed her few clothing items in the nearby dresser and her toiletry items in the bathroom connected to her bedroom. Making her way back to her bag, she pulled out a small picture frame of her parents and placed it gently on the bed stand. She then pulled out another item, a small glass jewelry box that her mother had given her, which had a small poem and inscription that her mother had etched inside. Evie gently moved her fingers across the poem and read it to herself:

Somewhere I have never travelled, gladly beyond
Any experience, your eyes have their silence:
In your most frail gestures are things which enclose me,
Or which I cannot touch because they are too near.
Love eternally, your Mother.

Evie moved her fingers away and closed the lid. She remembered her father telling her that it was a poem by E.E. Cummings, and she remembered him showing her the rest of this poem in one of his many collections of poetry. She then reached in her bag one last time and pulled out a small box and opened it. The box contained two gold rings; her parents' wedding bands. She held up her father's ring and looked at the inscription inside. She couldn't read it because it was in an old Gaelic language, but Evie always loved the way the writing looked. She then lifted her mother's small ring up. Like her father's ring, it was also inscribed with a language she didn't know. However, it wasn't the same Gaelic words as his; to Evie, it looked more like hieroglyphics found on Egyptian tombs. She had asked her father once what the inscriptions in the rings meant, but he said that he would let her know when she was older and tell her the magnificent story behind it; of course, he never got to. She placed both the rings back in their box and set them next to the jewelry box and picture frame on the bed stand. She then lifted the photo, kissed her parents, and said under her breath, *I think I can be happy now!* She placed the frame back down and made her way out of her room to go find David and Ruby.

As Evie made her way down the stairs, she thought about how lucky she was again to have Beth as her social worker. She remembered that in one of her foster homes, the foster mother tried to take away Evie's small treasures she had left of her parents. Beth quickly intervened and made sure that there was a clause written in her contract to protect Evie's personal belongings, which again was a huge relief since Barbara would have confiscated Evie's treasures as well if it weren't for Beth.

Evie finally found David and Ruby in a small kitchen in the back of the house. There was a huge bay window on the back wall, overlooking the garden, and a small potbelly stove in the corner, which she thought was probably something that was very useful in wintertime. The kitchen table stood in front of the bay window and was already set for three. Evie sat down as David took a seat next to her, while Ruby busily made last- minute preparations to dinner. The smells from the kitchen were wonderful. Ruby was soon finished fussing about in the kitchen and came to the table holding a large casserole dish. David got up and took it from her, placed it on the table, then held out the chair for his wife. Evie looked down at the covered hot steaming dish, and her stomach began to rumble. Ruby then said, "Beth was only able to tell us a few things about you—like your favorite color is yellow, and you love lasagna."

Evie smiled even bigger as she rubbed her belly, realizing how hungry she was. "I do. Thank you so much."

David then uncovered the casserole dish. As the delicious fumes rose into the air, he sat down, smiled, and pushed the dish close to Evie. "Dig in," he said, smiling from ear to ear.

Evie waited patiently at first, since she was never allowed to help herself to food in the past. David then pushed the dish a little closer to her. "Get it while it's hot."

He winked at Evie as she grabbed the serving spoon and plopped a huge portion on her plate. David then passed her some rolls and poured her a tall glass of ice tea. Evie began to eat greedily; she couldn't remember the last time she had a home-cooked meal. After a few more greedy bites, Evie slowed down, swallowed the food in her mouth, wiped her face, and said, "This is absolutely delicious."

David and Ruby both laughed when David said, "Compliments to the best chef in the world."

He placed his hand lovingly on his wife's hand. Ruby blushed. "Well I am now, but you should've seen my first attempts at making dinner when we first got married."

David let out a loud laugh. "Yes, my love. You've definitely improved."

Ruby giggled as the two began to tell Evie about Ruby's early attempts as a cook and their early years together. Evie smiled as they shared their stories and she admired how much love there was between them. Evie didn't talk much since she wasn't used to talking during meals, but David and Ruby prodded her into conversation until finally she was sharing stories of her own. After the meal was finished, Ruby nodded at David and he returned her a secretive wink. Evie didn't understand what the secret communication was, but she was full and happy, so she just finished telling David her story about the sea battles her father had told her about. Ruby went back into the kitchen and pulled something from the fridge when David said, "Close your eyes."

Evie hesitated for a minute but decided there was no reason not to trust them, since they had been so kind to her. She closed her eyes as she could hear David and Ruby talking quietly in the kitchen, and then she heard them slowly move over to the table. She then heard David say, "Open your eyes."

Evie slowly opened one eye and saw that they were both standing there with a large chocolate cake, covered with candles on the top. Evie then shot her other eye open and looked at both of them with wonderment. "We know it's not your birthday until next week," David smiled broadly, "but we thought we can have an early celebration for your birthday and to welcome you home."

Evie again became overwhelmed with happiness and began to cry. She could hear David chuckle as she wiped her tears away when Ruby said, "Make a wish."

Evie leaned over the cake and blew out the candles. She didn't even make a wish because her wish had already come true.

Chapter 3
A New Family

The next week flew by fast, and before Evie knew it, it was her fourteenth birthday. Ruby took her shopping early in the morning and let Evie pick out several outfits, shoes, accessories, as well as some art supplies and books. Evie felt a little guilty at first, but Ruby just held up her hand to stop Evie's protest about costs. "You can't start a new life without some basics." She then reached down and squeezed Evie's hand and held it as they stood in the checkout line.

Once they returned from their shopping trip, Ruby went to the kitchen to make birthday meal preparations as Evie went to her room to put up her new gifts. As Evie finished putting away her art supplies, she heard a crash outside her window and ran over to look. She could see David and a few other men struggling to get a large tent up. One man was holding on to a large pole as another grappled with the fabric over the edges. She watched David standing to the side, rubbing his hand over his chin. He analyzed the situation and made a few commands before the men started to pull the pieces together again. After a few more mishaps and struggles, the tent was finally pitched and standing, covering a large portion of the backyard. Evie then heard the doorbell ring, soon followed by loud voices and laughing children.

Evie cautiously made her way down the stairs and before she even got to the bottom, she was bombarded by two women and three children, all eager to introduce themselves to her. One of the women extended her hand out and said, "Hi, I'm Desi, David and Ruby's youngest daughter."

The other woman then extended her hand out saying, "I'm Jenny, the eldest daughter, and these are my rug rats, Todd, Nick, and David."

The three boys quickly shook Evie's hand and then dashed away toward the kitchen when Evie heard Ruby yell, "Now stop that. Get your hands out of the batter, boys. There will be plenty of treats later."

Desi and Jenny then escorted Evie through the kitchen where Ruby gave them a quick smile and waved her hand for them to go into the backyard. Jenny told her mother she would be back in a minute to help as they made their way to the patio.

Once again, Evie was greeted by four men, each of whom introduced himself. The first one was also named David (Jr.) and said he was the oldest. The next man was Steven, then there was Joe, and finally Michael. Evie quickly lost track of who was who. There were two small girls who had not been introduced yet. Lacy was Joe's daughter, and Kelly was Michael's daughter. David Jr. said that his wife and kids would soon be there as well. Evie then looked at Steven and realized he was looking intently at her when Evie felt a little weird, but she decided to break his stare and asked him, "Are your wife and kids coming too?"

Steven gave her a little chuckle and lightened his gaze. "Actually Evie, I don't have a wife, but you may know who my girlfriend is."

Steven took a pause as Evie gave him a curious look. Steven then said, "My girlfriend is Beth, your social worker. She thought you'd be a perfect fit for our family."

Steven was now giving Evie a wide smile. Evie instantly realized how lucky she was to have Beth and said, "You can't even know how happy I am that Beth decided I'd be a good fit for your family. You all are absolutely wonderful!"

Steven then walked closer to Evie and wrapped his arms around her. "We are so happy to have you too, kiddo."

Evie felt marvelous in his embrace and realized that she was loved by more people than she ever thought she would be. Evie then pulled back from Steven and was instantly towed away by the bouncing Desi as she took Evie around to meet more of the family. Evie was beginning to feel overwhelmed when Desi also mentioned that many of David and

Ruby's other children were coming with their kids too. Evie had no idea how she was going to keep this all straight. David seemed to sense her thoughts and feelings, hooked his elbow in hers, and gently began to lead her away from the tent and continued chaos, towards the back of the garden. When they finally reached the back, next to the vegetable bed, he took his arm out of hers and said, "I know this is a lot for you, sweetheart, and I know we have a very large family."

He paused for a moment as a serious looked crossed his face before he finished. "We have many children who we love, but you need to know, as I have told all my children, there is always room for more love. There is also a special place in mine and Ruby's hearts, just for you, Evie, and always will be."

He then leaned in towards Evie and gently kissed the top of her head. "You're a very special girl, and we're honored you're a part of our family now."

Evie felt overwhelmed again because she truly felt David meant his words, and she felt very loved for the first time in a very long time. David stood quietly as Evie collected herself before they made their way back towards the tent, where there was a ton of food being set out and lots of laughter.

Over the next couple hours, more and more people showed up. Evie was introduced to all of them. Desi had taken on the role of being her guide for the day and introducing her to everyone. Many of the people who had come were also children that David and Ruby had been foster parents to or even adopted themselves, adding more to their already large family. One of the women they had adopted was Leslie. Like Evie, she had been passed around from home to home before David and Ruby finally took her away from her awful life and gave her a new one. Leslie pulled Evie aside at one point and told her, "Evie, I know you might think that David and Ruby are too good to be true."

Evie thought about how delightful they were and how amazing everything had been so far and then nodded as Leslie continued. "The thing is, they're absolutely that incredible. I've watched them share their love with not only their own children and their foster and adoptive children, but so many others as well. They're a rare breed of people, just the most naturally kind and compassionate people that ever walked this Earth. Don't doubt for a minute that they don't love you or wouldn't do anything for you. I've seen it myself over and over again."

Evie smiled and thought, once again, she was truly lucky to have David, Ruby, and her new family.

As the party continued, Evie found a quiet place to sit back for a bit and watch. She could tell who were David and Ruby's biological children. All of their sons looked a lot like David, and their daughters definitely looked like Ruby. As she watched some more, she realized that all of their children, biological, foster, and adopted, were all very much older than herself. Evie started to wonder why David and Ruby would adopt someone so young, especially at their age. She told herself that maybe one day she would ask them about this, but pushed it aside as she watched some of the grandchildren play a game of Pin the Tail on the Donkey. One older boy rapidly spun a younger boy around and around in fast circles before pointing him in his direction. The younger boy took several stumbling steps as Evie and the others laughed, before David came in and helped guide the youngster in the right direction. Desi then appeared at Evie's side again, plopped down next to her, taking a big breath before handing Evie a glass of lemonade. Desi then turned to her and asked, "So, what do ya think?"

"It's a lot to take in," Evie answered and took a big drink before saying, "but I'm so happy and so grateful to be a part of your family."

Desi placed her hand over Evie's thigh and gave it a squeeze. "We're all happy you're here too...By the way, I absolutely love that hair of yours."

Evie blushed and tried to push her crazy red curls over her ears when Jenny and Leslie motioned for Evie and Desi to come over to a nearby table. The two got up and made their way over to the table. When Evie reached the table, she looked up and saw Joe and Steven carrying a large chocolate sheet cake with fourteen bright candles over to where she stood. Before they could even reach the table, everyone began to sing the happy birthday song loudly. They placed the cake gently down on the table as Evie leaned over, blew out all the candles, and made her wish...*I want to stay here forever.*

* * *

After her large and fantastic birthday party, the next few weeks were spent doing all the things Evie loved. She helped David and Ruby in the garden, found cozy spots in several places to curl up with a book, painted and drew as much as she could, and talked and laughed. Many of David and Ruby's children stopped by often. Desi took a real liking to Evie and took her to movies and coffee shops where they would talk or enjoy poems being read to the patrons. David taught Evie to fish and they went on several hikes in the beautiful mountains just outside of the town. Steven had a large pontoon boat, where the family would gather on Sundays to go swimming and fishing at the lake nearby followed by family barbeques. Evie was excited to see that Beth often joined them on family outings. Beth was just as excited to see how happy Evie was and how well Evie was fitting into her new life. Every day, Evie felt more and more at home with her new family.

Evie had also told Ruby she loved animals. Unfortunately, David had bad allergies, so they couldn't have animals in the house. Ruby decided to take Evie to a local veterinarian hospital, where Evie helped out with walking or playing with the dogs that were being boarded at the clinic. Evie loved spending time with the dogs and felt kindred spirits among her animal friends.

Before long, as summer was coming to an end, Ruby brought up a conversation about where Evie wanted to go to school. Evie had been so busy with her new life and family that she just said, "I haven't thought of it."

Ruby rubbed her hand over her cheek. "Well, there are couple of schools close by, but Desi told me there is a school here in town that focuses on the arts as well as other academics."

Evie looked up at Ruby and grinned. "I think I'd like that."

"Well, it's settled then," Ruby flashed Evie beautiful smile. "We can go there next Monday and take a tour to see if you like it."

David then came in, covered in grease, when Ruby told him the news. He clapped his hands together and said, "Fantastic, I think you'll enjoy it. You're an amazing artist."

He then kissed Ruby on the cheek, turned to Evie, and said, "Well, since schooling is out of the way, I think you need to learn a few other things every young girl should know." He paused and then added, "Go get on some clothes you don't mind getting dirty and meet me in the garage, kiddo."

He then made a little leap, winked at Evie, and headed out the door. Evie quickly ran upstairs to change, excited about what David might teach her. She looked at all her beautiful new clothes and didn't want to get them dirty, so she opened up her dresser and dug to the bottom, where she found her old clothes from the residential home. She had thought about throwing them away, but she decided to keep them as a reminder of her past life and just how lucky she was. She was now glad she kept them because she definitely didn't mind getting them dirty. She put them on and rushed downstairs. Right before she bolted out the back door to the garage, Ruby handed her two glasses of ice tea and gave her a quick kiss on the cheek before she said, "Don't let him go on one of his boring car rants."

Evie smiled and gave her a kiss back on the cheek and went out to the garage, where David was leaning over an old car, the hood popped up. Evie had no idea what kind of car it was, but she had watched the movie *Grease* once, and it looked like the kind of car they drove in that movie. She cleared her throat, which seemed to startled David because he hit his head on the top of the hood. He then turned around, rubbing his head, but before Evie could ask him if he was okay, he flashed a smile and said, "Every dang time."

David then took the glasses from her and moved towards the car, saying, "Everyone should know a few car basics. So today, I'm going to teach you how to change the oil and do the brakes. You ready to get dirty, kid?"

Evie smiled and laughed. "I think I'll enjoy this."

She was right, she did enjoy it, and over the next few hours David patiently taught her how to change the oil and brakes. He was also right about getting dirty. Evie was covered in grime almost minutes after they started. At one point, she missed the instructions David had told her about putting a pan under the oil tank before pulling the plug, and instantly, black oil started to pour all over the floor. Evie tried quickly to place the pan under the pouring liquid before it spilled too much. However, she definitely got covered in the slick black goo before she got the pan in place. Evie at first felt that this was it, she was going to finally get punished. Before she could think any further about the possible consequences, David let out a booming laugh. "That happened to Steven and Joe their first times too. No worries, kiddo, a little dirt and oil never hurt."

Evie felt relieved as she finished the task while David patiently instructed her through everything. After they finished the oil change, they sat on the front fender of the car looking out past the driveway in silence for a minute when David said, "I noticed you got scared there for minute when the oil leaked out. Why?"

Evie remained silent for a minute longer and then decided to tell him about her experiences at the residential home with Barbara. She told him of the punishments, chores, and strict rules that were enforced. She also told him of the incident where she broke all the plates and her punishment that followed. She said that after the plate incident, she was never allowed again to work with anything Barbara thought was a delicate task; she was left to do most of the gross and dirty work. She then realized she just did gross and dirty work with David and didn't want to offended him, so she quickly added, "But it wasn't fun like this. I liked getting dirty with you today."

David let out another loud laugh and then cleared his throat before saying, "I'm sorry you went through all of that, but I'm glad we finally found you. You will always be safe here."

Evie smiled but then thought about what he said: *Finally found you? Had they been looking for me?*

Before she could ask David about this, they heard Ruby holler from the kitchen that dinner was ready. David then clapped his hands. "Well, we better get cleaned up. If we come into the kitchen like this, I'll never hear the end of it."

David took Evie over to a small wash area in the garage and they washed as best as they could. They were on their way to the kitchen when they heard Ruby holler again from the back of the house. They made their way around to the back and saw that Ruby had placed dinner on the patio. She smiled and said, "I figured this would be a better place to eat tonight so you don't grease up my kitchen."

She flashed David a smile when he bent over, kissed her cheek, and again thanked her, and pulled out her chair. The three of them ate a wonderful dinner of fish, that David and Evie had caught, and a variety of beautiful red, orange, and golden veggies from the garden as they talked and laughed about their day and shared more wonderful stories.

Chapter 4

NIGHTMARES AND MYSTERY

The next week, Ruby and Evie visited Evie's new school, which Evie absolutely fell in love with. After their tour, Ruby took Evie to buy school supplies before they returned home. By the time they got back to the house, Evie wasn't feeling so well. Ruby placed her wrist on Evie's forehead and said that she felt hot. Ruby ushered Evie up to her room, where she took her temperature, and indeed Evie was running a fever. Ruby gave Evie some medicine and placed a cool washrag on her forehead before she said in a motherly tone, "You get some rest now. I don't want to see you up and about. If you need anything, I'll place this bell by your bed. You ring it and I'll come."

Evie thanked Ruby as Ruby went to place the bell on her bed stand. Ruby picked up the photo frame with Evie's parents' photograph, ran her fingers over their faces, and said, "They are just lovely, sweetheart."

Evie weakly smiled as Ruby placed the picture down and kissed the top of Evie's head before heading out of the room. Soon, Evie began to fall into a deep sleep…a deep dream.

* * *

A heavy fog rolled in through the darkness of her fevered slumber. Evie felt lost and an overwhelming despair filled her heart, but she couldn't wake herself up. She watched as her mind battled with constant lights, colors, and texture, endlessly materializing and breaking apart again, racing and dissolving in upon themselves. Then the darkness and racing lights began to change. She still couldn't make anything out clearly, but the emptiness around her began to harden like granite, and every new thought seemed to echo in her head like she was in an endless ice pit. She felt heavier than any living thing to have ever existed. She then watched as the color-changing fog slowly cleared away, only to find herself surrounded by the horrors of a battlefield and people screaming and dropping at her feet. Evie looked around for a direction to run but found that there was no way out as bloodied and dismembered bodies continued to drop all around her. To make matters worse, she began to notice something else too, flicking in and out of existence within the general swirl of bloodied chaos—random patterns of light so fleeting she couldn't focus on one point. Her mind was spinning, making her sick to her stomach. With mounting pain and bile beginning to form in her mouth, she watched the horrific movements flowing all around, the mutilated bodies and ever-changing shapes, the images flickering close and yet far, and the crackles of light and senseless trails of color. Her surroundings and mind were in complete pandemonium. She then saw a flash of light form ahead of her, and she knew that somehow this light was something good in this evil place; she began to run through the fallen bodies towards the light. The shrilling panic and the cries of the wounded people on the ground filled her head as she ran forward. Arms and legs reached up from the fallen bodies trying to pull Evie down to the ground, which made it hard for her to run, but she knew she must keep running towards the light. Evie could feel the desperation and pain from the dying people deep in her heart. Then, somewhere in the chaos, she heard a voice screech, "KILL THEM ALL."

Evie's heart began to pound even more to the point where she could only hear the rapid movement of blood through her head and her labored breathing as she got closer to the light. Before she could reach her goal, the ground began to violently shake and she saw a blast of fire come tumbling from the far side of the battlefield, moving rapidly over the fallen bodies. The few remaining souls that were still somehow standing were burned where they stood. Evie desperately heaved her body forward and reached her arms out, touching the boundaries of the light before the fire could engulf her too. The tips of her fingers finally touched the edges of the light and in that moment, she heard a woman's voice say, "Please find me, girl. I am here."

* * *

Evie found herself awake, sitting upright in her bed, with her arms still stretched out into the darkness of her room. She sat shaking and trembling in the dark silence for a minute, too scared to even breathe as she tried to remind herself that it was only a dream, only to ask herself, *Was it really a dream? It felt so real!*

Evie shook her head, trying to forget the nightmare. She felt her forehead and realized it was still very hot, so she chalked up the nightmare to having a fever. Although she had vivid dreams in the past that seemed real, this one felt more real than any other dream before. But again, she decided it was because of her fever. She rubbed her eyes and when she removed her hands, she could see through the window it was dark out; even though Ruby had told her to ring the bell if she needed anything, Evie didn't want to wake her up. Through her haggard exhaustion, she slowly moved her aching legs over the edge of her bed and painfully lifted herself to a standing position. As Evie inched her way towards her bathroom, she could hear voices outside her room. She quietly opened her door and could hear David's and Ruby's voices coming from the room down the hall. Evie then made her way down the hallway to the room where she heard their voices, trying not to walk on floorboards that creaked. The house was old, so many of the floorboards were squeaky, but Evie had found a few paths along the hallway where the floor didn't make sounds.

As she neared the door to Ruby's craft room, she also heard another voice and immediately recognized it as Steven's. She wondered what he was doing here so late and hoped that everything was okay. As she leaned her ear up to the door, she began to make out what they were saying when she heard Ruby say, "Now is not the time. We just got her here and she needs time to settle into her new life."

She then heard Steven say, "It took us a long time to find her. We thought she was lost and we have already lost so much time."

Evie then heard David clear his throat before he said, "Our job is to keep her safe. There is nothing else we can do until we are told otherwise, and there has been no word since we found her."

Evie suddenly realized they were talking about her and tried to move in closer to the door crack to see if she could hear better when the floor let out a loud popping noise. The voices in the room stopped as she heard footsteps coming towards the door. Evie quickly dashed back the way she came, ran to her room, and jumped in bed, pulling the covers over her. A minute later, she heard her door open and heard David whisper, "Evie. You awake?"

Evie didn't respond; she didn't know how to process what she had just heard or what she would even say. She heard David say her name one more time. Again, she didn't respond. She then heard her door pull shut and David's footsteps fall away. Evie lay in her bed for a while longer, thinking about the conversation she had overheard and about her nightmare. She felt an odd shiver go up her back, but before she could think more about what she heard or her dream, she felt the fever begin to take over again. She wrapped the blanket up over her to where it was almost covering her head completely and slowly drifted back to sleep.

* * *

The next morning, Evie was feeling a little better and made her way down to breakfast. David and Steven were at the table when Ruby reached Evie and began to fuss over her again. Evie saw Steven giving her an odd look from the corner of her eye. Ruby quickly pushed a glass of orange juice in Evie's hands telling her she needed to have fluids, blocking Steven's gaze from Evie's view. Evie then joined Steven and David at the table as Ruby finished making breakfast. David and Steven continued talking, but the conversation seemed normal enough. Evie thought maybe she had been mistaken about what she heard last night and decided it was just her fever that was in question, not them.

After breakfast, Evie began to feel weak again, so Ruby made her go to bed, forcing another glass of orange juice in her hand and telling her to finish it. Evie made her way to her room, Ruby following just behind. Once Evie was back in bed, Ruby pulled the covers up over her when Evie asked, "Do you ever dream, Ruby?"

Ruby tucked the last corner over her shoulder and sighed. "Of course, honey. Everyone dreams."

Evie gave her a weak smile and asked, "Do you ever think your dreams are real?"

Ruby rested her hand on Evie's shoulder and smiled before she said, "Some dreams are more real than we'll ever know."

Evie smiled and began to close her eyes. As her eyes began to flutter shut, she saw Ruby's smiling face turn slowly into a worried expression. Evie's eyelids felt heavy, and before she could ask Ruby any more questions, she fell back asleep.

Chapter 5
THE NORMAL LIFE

✦•━━━━━━━ ● ━━━━━━━•✦

Again, the next few weeks flew by, and before she knew, it was Evie's first day of school. Evie loved her new school. Many of the classes were focused on art, music, dance, and theatre. She excelled in all classes except for dance; she was naturally cursed with clumsiness, so graceful movements required in dance were definitely a challenge. She also loved many of her academic classes, but loved her literature teacher the most. Mr. Heath was a younger man with thin wire-framed glasses and crazy, disheveled blond hair. She loved the way he would talk about books and poems and tell animated tales of the authors' and writers' histories. His stories also reminded Evie of how her father used to tell stories. She also loved her history teacher, Ms. Bell. She was a middle-aged woman who wore a tight bun, pulling her brown hair back, that reminded Evie of a librarian. Ms. Bell was a very quiet person and deep thinker. Every time a student asked a question, Ms. Bell would pause and say, "That's an interesting question. Why do you think that is?"

This also reminded Evie of her father in the way he would always make her think before providing an answer to her question. Oftentimes, he wouldn't even provide an answer and would just tell Evie she would have to find out what she thought on her own. It would frustrate Evie when he responded this way, but it also helped Evie explore her own ideas, which she guessed was his intent.

She also made several new friends, but she would often think of Jessie and wished that she could be here too. One girl she met, Rebecca, soon became a close friend, and Evie spent a lot of time with her outside of school as well. Evie loved how normal her new life was, how her conversations and time with

Rebecca were things normal girls would do, and they didn't have to hide their friendship from anyone like she had to with Jessie.

The next year flew by fast, and before she knew it, summer had come again and she was celebrating her one-year anniversary and fifteenth birthday with her new friends and family. Towards the end of the summer, Evie was helping Ruby in the garden when Ruby mentioned how happy she was that Evie had been healthy for the last year and she hadn't even had as much as the sniffles since Evie's last fever a year ago. Suddenly, Evie remembered the conversation she overheard a year ago during her fever and she thought about asking Ruby about the conversation; but felt ashamed that she had been eavesdropping. Evie wanted to know why they had been talking about her but decided to wait for a better opportunity to ask questions; so, she pushed it aside once again. Besides, she had never heard anything else in regard to that late-night conversation. Evie thought maybe it was because they knew she overheard them, and they were being more careful about what they talked about, or maybe it was just the fever.

Evie also started to think about how intense her dreams had become over the last year. She first assumed that the nightmare she had the night she overheard the conversation was due to her fever. However, the nightmares had been getting worse and worse with each passing week. Each dream had been more horrific than the fevered nightmare. Not only were the nightmares vivid and awful, but the flickering lights and colors in the chaos always made her feel sick and lost. When she woke from her terrifying night terrors, her head would pound and hurt for days. She also noticed in several of her dreams, a solid bright light would appear, followed by a woman's voice in the distance, which Evie could never locate the source of. Every time, the light and the voice seemed to be guiding her or helping her, so she always tried to find either one in the frantic and chaotic dreams.

Evie then thought back to the dreams she had while she was in foster homes and the residential home and wondered why her dreams were more intense now. She still dreamt during her time there but decided that maybe her real-life chaos and pain stifled the vividness or meanings of her dreams in the past. Now, since her life with David and Ruby was normal and happy, her dreams seemed to take on a life of their own. They became more and more vivid, and unfortunately, more and more awful.

Evie wondered why her dreams were doing this now that her life was normal and happy. *Why were they becoming more real and more terrifying?* Over the last year, Evie had woken up several times in the middle of most nights, finding herself crying out in the darkness of her room. David would always come running to her room to console her. Like her father had done, David would tell her that whether it is a dream or real life, there is always a way to defeat the darkness and evil that looms in the world. Evie also noticed that after David had consoled her to a point where she felt better, she could see a deep worried look in his eyes, but he always tried to hide it from her and would hurry out of her room.

Evie pushed her thoughts aside about the late-night conversation and her awful night terrors. She reminded herself she was just lucky to have such amazing people take care of her, so she focused her attention back to the garden work with Ruby and decided not to bring up the conversation she overheard.

* * *

Another summer and another birthday celebration came, her sixteenth birthday to be exact. At this party, Evie was presented a small envelope as her gift. She slowly opened it up and there was a birthday card signed by all of her family. There was also another envelope wrapped inside the card. Evie opened the next envelope and saw it was a plane ticket to Ireland, with a date set for the following summer.

Evie looked up at all the smiling faces around her. She didn't know what to say. She had always wanted to go to Ireland, and her father always said they would go, but again, they never got to. Before she could even get a word out to thank everyone for the wonderful gift, Desi blurted out, "We all pitched in. You always talk about wanting to see where your dad grew up. So, we figured that this would be a perfect gift for you."

Evie's eyes filled with tears as one by one her family members gave her hugs and she thanked each and every one of them. When David and Ruby reached her, David said, "We did a little hunting around about your parents. It was hard to find anything, but we did find your father's birthplace. Ruby and I will take you to Ireland and show all that we have learned about your father."

Evie fell into David's arms as sobs shook her body. She felt his arms wrap around her followed by Ruby's arms wrapping around them both. She just continued to sob and tried to say thank you through her shaky voice.

* * *

The whole next school year, Evie checked the calendar each and every day and would yell out before she left for school, "One more day closer!"

David had also spent the first half of the school year teaching Evie how to drive. Joe had graciously given Evie an old car of his. The car was pretty beaten up and looked awful. Joe told her as he handed her the keys, "Everyone's first car should be memorable. It may not look like much, but it works. I'll bet you'll have some great memories with it."

Joe was right, it worked, but the car was definitely finicky. It took forever to warm up in the winter, and the driver's side window always got stuck. Sometimes, when she would shift gears, the clutch would pop out of place and the car would die in the middle of traffic, horns honking all around Evie as she tried to get it started again. There was also a weird smell to the car and when she asked Joe about it, he laughed and said, "Yeah, I don't know what that is. I could never figure it out either."

The rest of the school year went by slowly. Evie assumed it was time punishing her for being so eager to go on her trip, but she got through it. Meanwhile, her dreams became worse than ever. The nightmares got to the point where David and Ruby thought about sending Evie to a therapist. Evie didn't like that idea and told them she was fine. She did her best not to worry them about her dreams as much as she could. The only times that her dreams were brought up again was when she woke to find David sitting on the edge of her bed trying to calm her down from another nightmare.

The school year finally ended, and the next morning after the last day of school, Evie ran excitedly down the stairs. She missed a step and fell to the bottom of the stairs, hitting her knee hard on the last step. She sat, holding her painful knee, when Ruby came rushing around the corner asking Evie if she was okay. Once Ruby realized that Evie was fine, she helped Evie up. It wasn't the first time Evie had fallen down the stairs or hurt herself doing something else. Her clumsiness was definitely her ultimate curse, and by now, David and Ruby were used to Evie holding some part of her body that was wounded from her never-ending battles with gravity.

Evie then dashed past Ruby after she pulled herself together and ran to the kitchen, marked the calendar, and yelled out, "One more week!"

89

David was now entering the kitchen and started laughing when Ruby came in the room laughing as well. They all ate breakfast and began discussing their travel plans. As the planning wrapped up, David got silent for a minute and then asked, "Evie, do you know much else about your parents?"

"Only what I've told you." She paused and then said, "After they died, Beth and a few other people who tried to help me couldn't find any other family members. Every time I asked about my parents, nobody really knew much else either."

David rubbed his chin. "Well, I hope our trip will have some answers for you."

Evie smiled at David, but before he turned to get up, she saw another worried look cross his face. Evie wanted to ask him why he seemed so worried but pushed it aside and said to herself, *One more week!*

Chapter 6
TO IRELAND

he plane ride was awful. Evie quickly realized that she didn't like flying. Between her excitement about going to Ireland and her anxiety of flying, the trip seemed to take longer than Evie thought it should. Halfway over the Atlantic Ocean, Evie finally began to feel less anxious and tried to fall asleep. It was difficult at first because the plane seats were so uncomfortable, but she finally felt exhaustion win over. As she fell asleep, another dream began to enter her head.

* * *

Evie could feel the nightmare coming but couldn't wake herself up. She reminded herself of her father's and David's words and told her dream self, *I can always find good too.* She kept repeating these words over and over as she felt herself slip further and further into the dream fog. As bright lights flickered in and out of existence in the surrounding fog, Evie patiently watched. She learned not to focus too much on the lights, since they always made her head hurt, so she would just float with detached curiosity until the lights and fog would fade away. When the fog finally lifted, Evie braced herself for another horrific scene to unfold; however, this time, the dream did something else.

Evie found herself drifting on a ship surrounded by a dark blue sea that sparkled with stars. Her anxiety faded when she realized this wasn't a nightmare—so far—and she began to explore the new dream with curiosity. Evie noticed the ship was also sparkling and shimmering, flickering with faint yet lustrous blues and whites, matching the starry water below. As Evie looked up, her gaze was caught by the broad sails waving and shimmering like twilight wings in the dark sky. As she looked over the sails to the sky above, she noticed that there was a large white planet in the sky, shining vibrantly in the thick starry, sapphire night. Evie shook her head and looked back down, expecting to see the large planet's reflection in the water, but it wasn't there. She looked back up and then down at the water again, baffled that the planet's reflection still wasn't there. She then realized she wasn't on water but what looked like a river of slow stirring stars.

Evie rubbed her eyes, looked around, and quickly realized that the ship wasn't on a body of water but floating in the night sky far beyond any earthly surface. Completely shocked by her new dream surroundings, she looked back up again at the large white planet and tried to figure out what planet it was. Besides all the things Evie loved to do, she also loved anything having to do with space. David had bought a telescope, and they had spent many nights in the mountains looking at the stars. David would point out different planets and stars in the night sky while explaining to Evie all the wonders of space. Evie realized that this planet and the surrounding stars were none of the ones David had told her about, and she was baffled once again by what was happening.

She looked around some more to see if there was anyone on the ship with her, hoping there might be someone who could tell her where she was, but she was alone. Evie walked the top deck to find different spots to peer over the edge, but all she saw was more vibrant stars and deep blue space. Again, she saw bright lights flickering all around her, but they were slow and patient flickers, unlike the rapid and chaotic lights in her nightmares. She watched as the colors from the lights would form together, then split, melt away, and merge with stars. As Evie watched this endless scene of dark space, bright stars, and flickering light, she began to feel lost and alone; but also, a strange feeling slowly filled her body and mind, like she belonged here. She felt like a sailor who had been lost at sea, finding his way by following familiar patterns in the night sky to lead him home. Although she didn't recognize the stars, something about them made her feel like they were leading her home.

Evie felt a calm familiarity with her unusual surroundings, and the more she walked the deck, the more peaceful she became. At one point, she thought she heard a woman's voice in the distance but couldn't find where it was coming from. Evie remembered again, in many of her dreams and nightmares, she would often hear this same woman's voice but could never seem to find her. Evie shrugged the thought off and once more looked up to the space above, taking in the majestic view when she started to feel a tug on her body. She fought the tug because she didn't want to leave just yet. However, the pull became stronger, and soon the stars, lights, and ship began to fade away. Evie then slowly woke to David shaking her arm with a huge smile across his face. He whispered, "We're here, sweetheart!"

* * *

Ireland was absolutely beautiful. After they landed at the Dublin airport, they took a rental car and began to drive north. David said Evie's father was from Donegal, Ireland, which was in the northern part of the country. The drive through the countryside was amazing. It was covered in green rolling hills, small patches of white flowers growing across the expansive greenness, and several small villages that had been built hundreds of years ago.

They finally reached Donegal and spent the next few days exploring and taking in all the views. David had learned a few things about her father's past. He would show her where he was told Collin went to school and where her father had his first job. However, there wasn't much else that David had learned, so instead the trip was full of other facts about the city and Ireland.

One day, they made a trip outside of Donegal, to a small country village on the outskirts. David believed that this was another area her father had frequented, but as they walked around, there wasn't much else David could tell her other than Collin had been to this town a few times. As evening came, David, Ruby, and Evie found a small pub on the outside of the small village and decided to get something to eat and drink before calling it a night. The pub looked like it had been around for a hundred years or more. It smelled of moss and dirt. When they walked in, there were only a few patrons in the pub, who were older and obviously had already been drinking for a while.

David, Ruby, and Evie scoped out the whole pub and found a small table in the corner to sit. After a few minutes of waiting, a server finally came over and brought them a menu with only a few items on it. As they looked over the menu, the pub suddenly became oddly quiet. Evie looked up to see a very old woman come in from the back of the pub and head over to a table close by. As the ancient woman sat down, the patrons began to talk again but much more quietly than before. A few of the patrons also seemed to keep an eye on the old woman, but when the old woman would look in their direction, they quickly darted their eyes back to their drinks.

Evie felt a nervous energy overcome her, but it wasn't necessarily a bad energy. She simply felt that there was something just out of her grasp she needed to know. Evie could also feel the nervous energy from David and Ruby, but it passed as the server brought them their dinner. David and Ruby began to talk and Evie tried her hardest to join the conversation, but somehow the woman's presence still consumed her thoughts. There was something about this person Evie could just not pinpoint.

After a few more minutes, the server brought a small plate and drink and placed it on the table in front of the mystery woman as Evie took in the woman's features. The mystery woman had long, moon-silver hair that flowed carelessly down her back and shoulders. Evie could tell the woman's hair was most likely red in her younger days because there were a few bright reddish streaks left. Even seated, she was taller than Evie and was a little plump, but Evie could tell she used to be much thinner in her younger days. She had light skin, thin lips, and a shallow facial structure. However, her deep green eyes stood out to Evie the most.

Evie couldn't figure out why, but this woman seemed very familiar to her, as if Evie knew who she was but didn't know how.

The old woman was still looking down at her food. At length, she looked up and made eye contact directly with Evie. Evie froze as their eyes locked. Evie could feel something overcome her body and mind; once again, she felt she knew who this woman was. The exchange between the two seemed to freeze them both, and Evie thought that the woman was trying to figure out who Evie was as well. Their eyes stayed locked, and Evie began to feel like her mind was piecing together a memory of this woman.

Before Evie could organize her scattered thoughts, a sudden flash of a memory entered her mind while she looked into the depths of the old woman's ancient eyes. It was the most powerful feeling that Evie had ever experienced in her waking life or in her dream life. The feeling physically jolted her body as the flood of memory began to invade Evie's mind. The memory became so powerful that Evie began to feel faint and fell. As she hit the floor, the memory finally emerged in her mind: it was of a large man in an opaque cloud saying, "You are the one, trust me." Evie then screamed out the name "Magnus" before completely passing out.

* * *

Evie woke the next morning to find that her head was pounding and her whole body felt as heavy as a boulder. She tried to get out of bed but couldn't. Ruby must've been close by because she was soon by Evie's bedside telling Evie to remain still. Evie dismissed Ruby's request and slowly pulled herself upright. She then asked Ruby, "What happened?"

Ruby looked at Evie with a concerned expression. "I don't know. Hush now and get some sleep."

Evie looked at Ruby and could see that Ruby was desperately searching for something in her own thoughts. Evie said, "Ruby, it was like my dreams, but it happened in real life. What's wrong with me?"

Ruby leaned over and began to stroke Evie's hair. "I'm not sure, honey, but David is out right now trying to gather some information. We're not exactly sure what happened, but we think we might have an idea."

Evie looked at Ruby and was baffled by her response when she asked, "What do you mean, 'might have an idea'?"

Ruby looked around the room nervously and then said, "I really don't know how to answer anything right now. Please just wait until David gets back and hopefully we might have more answers for you."

Ruby stroked the top of Evie's head and gave her another worried look before Evie asked, "Does this have anything to do with why you were talking about me late at night with Steven a few years ago?"

Ruby flashed her a look of shock then shook her head. "Oh, honey, there is so much to tell you and so little I know. Please try and get some rest before David comes back. I believe that you may need your rest and strength for later." She paused and said,

"Please don't ask me any more questions until he gets back. Promise me."

Evie didn't know what to think but could see the plea and fear in Ruby's eyes. Evie slowly nodded. "I promise."

Ruby gave her a weak smile and began to stroke Evie's head once again, humming her beautiful lullaby under her breath as Evie slowly fell back asleep.

Chapter 7
MARINA AND THE KEEPER'S ORDER

***

The old woman dashed out the pub door after the young girl collapsed on the floor. As she raced across the dark fields and through the thick forest to her home, she thought, *It cannot be true, it cannot be real. Did she really yell my father's name before she fainted?*

Marina quickly found her way home through the night and went directly to the tall tower in her castle that she had locked up years ago. As she waved her hand over the heavy locks across the door, she whispered, "*aoratis anoxis,*" and it slowly opened with a loud creak. A wave of air blasted out from behind the door, almost knocking Marina to the ground. She held herself steady for a moment and then rushed into the dark room, bumping into a few chairs that were scattered about before she found what she was looking for. On the large table, she reached her hand out into the darkness and searched for the item she had left there many, many years ago. Her hand finally bumped a small round object. Marina grabbed it and rubbed her hands gently over the round ball. The ball soon began to spark with light. As the glow steadied, Marina threw the ball up into the air above her head, where it began to spiral and spin, growing brighter and brighter with each turn. Soon, the whole room was visible.

Marina looked around at the scattered books, scrolls, maps, and hundreds of ancient artifacts across the room. She then began her search once again, for the first time in a hundred years.

* * *

After David had carried Evie to a small local inn, he went back to the pub to begin asking the patrons about the old woman who had locked eyes with Evie before she fell to the ground. David wasn't sure whether this woman was the cause of Evie's fainting episode, but he had a strong feeling she knew something, and he needed her help. The way Evie had locked eyes with that woman was so powerful that David couldn't break Evie's attention, which made him believe that this woman might know about the past that he and Ruby had been trying to figure out since they found Evie.

Several years ago, David had been contacted by a man who said he had to remain anonymous. Mr. Anonymous told David to find a young girl who was close to where he and Ruby lived. The man mentioned that he was part of The Keeper's Order, of which David and Ruby had been members for several years. The purpose of The Order was to protect secret knowledge and information concerning Earth's true history.

Although David and Ruby weren't high-ranking members in The Order, and they didn't know much about the secrets The Order protected, they were always willing to help when needed. When they were contacted by this mystery man, he said they must find this child who needed their protection to preserve The Order's ultimate mission. The nameless man had told them that the child's parents had died and she was supposed to be given to an Order member named Dermot Kelley. David actually knew Dermot, who had first contacted him when David was much younger. It was Dermot who enlisted him and Ruby into The Order. They didn't have much contact with Dermot through the years, but he would occasionally reach out to David and Ruby, providing them bits of information to help with greater tasks of The Keeper's Order. This Mr. Anonymous told David that he heard of the deaths of the child's parents, and he tried to tell Dermot only to discover that Dermot had been murdered. Mr. Anonymous also told David that the girl's parents' deaths were most likely not an accident either. The mysterious man didn't have much more information to give David other than that he and Ruby needed to find this child, and that whatever Dermot knew about this girl, he took to the grave. David had very little information to help him in his search for this child.

David and Ruby searched for years for the young girl but couldn't find her. Finally, they got a break when their son Steven, who was also enlisted into The Order, found out where she was.

David knew that Steven met a woman named Beth, who was a case worker for foster children. Beth hadn't worked with David and Ruby yet, since they hadn't fostered a child in years, but Steven and Beth had developed a close relationship. As Steven and Beth's relationship deepened, they became romantically involved and eventually learned they were part of The Keeper's Order. During one late-night conversation, Steven told Beth about David and Ruby's struggles to find a young girl who needed protection. Beth had been assigned to be a case worker for a young girl a couple of years prior, and as she and Steven compared notes, she realized that Evie might be the girl they were looking for. They both reached out to The Order once more, but they couldn't make contact. However, even with no contact made, they came to the conclusion that Evie must be the girl The Order was trying to protect. Beth quickly transferred Evie into David and Ruby's home, knowing the young girl would be in safe hands until they were told otherwise. Once Evie was in David and Ruby's home, no contact was made and no information was given to them about what they were supposed to do with the girl.

When David and Ruby first brought Evie to their home, Steven insisted that they try to find the anonymous man who had contacted them, but Ruby protested. She pointed out that they didn't know who this man was and they still had very little information. Ruby wanted to keep Evie as safe as possible, for as long as possible, and told Steven and David they should at least wait for more information before doing anything further. Ruby also indicated that she wanted more information to ensure she wouldn't be putting Evie—whom she had come to love deeply in a short time—into the hands of someone they didn't know. David agreed with Ruby and also decided it would be best to wait until they were contacted again before they made any decisions. Years went by, but no word was received about what to do with Evie, so they decided to let it go.

A few months before Evie's sixteenth birthday, David received a letter that said, *Take the girl to Donegal in Ireland, her father's home, before she reaches seventeen.* That was all—no other information, no other guidance on what to do afterwards. David did his best to find any information that would help them once they got to Ireland. He still couldn't find much and just hoped that someone would reach out to them once they got there.

For the whole stay in Ireland, David asked as many people as he could about Collin, Evie's father, but no one seemed to know anything. However, David was careful not to provide too much information to those he asked about Collin. He didn't want to jeopardize The Order's mission or Evie. With no contact made, and their trip coming to an end, David decided that whatever the plan was, it might not come to fruition. However, the interaction between Evie and the old woman led David to believe this encounter wasn't a coincidence.

As David entered the pub again, many of the people he talked to didn't seem very willing to answer his questions. A few people even laughed and said, "Why d'yeh want to find that witch anyway?"

A few others he asked seemed frightened and ignored his questions. Finally, the young server girl who had been waiting on them and the old woman gestured her hand towards David to follow her to the back. David made his way to the back of the pub when the girl looked nervously around and said, "I 'eard yeh tryin' to find the witch?"

David nodded. "If you mean the old woman, then yes, I am."

The girl looked around nervously again. "Well, 'er house is back in the forest, a few miles from 'ere, right before yeh get to the hills." She paused, "But be careful. People say the forest is haunted, an' that the witch will place a curse on anyone who comes near 'er home."

David looked at the girl with worried eyes and asked, "Can you give me directions?"

The girl just shook her head and pointed at an east-facing wall. "Just 'ead that way. Go into the forest fer a bit. I'm told yeh can't miss it; the witch's home is very big."

"Thank you," David said and nodded at the girl once more.

Before David left, he added, "Please don't let anyone know about our conversation."

The girl nodded vigorously. "I promise. Besides, I don't think anyone would be brave enough to follow yeh or ask 'bout the witch anyway."

David gave her a weak smile and then headed back to the inn, thinking about what he would do next.

* * *

Marina finally seemed to find what she was looking for. She opened the old scroll, closed her eyes, and concentrated on the depths of her mind. For the last few years, she had been dreaming of a young girl. She could feel the girl's pain and suffering in her dreams and would call out to the child in the hopes of helping her. However, the child never got close enough and Marina could never reach out to her completely. Marina had decided that she was going to give up, when the child from her dreams sat directly in front of her at the pub. Marina was baffled to see that the child was real, but even more confused by the feelings and thoughts that began to overwhelm her mind as the child looked deep into her eyes. Marina herself couldn't break the deep gaze and before she could say anything, the child began to sway in her seat then yelled out "Magnus!" right as she hit the ground. This frightened Marina. While she wanted to help, she didn't know how and fled the pub.

What frightened Marina the most was that the child yelled out her father's name before she lost consciousness—her father, Magnus, who had been dead for centuries. She had tried for hundreds of years herself to decipher her father's secrets and what they might mean but never could determine anything with certainty. She had even been in contact with The Keeper's Order that her father had built before his death, but still, information was scarce and vague.

Somehow, she knew this child was the key, the one who would unlock the secrets, unlock the past, unlock the dreams.

Chapter 8
CONTACTING MARINA

◆•————————•————————•◆

David made it back to the inn and made a quick phone call before he headed back to the room where he left Ruby and Evie. As he entered the room, he found that Evie was still sound asleep. Ruby was sitting on the edge of her bed, stroking the child's head and singing the lullaby that had been taught to her by The Keeper's Order. Ruby turned her head towards David and said, "I hope the lullaby will bring her some peace. Since she has been asleep, she hasn't seemed to have any awful dreams yet."

David nodded and then motioned his hand for his wife to follow him. They both stepped outside the door. David then said, "I believe we have to extend our trip for a little longer. I just called Steven and he is on his way. Hopefully when he gets here, we can start looking for more answers."

Ruby nodded and then, in a worried and shaky voice, said, "Oh David, I just can't let her go. I don't know what all these secrets are and what they have to do with her, but the poor child has had such a hard life already. I just don't think it's a good idea to try and figure out why The Order needs her so much."

David placed his hand around his wife's shoulder and pulled her into his chest. "I know, love, but if we don't get some answers, I'm afraid the nightmares that consume Evie's dreams will eventually become worse. I don't want her to suffer anymore either. I just hope we can find a way to help her."

Ruby began to sob as she leaned her head against David's chest and said, "I know you're right, but I'm just so scared for her."

David rubbed the top of her head, kissed it gently, and sighed. "I know, I'm scared too."

They went back into the room where Evie was still sleeping and as Ruby approached the bed once more, Evie began to mumble and toss in her sleep. Ruby looked back at David and said, "I think she's having another dream. Should we wake her?"

David came over to Evie's bedside and looked down at the beautiful young girl; he admired her bright red hair and delicate features, watching as she continued to talk in her sleep. Her head moved back and forth, like she was trying to look for something lost in her dreams. She didn't seem to be frightened or suffering as he had seen many times in the past when he went to her bedside to rescue her from a nightmare.

He bent down next to the bed, held Evie's hand, and said to Ruby, "I think she's fine for now. Maybe her dreams are really telling her something. Let's hope she finds some answers. We'll stay here and wake her if anything happens."

Ruby nodded and once again began to sing her lullaby as David stroked Evie's hand, keeping an eye on her in case there were any changes.

* * *

As Marina found the passage in the scroll she was looking for, she remembered how she had found the scrolls in the first place...

Marina was the child of Magnus and Seraphina from Northern Ireland. Her mother came from a line of royalty, so Marina was born into wealth. Magnus claimed he wasn't from Earth originally and said he was a man from an ancient galaxy, one of great unknown powers in the universe. Marina was never sure of Magnus's story when she was younger, but came to realize the truth years after her father had passed away. Her father, herself, and many others who came from Magnus's bloodline lived much longer lives than anyone else on Earth. Marina herself had been alive since the year 1018 A.D.

Her longer life span was enough to convince her that there was something special about her father. With Marina's inherited wealth from her royal mother and inherited long life from Magnus, she was able to live on Earth for many years, changing her identity every generation to remain undetected, as did her father and others in his bloodline. Besides herself, there were her two brothers, who were also very powerful. Marina watched them rise to positions of influence, but they were ultimately destroyed by what they created.

Even though Marina didn't desire the power of her siblings, she became selfish and vain—qualities that over centuries began to destroy her. Then one day, long after her father had passed, she came across some of his ancient texts. Although she couldn't read them at first, there were pictures in the texts that allowed her to decipher some of the meanings behind them. Slowly, some of the words and symbols also became clearer as she continued to read the texts. While deciphering the pictures and texts, suppressed memories of her father's stories also began to resurface.

Marina came to the understanding that Earth, also called Terran, was a lost planet, cast out of a distant galaxy, and there would be a person of true heart born into Magnus's bloodline who would return Terran to its lost system. She knew that it was too late for her, so she began her search for others in Magnus's bloodline who could possibly be true of heart.

She also discovered in the ancient texts that there was a way to reach out to others through dreams. Before her father died, he told her to remember her dreams. Again, she didn't understand this at first, but as she began to search through her father's belongings, she began to understand her own vivid dreams held meanings and connections to her father's past and memories. She practiced for a long time reading the scrolls and learned how to find paths and meanings through her dreams. She eventually became strong enough to navigate the "dream state" her father's scrolls spoke about and she was able to reach out to others in Magnus's bloodline though her own dreams. Marina searched for many years in the dream state and found many of Magnus's lost relatives. However, like all the others before them, they were lost to power and greed.

After many more years of searching and not finding anyone worthy of Magnus's words, she felt defeated and a hundred years ago, she finally had given up. However, she began to have dreams over the last few years of a child while not in the dream state, but during regular slumber. The dreams were often vague and stifled by something that Marina couldn't penetrate.

She tried several times to reach out to the child, but she could never connect with her. Then, a few years ago, the dreams became stronger and she began to see the face of the child. She still had no name, but this renewed her efforts. In Marina's dreams, she could see the kindness and purity of the child, which brought her great joy. There seemed to be breaks in the dreams where Marina thought the child could hear her, but again, she was never able to reach out the way she had with others in the past. Again, she knew Magnus had written that a true-hearted heir could save them and unlock their past. Although Marina was unsure what this true past was and didn't know what they needed to be saved from, somehow Marina knew, after seeing the girl, that this was Magnus's true-hearted heir, and she needed to reach her again.

Marina looked over the scroll once more and recited the passage in her head. After she was sure she remembered the words correctly, she closed her eyes and fell into a trance as she entered the dream state once again.

The fog rolled in and Marina could feel the young girl's presence even stronger than she had in the past. She hoped it was because the girl was still close by, so she began to focus on the girl's face. The fog soon began to fade away and Marina found herself hovering over a small bed where the girl slept. Marina began to talk and hoped that this time she could reach the girl.

Marina drew closer to the child and said, "Girl, I am here."

She could see the girl move her head and mumble something under her breath as Marina, once again, said, "You need to come find me, girl. There is much we need to discuss."

The fog began to get thicker around the girl and Marina began to think that she would start to lose contact, so she pushed harder than she ever had. As she concentrated with all her might, she felt herself drifting away. However, Marina could still feel the girl's presence, as if she was taking the child with her into the fog. Marina soon found herself in a white empty space, as a small shadowy figure began to move towards her. Marina then heard the figure ask, "Is this a dream?"

Marina realized it was the girl's voice and, in a soft tone, replied, "My name is Marina. I am real, not just a dream, child."

Soon the white empty space began to faded away, and Marina could see the girl standing in front of her.

* * *

Evie could see the flashing lights of the dream coming again, but this time she didn't feel it was a nightmare, so she tried to focus through the flickering lights and thick fog that spun around in her mind. The lights slowly blinked out, the fog began to shift, and soon she saw a shadow form in the haze. Evie felt scared at first but stayed focused on the shadow as it moved towards her. The fog began to fade and Evie could see a vague image of a woman standing in front of her now. Although the woman wasn't clear, Evie could see her piercing green eyes through the fog. As the woman moved closer to her, the fog cleared some more and the figure came completely into view. Evie gasped. She realized instantly that it was the old woman from the pub. Evie shook her head, moved forward, approached the old woman, and asked if she was dreaming. The woman reassured Evie that she was real, told Evie her name was Marina, and said it was important for Evie to come find her. Evie was still not sure if this was real, but she knew that she had to find the woman—Marina.

"Where do I find you?" Evie asked.

Marina then started to flicker as the fog began to thicken around her again. Evie thought she might lose the woman, so she stepped closer. "Please, you must tell me where to find you. I need help."

Evie somehow knew that this woman would be able to help her, if only to stop her awful nightmares.

She didn't know how, but deep down, she knew that this woman was the voice from her dreams that had always been calling out to her, trying to help Evie in her nightmares. The woman flickered once more and, in an accent Evie couldn't identify, said, "I am not sure how much longer I can hold this. I am feeling weak. You can find me on the other side of the forest next to the pub where we met last night."

Before Evie could ask anything further, the woman began to fade back into the fog as Evie remained there in the darkness and empty space, alone and afraid. However, she knew she must find this woman and now she knew where to start.

* * *

Evie woke to voices coming outside of the door. She recognized the voices as David, Ruby, and Steven. Evie was still sore and her head still hurt terribly as she made her way out of bed and to the door. She slowly opened the door to find David, Ruby, and Steven all talking in the hallway. Ruby immediately rushed over to Evie and hugged her, followed by David and Steven, who said, "It's good to see you up. How are you feeling?"

"I feel a little weak, but much better," Evie replied, and gave them a smile as she rubbed her head.

The threesome gave her a worried look when Steven turned to David and said, "I think it would be best to finish our conversation downstairs and let Evie get some sleep."

Evie suddenly felt angry and before she knew it, she shouted, "NO!"

The threesome turned to look at her, stunned by her protest. Evie felt a little bad for her outburst, but she knew that whatever they had to talk about had to do with her, and she was no longer going to be kept in the dark. She turned, stared at Steven, and said, "Whatever you have to say, you can tell me. I know that this is all about me and I deserve to be a part of this."

Steven gave her a stern stare but before he could say anything, David interjected, "She's right, Steven.

Whether we like it or not, we can't protect her if she doesn't know our concerns and why we worry."

Steven's gaze softened and he looked at Evie this time with more concern than sternness. "Okay," he said, "you're right. However, whatever we find or do, you must understand we only are trying to do what is best. So please trust us if there are some things we have to say no to."

Evie nodded in agreement and then remembered her dream last night. "I agree," she replied, "but I think I might have an answer that will help us."

David and Steven gave her a curious look when Ruby interrupted, looking a little angry. "We can discuss this after breakfast. We all need to get some food in us first, before we discuss heavy matters."

David smiled at his wife and kissed her flushed cheek. "You're right, my love. We'll talk some more after we eat."

The foursome made their way downstairs and ate; however, there was little conversation, and it wasn't as happy and upbeat as usual. Once they finished their meal, they headed back up to the room

Steven had rented. It was slightly bigger than Evie's room and had a few chairs for everyone to sit in. They all sat down. Before Steven could say anything, David asked, "I'm curious, sweetheart; what do you think you've learned that might be able to help us… help you?"

Evie fidgeted in her seat for a minute before she began to describe the dream she had of Marina and where they might be able to find her. After she finished, David and Steven were both rubbing their chins, thinking deeply. Ruby looked directly at her husband and son and in a baffled tone said, "That's the woman you two were looking for and exactly where you were told to find her."

Ruby then turned to Evie and asked, "You dreamt this, honey?"

Evie blushed a little bit to think about how ridiculous it must sound to tell them to follow a dream. However, she could tell from the expressions on the others' faces that her dream was actually accurate. She shook her head at her own extravagant thought and realized, *Oh my gosh, my dream was real!*

Evie shook her head once again at this realization. Steven finally said, "Dad and I will go check this place out to see if it's safe before we bring you."

Before Evie could even protest, Ruby stood up and said, "No, we'll all go. Besides, if the townspeople are right, this woman may not be happy to have strangers on her property. At least if we bring Evie, maybe the old woman will know we're not a threat, and we can get some answers."

She then moved over and placed her hand on Evie's shoulder, holding her head high. "Witches, dreams that come true, and the mystery behind Evie's past. It all seems absolutely crazy, but we do this together or not at all, and that's final."

David smiled at his wife, then stood up, walked to Evie's other side, placed his hand on her other shoulder, and turned to Steven. "Your mother's right, Steven. We're all in this adventure together."

Steven shrugged his shoulders and, realizing he'd lost the battle, let out a big sigh and said, "Okay then, let's finish getting ready and go find this witch's house."

Chapter 9
FINDING MARINA

◆•————————●————————•◆

David, Ruby, Evie, and Steven packed a small bag of food and supplies and headed towards the forest outside of the pub. As they neared the forest's edge, Evie could feel a tingle run down her spine and spread across her body. She had feelings of being surrounded by the unseen, but she shook her head to throw off the swift chill of dread and took a step forward. The others were still standing behind her when Ruby said, "I don't like the feeling of this."

Evie realized that the others all seemed to feel the same way she did and began to wonder whether this was a good idea. The fear was powerful to all of them, but for the first time in all her life, she felt this was right. It was as if a shadow at the corner of her eye needed to be confronted—to finally answer what had been lurking behind her dreams all this time. She shook off another shiver. "We have to try. We'll never find out anything unless we find Marina." Evie paused and added, "I don't think she will hurt us; I really do believe she wants to help."

The others all mumbled in agreement and began to make their way through the trees. Although it was still early morning, as they walked further into the trees, it began to get darker and darker. They all began to feel a little nervous again, but they kept moving forward. Soon, the whole forest was black as night and Steven mentioned turning around when Evie saw a light shining through the trees and pointed. "Look, there's light ahead. Maybe we're almost there."

The others looked where Evie was pointing and agreed to head towards the light. As they got closer, the forest around them began to brighten, and soon they found themselves in a large clearing at the edge of an expansive and beautiful garden.

An enormous castle stood at the opposite edge of the garden, and even though Evie knew it had to be a very old castle, she was surprised to see that it was in pristine condition. Evie looked in awe at the castle and surroundings, and noticed rocky peaks that surrounded the edge of the beautiful clearing. After a brief moment to take in the view, they moved from the forest's edge towards the castle by following a small garden trail. Evie was once again surprised to see that the garden, though larger than Ruby's or her mother's, had the same layout. Evie mentioned this to Ruby. Ruby smiled and replied, "I was taught by The Keeper's Order how to build a garden that maximizes the growth of the plants."

Evie gave her a curious look and asked, "What's The Keeper's Order? Was my mother a part of that?"

Ruby smiled again. "I will explain later," she answered and then added, "I'm not sure about your mother, sweetheart, but as you said, maybe we'll find some answers from this woman we seek."

Evie shrugged and decided that there was already so much going on, she didn't have room in her mind for yet another mystery. As they made their way through the garden, Evie was awed again by all the beautiful plants and flowers—although there were some Evie didn't recognize. As they neared the castle, there was a small patch of flowers that seemed to glisten in the light and change colors. Evie shook her head once again but decided it was best not to get too curious about these flowers; she was on a mission and needed to focus on that.

As they got closer to the castle, Evie thought she saw the structure shift. A window she had been looking at seemed to move from one place to another. Again, Evie shook herself and thought that was crazy; so, she continued walking trying not to think about it.

The garden trail finally ended next to a door on the back side of the castle. They all stood there like some grim deity waited for them on the other side. Steven slowly approached the door, but before he could knock, the door opened and they heard a woman's voice say, "Please, come in."

They entered and found themselves in a kitchen where Marina was already sitting, with four other chairs around the table and a drink at each spot, as if she had been anticipating their arrival. They all slowly sat down and Evie could tell everyone was nervous to speak first. When it came to the point that the silence was too uncomfortable for Evie, she decided she would start the conversation, just as Marina asked, "Tell me about your dreams, child."

Evie sat there for a moment because she wasn't sure how to tell this stranger about her dreams, especially since most of her life, no one had really taken them seriously. Instead of explaining them, Evie simply answered, "I've had them as long as I can remember. How can this meeting be real if they were only dreams?"

After a long pause, Marina began telling them her story. She described her past and explained how she lives longer than others on Earth. She then went into detail about her father, Magnus, and where he claimed he was from. Marina told them how her father, and others like him, had special powers, making them live longer than others. She also provided information about Earth being a lost planet, cast out from a distance galaxy, where something had gone horribly wrong. However, Marina said she wasn't sure why or what had happened.

Evie was overwhelmed and couldn't believe what she was hearing. She had so many questions, but didn't even know where to start. She sat again for a long period in silence, taking it in, when she finally asked Marina, "How did you use dreams to find me?"

Marina took a deep breath. "You, too, are a descendant of Magnus, and his blood runs in your veins. You and I have special powers to navigate dreams. I was able to find you because I remembered my father's stories and his texts showed me how."

Again, Evie sat there completely baffled and thought that this meeting itself might be a dream. Marina then stated, "I have lost the ability to make true meaning and connection from the dreams due to my vanity and selfishness, but I believe I have found the hope I was looking for in you."

After another long silence, Evie asked, "What am I supposed to do with this? How are my dreams and my lineage supposed to help us now?"

Marina let out a long sigh. "I am not sure because I have lost so much of my purity, but I would like for you to stay here with me and look over what I have. Maybe that would be a start."

Again, the room was silent as everyone tried to process what Marina had just told them. Finally, Steven asked, "Is this what The Keeper's Order was trying to protect?"

"Yes, to a certain extent." Marina nodded and continued, "The Keeper's Order does not have powers like my father or myself, but Magnus created The Order to preserve knowledge so that when the time came, they could help us return and help Magnus's heir." She paused and added, "Unfortunately, much of the knowledge has nevertheless been lost, and many of the people in The Order have also been lost, or were killed for what they knew."

She took another deep breath and went on, "The head of The Keeper's Order was the only one who knew about Magnus's heir—about Evie. Other members only help store knowledge. However, the head of The Order was murdered, so I thought

Magnus's true-of-heart heir was lost forever, until my dreams became more powerful."

David took a deep breath before asking, "Dermot knew about Evie? Did he know about her parents?"

Evie looked over at David in shock, but before she could ask anything, Marina replied, "Unfortunately, I am not sure what Dermot knew, but whatever it was, he was killed for it, and everything he knew went with him. What he might have known about Evie's parents, I am not sure we will ever know, but hopefully, if you will allow Evie to stay here with me, maybe we can figure things out."

Ruby immediately protested. "I'm not just going to leave Evie with a stranger. I'm staying too!"

Marina looked at Ruby and gently said, "What I must do with Evie, must be done alone. I am unsure of what we will find, but I do know that there are aspects of knowledge and powers she must learn on her own. I am afraid that if there are others who do not share Magnus's bloodline while she discovers her past, their presence may interfere with what she has to do for herself—for her future."

Ruby went to protest again when Steven interjected. "My mother's right. We can't leave her alone, but I understand that we also can't impede Evie from finding herself. Is there any way we can help without leaving Evie from our care?"

Marina rubbed her hands together before saying, "Yes, I believe so. Since we have lost Dermot, there has been no one to lead The Keeper's Order. I believe that the best way you can help is to use some of the information I have to restore what we have lost. Maybe you can pull together the members who have scattered since Dermot's death."

She paused and went on, "If Evie and I are able to find what she needs to know, having The Order restored will perhaps renew our efforts in collecting and finding knowledge Magnus left us. This may be exactly what we need to move forward with whatever might happen next."

Steven and David agreed. Ruby still looked a little defensive, but then said, "Anything we can do to help Evie."

Chapter 10
LEAVING EVIE

In the days following the initial meeting, David and Steven combed through several books and scrolls that Marina had given them to restore The Keeper's Order. Marina also gave Ruby several books on plants, flowers, and herbs that could be used for various purposes, but Ruby was especially interested in an old book on healing remedies. Ruby was in Marina's garden often trying to find what she needed and also took over Marina's kitchen to make her healing concoctions. Evie occasionally helped the others in their endeavors but spent most of her time with Marina discussing as many things as possible before they made a plan. It was one Evie was sure Ruby wouldn't like. She thought several times about pulling Ruby aside and telling her what she had planned with Marina but couldn't find the courage to do so. In the end, Evie left it alone until she finally had to tell the others of her decision.

David and Steven found a man in Egypt who said he was part of The Order and was willing to help them, but he wasn't willing to talk on the phone. He told David and Steven that if they wanted to talk, they needed to come to him. Steven found this man when he was going through a list Marina had of people in The Keeper's Order. Although the list had several names, there was very little contact information on any of the people. Since Steven brought his cell phone, he was able to do a search and found only three people on The Order's list who had a phone number. Steven asked Marina if she knew anything else about the people on the list or how to reach them, but Marina told him that unfortunately, after Dermot died, she had no idea how to contact the others.

Steven and David were frustrated with their search, but were happy they were at least able to find and reach one person.

While Steven did his search, David pored over other texts Marina had given him. One book he came across worried him. The book said that to train a person in Magnus's bloodline, the person being trained had to work alone and only with a person in Magnus's bloodline. Otherwise, the person being trained wouldn't be able to find their absolute strength. David realized that if Evie was going to be able to find herself, they may have to leave her alone with this strange woman after all. David didn't like the idea of leaving Evie—and he knew Ruby definitely wouldn't. So, he decided that he would spend the rest of his time while they were there getting to know Marina as best as he could. This way, if they did have to leave Evie, he would feel better about leaving her with Marina.

David didn't express his concerns to Ruby. He didn't like to keep anything from her, but he knew Ruby would protest, and everything they were working on to help save Evie might come to an end before they could find any answers. David thought that maybe this wasn't a good idea after all. However, before he could think on it any further, Steven approached him, rubbing his chin, and said, "Dad, I've found something that makes me believe that we have to restore this Order."

David gave his son a concerned look, knowing that his son only rubbed his chin when he was troubled, and asked, "What did you find?"

Steven then held out a book so old that David thought it would crumble apart as Steven opened it. Once Steven opened the text, David was surprised to see that most of it was in English. There were parts of the text that were in another unidentifiable script, like some of the other things they'd been trying to figure out, but for the most part, David and Steven could read it.

"It seems that this man Magnus, Marina's father, stored some knowledge about protecting Earth," Steven answered then paused before adding on, "Apparently, Magnus was able to hide Earth from an evil man who has been destroying galaxies all over the universe. The text says that although Magnus was able to hide Earth from this man and his powers, the protection Magnus placed over Earth has a limited time frame."

David looked at his son, shook his head, and asked, "How long before it doesn't work anymore?"

Steven gave him a worried look before answering. "If Marina is right, Magnus placed this protection over Earth in the year 1018 A.D. He also wrote that the protection spell he placed on Earth would start to break and fall apart in a thousand years."

David realized why Steven was so worried and said, "It's the twenty-first century. It has been longer than a thousand years since this was cast."

"I know, and there's more." Steven paused and said, "Magnus wrote that when the spell starts to fall apart, there would be signs here on Earth that would begin around the planet indicating the end of the protection. These signs would not only indicate the spell was breaking, but also that there would be chaos on Earth. This evil man Magnus hid us from will eventually notice the chaos and find Earth if we don't stop him."

David sighed and shook his head again before asking, "What signs?"

Steven shook his head as well and went on, "Magnus wrote that a hundred years before the spell breaks, there would be increases in wars, famine, diseases, and pollution. He also noted that there would be extreme differences among ideologies, science, and religion that would cause Earth's occupants to fight among themselves and divide and separate us further from the truth."

David sighed. "It's like a prophecy that's coming true. This is so unreal."

Steven then continued saying, "Magnus also wrote that mankind will begin to explore space around Earth, and that our exploration of our system is also another thing that will show this evil man where we are. He also wrote that he or his heir would be the only one who could bring the people of Earth together to help them stop this man…this evil."

"Magnus is dead." David rubbed his temples as if the news was creating a terrible pain. "That means, if Marina is right, Evie is the only one who can take his place. Do we even know what this evil man is capable of?"

"No. Neither the text nor anything else that I could find mentions anything further on this subject. But," Steven took another deep breath and went on, "it seems that if Evie is really the one to help stop this, she'll have to work alone with Marina to be able to figure out her powers."

"I know." David sighed. "I deduced this too while reading some of the books. Your mother will not like this idea."

"I know." Steven then also rubbed his head as if it hurt too. "We will really have to get to know Marina if mom is ever going to trust her enough to leave Evie alone with her."

David sighed again. "I think the same thing."

After David and Steven finished their conversation, they decided to go find Marina to get to know more about her. They found Marina in the kitchen helping Ruby with a healing remedy she was working on. David assumed Evie was off gathering more flowers or reading in the side room where she had been spending most of her time since they arrived. So, he figured it would be a good time to get to know Marina. As David and Steven approached the table, Marina and Ruby were laughing about something. David felt relieved about this; Ruby seemed to like Marina, so hopefully it would be easier to convince Ruby to leave Evie. David and Steven took a seat at the kitchen table, when David asked, "What's so funny?"

Ruby wiped some sweat from her forehead. "Oh nothing. Just before you came in here, I poured a glass of crushed flowers into the pot, and I think I put too much in because it shot up my nose as soon as I dropped the flowers in."

David smiled at his wife and jokingly said, "Well, I hope it was nothing that would turn you into a frog."

Ruby and Marina laughed when Marina said, "No. It is just a special drink that helps restore energy." She laughed again and said, "Most people think I am a witch, but do not worry, I am not the kind of witch that turns people into frogs."

Marina chuckled again. David, with a bit more concern in his voice, then asked, "Well, what kind of witch are you?"

Marina stopped chuckling and smiled. "I know it is funny to think I am a witch; however, I am not—that is just what people like to think—but I can tell you are concerned about something." Marina paused and continued, "Please, ask me anything you would like. I know how hard it must be for you to trust a stranger."

David wondered if Marina knew that he had discovered that they needed to leave Evie alone with her. He thought, *She must know, because, after all, it's her books we are studying.* David then looked at his wife, who was still chuckling a bit, when he said, "I would just like to know more about you besides what you have told us already."

"Fair enough." Marina nodded. "What do you want to know?"

David asked Marina why she wasn't the one person true-hearted enough to be the heir Magnus had waited for, and why Evie was. Marina then said,

"As I told you, I was not eager for power or money like others in Magnus's bloodlines, but I was once a very beautiful woman. I became vain and selfish when I was younger. I spent many years only caring about myself and worrying about keeping my beauty. When I learned we live longer lives than others, I spent many years creating remedies to hold on to my youth and beauty." She paused and said, "I was so self-involved that when my brothers reached out to me for help, I refused, since I was only concerned with my future."

David then asked, "Why did they ask you for help?"

"My brothers became very powerful men with much influence over great rulers. With so much power, they eventually became corrupt and greedy." Marina lower her head and said, "When they came to ask me for help in keeping their power and influence, I refused."

Marina then paused and went on, "I learned about special herbs and flowers that could help a person maintain power, like I could do with my beauty. When my brothers asked for help, I believed they were still good and fair people, but I refused to help them since I did not want to share my potions, herbs, and flowers with them for the concoctions that they needed."

Marina sighed before finishing. "Not only did I not want to share my potions and plants, but I justified not helping them because the men they had influence over were not good or kind. Without my help, my brothers eventually became evil and corrupt like the men they served, and eventually they all died, murdered by the people they served."

Steven looked nervously at the others before saying, "I'm sorry, but this story of yours doesn't make us really trust you."

"I would not have trusted me either at that point." Marina nodded. "However, after I lost my brothers, I was devastated and realized that losing people I love because of my selfishness was not something I ever wanted to happen again. I gave up my efforts to keep myself young and beautiful and began to search for other members of my family so I could help them."

Marina made a sniffing noise before saying, "I told you I found many who had been lost to power and greed, but I also found others whom I came to love so deeply that I did everything I could to help them." She paused and the others could see the sadness in her eyes as she went on, "Unfortunately, even among those I loved, many became corrupt to the evils of this world. So, with great regret, I had to let them go so they would not learn about the powers and knowledge Magnus left us and use it for more destruction and deception."

Marina's eyes were filling up with tears when she sucked in a deep breath and finished. "You have no idea how much it hurts to walk away from those you love and to realize there is nothing you can do for them. So, I reached out to The Keeper's Order to ensure that those I had to let go would stay protected."

David then asked, "Is that why Dermot enlisted us?"

Marina looked at them intently before she answered, "Dermot became head of The Order long after I enlisted The Order to protect my family.

The Order's original mission was to only protect knowledge, but when I reached out to The Keeper's Order a hundred years ago, I made clear that it was also their job to ensure that anyone in my bloodline would also be protected." She paused and then added, "That is why Dermot found people throughout the world and enlisted them into The Order as people who could protect my family when I could not."

Ruby looked shocked but then asked, "That's why he enlisted us then, to help you protect your family?"

"Yes." Marina nodded. "There are many people in my family I do not even know, but I would do anything for my family, absolutely anything to protect them and make sure they are safe."

Marina then looked sympathetically at David, Ruby, and Steven before adding, "Evie is my family. I will do anything to protect her. I promise that now and for as long as she lives."

They were all silent for a while, thinking deeply about Marina's words, when Ruby finally asked, "Will Evie live a long time too?"

"Yes," Marina answered. "Once someone on Earth in Magnus's bloodline reaches the age of eighteen, they begin to slow down in the aging process. Evie will live much longer than all of you. This is another reason why it was so important for me to have The Order protect my family and why it is so important that I found Evie, so I can be sure to find a way to protect her as long as she lives."

Ruby then looked at Marina and nodded before saying, "Marina, we trust you."

Marina then smiled as tears began to well up in her eyes. "That means more to me than you know. I know I just met Evie, but I love her already. She is an amazing child. Even if she is not the one we need, I promise I will never leave her and never abandon her. She is my family."

* * *

After a few more days went by, David and Steven believed that they finally had enough information to get started. After dinner that night, when David and Steven told the others of their plans to leave for Egypt, Ruby looked around and said, "I hate to not go with you guys." She placed her hand on David's hand and finished saying, "We've been by each other's side since we were teenagers, but I think I have to stay here with Evie."

Marina gave Evie a knowing look. Evie nodded and then cleared her throat before nervously saying, "Ruby. You have to go with David and Steven. I've learned a lot from Marina these last few days, and I believe she's right. There are things I have to do by myself."

Ruby's face began to turn red and Evie knew she was going to protest. Evie then quickly got up, bent down on her knees in front of Ruby's chair, reached out, and grabbed Ruby's hands. "Please, Ruby. I need to do this. I need to find out who I am. I need to find out about my parents. I need to end my nightmares."

She paused before continuing her plea, "Please, Ruby. I love you so much and I promise I'll be safe and be back by your side before you know it. Please let me do this."

Ruby's redness faded as tears began to run down her face. Evie could tell she wanted to protest again, but Ruby finally took a deep breath, sat up straight, and stated, "I love you so much. I just want you to be happy."

Evie smiled and nodded. "I know, but I think this is what needs to be done for that to happen."

Ruby bent over and kissed the top of Evie's head, grabbed Evie's hands tighter, and said, "Okay, I know this is what you need to do. I love you so much, my brave beautiful girl."

She then wiped another tear from her cheek and gave a hard look at Marina. "You take care of my girl. I swear, if you let anything happen to her, I don't care what magic or powers you have, I'll make you regret everything."

Marina nodded gently at Ruby before saying, "I promise, Ruby. Evie is my family too, and I will do anything for my family...anything for the people I love as well."

Ruby nodded again, not taking her eyes off Marina, and in the sternest voice she had ever used, said, "I know I said I trust you, but promise me you will keep your word and not let anything happen to her."

Marina gave Ruby a worried look before saying, "Ruby, I promise you that I will do anything for Evie."

Ruby gave Marina a frail smile, choked up a sob, cleared her throat, and weakly said, "Good."

Ruby then got up and made her way out the back door to the garden as David followed. Evie looked out the window and could see David holding his crying wife in his arms, trying to console her. Steven then cleared his throat and said to Evie, "Please do everything you can to stay safe. It will break their hearts if anything happens to you."

Evie felt a wave of guilt wash over her and thought about changing her mind and keeping Ruby with her, but she knew that she really did have to do this on her own. She looked at Steven and said, "I promise. You have all been so kind and so helpful. My life is wonderful because of your parents and your family. I love you all so very much."

Steven nodded, got up, wrapped his arms around Evie, and gave her a kiss on the cheek before joining his parents in the garden, trying to help his father console Ruby.

The rest of the week flew by. Before Evie knew it, she was saying tear-filled goodbyes to David, Ruby, and Steven. Evie watched them as they made their way back through the garden and finally fell out of sight into the dark forest. She felt alone and lost again for the first time in years. Evie then turned to see Marina standing behind her when instantly tears began to pour down Evie's face and she rushed into the arms of Marina, who began to console her. Evie eventually felt exhausted, so Marina led Evie up to a bedroom, and Evie cried herself to sleep.

Part Two

◆———————●———————◆

THE SEARCH

Chapter 11
EVIE AND MARINA

vie woke up hours later in a small dark room with the only light coming from a tiny crack through the curtains. Her head was pounding and she still felt light-headed and thought that maybe she had a bad night terror but realized she had only cried herself to sleep the night before. She opened her eyes further and began to sit up. Even though she was in a new room she hadn't been in before, she realized she was in a familiar place and this wasn't a dream. Evie started to sluggishly move around and eventually gained enough strength to look out the window. Outside the window was the familiar rugged countryside and she could see rocky hills in the distance. It had to be early morning because there was still dew on the ground and window panes, and a sliver of sunlight was peeking over the horizon.

She could smell wood burning and a faint whiff of biscuits and tea being brewed. She could also hear someone shuffling downstairs, but it was a quiet slow shuffle. Evie slowly cracked the door to the room she was in and peeked out. At the top of the steps, the smells from below became more potent and the slow shuffling she heard became louder, less slow, and more at the pace of someone cooking in the kitchen. Evie realized how hungry she was and the smells of food eventually overpowered her, so she headed down the stairs to where the smells where coming from. Her nose led her to the kitchen after passing many different doors and hallways, where she found Marina making breakfast. She took a moment again to analyze the kitchen and Marina before entering. She noticed Marina always seemed to wear the same type of clothing; she dressed as though she was in mourning. Before she could think about this any longer, Marina turned and noticed her. "Good morning. How are you feeling today?"

"I still feel a little light-headed from all the crying, but good," Evie replied.

Marina smiled and nodded. "Do not worry. It was a lot to take in all at once."

Evie then looked at the food on the table and said, "The food smells good."

Marina gave her a small smile and waved her hand at the table. "Sit down, eat, and regain your energy. We can start talking some more once you feel up to it."

Evie felt a rumble in her stomach, so she sat down and said, "Thank you so much."

Evie began eating a simple meal of biscuits, butter, and dark tea. It wasn't much, but she ate it up and had seconds. While she was eating, she watched Marina shuffle around the kitchen some more and grab certain items, look at them for a bit, then shake her head and continue her shuffle. Just as Evie was about to break the silence and ask Marina a question about what she was looking for, Marina chimed in saying, "Do you remember what you shouted out right before you passed out the night at the pub?"

Evie thought for a minute and shook her head. Marina paused for a minute and then asked, "Do you remember why you passed out or what you saw when you passed out?"

Evie rubbed the top of her head, trying to remember, but she still felt weak, so she just answered, "I just remember that I felt very dizzy and like my body was just giving up."

Marina looked at her with concern and asked, "Was there anything else?"

Evie sat there for a minute again, trying to remember, when suddenly she said, "Oh yeah! I remember a man in a cloud saying to trust him, that I am the one, I think?"

"That makes sense." Marina paused for a second with a far-off look on her face.

Evie shot her a confused look and asked, "What makes sense?"

"Right before you lost consciousness," Marina answered, "you yelled out my father's name."

Evie, still very confused, asked, "What does that mean?"

Marina gave her another concerned look before answering, "I am not sure, but maybe today, if you are feeling up to it, we can try and find some answers. Now eat up and get yourself cleaned up so we can get started."

Evie complied, finished her breakfast, and made her way up back the way she came—almost getting lost a few times because Marina's castle seemed to have a million doors and hallways. She had been there for days, but she had been sharing a room close by the kitchen with David and Ruby, so this path was completely new to her. Once back in her new room, she took a bath and got herself cleaned up. After a fresh set of clothes, a bath, and food in her belly, she felt she was ready and went back downstairs to the kitchen to find Marina. When she got to the kitchen, she didn't see Marina, so she decided to wait for a while until she came back. After a long period of sitting in the kitchen, Evie realized that Marina might not be coming back and was beginning to get impatient, so she decided to find her.

Marina's castle was even more confusing to navigate and a lot bigger than Evie first thought.

While David, Ruby, and Steven where there, there were only a few rooms that Marina had shown them, so the rest of the castle was still a mystery. There were several doors that were locked and several hallways that looked almost too dangerous to enter. Evie had also forgotten how to get back to the kitchen or her room at this point—the task of finding Marina in this massive castle became a little more daunting than Evie thought it would be.

As Evie continued her search for Marina, the kitchen, or her room, she passed a dark, ominous hallway that gave her the chills; however, for some reason, she couldn't leave the entryway of this hall. As she stood there looking down this new path, strange feelings of distant memories she couldn't reach in the back of her mind and a tingly light-headedness started to consume her. However, she couldn't move away, almost as if something was pushing her to go down this particular path. After a while, Evie gathered her courage and began to take small fretful steps down the hall.

Unlike the other mazy and echoing hallways that had multitude of doors down on either side, this one didn't have any doors and the walls seemed to move and shimmer as she passed. At times, the hallway almost seemed to move as well, creating turns that weren't there before. At one point, Evie looked back and couldn't see the start of the hallway. This frightened her, but there was still an overwhelming feeling that she must continue down the path.

She walked for a while longer when she finally saw a faint light. When she reached it, there was a large door with several locks on it, but none of them were locked and the door was slightly open, leaking out the faint light. There was something about the door that scared Evie, but the urge to push it open was too powerful. As Evie slowly pushed open the door, she made her way to an enormous room filled with books, scrolls, art, weird artifacts, and dusty old crap that must have been there for hundreds of years or more—if Marina was telling the truth. Evie couldn't figure out what the light source was for the room since there were no windows, lamps, or even candlelight. As she looked around, she saw a massive ball that must have been five stories up, glowing and moving like a sun in miniature.

Evie continued to look around casually, afraid to touch anything and, since she figured that she couldn't explain the glowing ball of light that lit up the room, she thought there might be other things she shouldn't touch that weren't easily explained—according to her knowledge of the world.

As Evie was investigating a stack of old books, Marina came around the corner of another stack of books, piled so high it could cover two buses. When Marina saw Evie, she said, "Oh good, I am glad you found me. I did not know for sure if you would."

Evie gave Marina a curious look, wondering if Marina had left her to navigate on her own for a reason, but shook her head and said, "It was a bit difficult because your castle is so big, but something made me pick this hallway and this room was at the end of it."

Marina chuckled a bit and mumbled something under her breath that Evie couldn't hear, but before Evie could ask a question, Marina stated, "Should we get started?"

Evie nodded and watched Marina fumble around some more with an old stack of scrolls, mumbling to herself as she picked something up, looked it over, scoffed a bit, and continued her search. Finally, Marina seemed to find what she was looking for. "Here it is!"

Evie looked at her arms trying to figure out what she had and asked, "What is it?"

Marina slowly and carefully unrolled a scroll that was so old Evie thought it would turn into dust at any moment. Marina placed the open scroll in front of Evie and asked, "What do you see?"

Evie leaned over the scroll and, at first, saw nothing but a bunch of marks and drawings that to her seemed completely foreign. "I'm not sure what I'm supposed to be looking at here," Evie replied while looking at the mysterious scroll.

Marina looked at Evie and nodded towards the scroll again. "Take your time and really look."

Evie proceeded to look even closer at the scroll and, as she examined it, she began to feel light-headed again and the scroll seemed to become blurry. However, right as she was about to give up because her head was starting to hurt again, the symbols and drawings on the page moved and then seemed to start rearranging themselves into a pattern. Evie was shocked to see the scroll was moving, but before she could think about this weird phenomenon, Evie recognized the swirling patterns and symbols as something vaguely familiar. At first, the symbols didn't seem to make sense and her head was beginning to hurt even more. So, she pushed through the pain and continued to focus even harder. Suddenly, the symbols and drawings stopped moving around and almost looked as though they were slightly levitating off the page, like the scroll had become three-dimensional. Evie was stunned by this, but soon she was able to make out pieces of what the scroll had on it: what looked like a partial map and key, along with some writing on the sides. The scroll also seemed to label and provide descriptions along the sides of some of the drawings. Before Evie could think about the strangeness of it all, she excitedly shouted out, "I think it's a map."

Marina's usual straight thin-lipped mouth turned up into a giant smile and her deep green eyes sparkled like a child's on Christmas Day. Marina loudly exclaimed, "I knew you would get it!" Marina's smile widened and in a lower tone, she stated, "Now, I only have three of these scrolls as far as I can tell, and they all seem to be a partial fit to something. However, I could not decipher two of them, including this one. The one I was able to somewhat decipher was the one that told me to look for you in dream state. Would you like to see the others?"

Evie saw the excitement in Marina's eyes and said, "Yes, I think I'd like that, but I need something to drink first, please."

Marina looked at her with concern and replied, "I will run and get you something to drink. It is very common for someone in my father's bloodline to feel depleted after a decipher."

Before Marina left the room, she put down the two additional scrolls on the table in front of Evie and said, "Wait until I get back with your drink."

Then, she scurried out of the room and back down the long never-ending hallway.

Evie looked back down at the table at the two rolled-up scrolls and the one she had already examined. She looked at the open scroll again and her head started to hurt, so she thought it would be best to wait for Marina in case she passed out as she had at the pub. As Marina was searching for a drink, Evie started to explore the rest of the colossal tower room. She looked up at the large light orb to try and figure out what it was and how it worked. She estimated that this room had to be much higher than she originally thought. As the orb was so bright, she thought the room was about five stories high. Upon closer examination, she realized the room extended even higher than the orb, making the room at least ten stories high, with books and artifacts extending along the expansive walls on all sides. After looking up for a while, her neck began to hurt, so she decided to explore the rest of the room that wouldn't make her have to look up so high.

When she first walked in, she noticed all the stacks of books, scrolls, drawings, maps, and artifacts, and upon closer examination, many of these items in the room reminded her of being in a museum. She remembered watching an episode on TV where two researchers were exploring tombs of ancient civilizations and Marina's room reminded her of some of the things they found in these tombs. Evie was always fascinated by the past and often found herself interested in ancient times. When reading or watching things about the past, she remembered she would always laugh a little bit about the conclusions people came to, thinking that they missed something in their interpretations. However, Evie could never figure out why she thought they might be wrong. She pushed this thought out of her head and continued to explore some more.

She wandered the labyrinthine room and saw several large stacks of books; many of the titles were in languages she couldn't read, and some of the titles seemed to move around like the symbols on the scroll. As she circled the corner around another large stack of books, there was a small clearing down a long aisle, so she decided to see what was at the end. At the beginning of the aisle, there were two large statues of giant dogs that looked as though they might even be guarding the aisle. When she walked by the statues, the dogs' eyes almost seemed to follow her; however, she felt more comforted by the statues' gaze than nervous.

As she walked down the aisle, she thought she heard whispers coming from the stacks. She shouted out, "Is anybody there?" No response.

She then peeked her head through a gap in one of the stacks to see if there was anybody on the other side, but all she saw were more books and scrolls. She decided to press on, and as she got closer to the clearing, the whispers got even louder, so once again she called out and looked through another gap. Still nothing. As she took a step into the clearing, the whispers instantly ceased, and the quietness of the clearing became almost eerie.

She took a long pause and examined the clearing from the end of the aisle. It was covered in maps of places and areas she'd never seen before. There were drawings of swords and ships on the edges of the clearing that she didn't recognize from all the history shows she watched and books she read, but somehow they looked familiar. All the maps and drawings had symbols and words on them that looked similar to those on the scroll she first read but seemed slightly different and they didn't move around like the ones on the scroll. In the center of the clearing was a map laid out on a large table. She moved over to the table to see the map: it looked like it was a map of a galaxy, one she'd also never seen before. Besides loving to watch shows about history and ancient artifacts, Evie was an avid reader of anything having to do with science and space. She considered herself a novice astronomer and was always looking at the stars and sky since David had taught her many things about space. She searched her head again to try and remember if she had ever seen this galaxy before, but she couldn't remember if she had; however, like everything else in the room, it seemed to have something vaguely familiar to it.

She decided to examine the map a little more to see if it would trigger what galaxy it might be. When she looked down at the map, once again, her head began to hurt, and she started feeling dizzy right as the map began to move and the symbols began to switch places. She thought, *I can power through this like I did when reading the scroll!*

Evie then began to focus harder and push through the pain. The map and symbols continued to move around, but unlike before, they didn't seem to stop. It was almost as if the map was searching for something. Her head began to hurt even more and she thought of turning away, when suddenly, in the top right corner of the map, two words levitated off the map and became crystal clear: *Callais and Antillis.*

As soon as Evie saw the words, her head hurt so badly and she felt she might lose consciousness again, so she turned away. Before she could look again, she heard a loud boom coming from somewhere outside of Marina's castle. Evie jumped, quickly ran back down the aisle, navigated herself through several piles of books and scrolls, and eventually found where Marina had left her. As she reached the table with the scrolls, Marina came scurrying down the hallway and yelled, "Evie, hide!"

Chapter 12

ELLIS

Evie looked at Marina with confusion but then figured it would be best if she followed Marina's instructions. Evie ducked down behind a large stack of books and tried to be as quiet as possible. Down the long hallway, Evie could hear someone calling out Marina's name. Marina didn't answer, but it wasn't long before the voice found Marina's location. Evie thought, *How did this person find Marina in this maze of a castle?* She pushed the thought out of her head and continued to listen.

Then, a man came in and started yelling at Marina, which didn't make any sense to Evie, since it sounded like the man was yelling in another language.

Evie then positioned herself in her hiding spot so she could see through a small crack in between the stack she was hiding behind and another stack close by. At first, she was able to see only the back of a large man with curly red hair. The man was so huge that he blocked out most of what Evie could see. He was still yelling in another language when Evie heard Marina calmly say, "Hello, Ellis. Please take a seat and calm down."

The large man, Ellis, although very upset, grumbled a bit and proceeded to sit down. Evie wondered if this man respected Marina or maybe feared her since he complied with her request so quickly. Ellis then sat down in a chair that didn't look like it could support his frame. Once he sat, Evie was able to see the man from the side and noticed he had a big red curly beard that reminded her of her father's. As a matter of fact, even his face seemed to remind Evie of her father. She almost wanted to jump out and hug him, but she pushed this thought out of her head and reminded herself she had to stay focused because he seemed furious.

After he sat down, Evie could see the rest of the room and watched Marina sit in a chair across from him, close to the table with the scrolls on it. Marina then looked intently at Ellis and asked, "What can I do for you?"

Ellis began to talk, but in English this time, with a thick Irish accent. Again, Evie wondered if he was doing this for Marina, because she assumed Marina knew other languages (since most of the books weren't written in English). At first, it was hard for Evie to hear what Ellis was saying because he began talking in a calmer tone. Evie still couldn't hear him clearly, so she quietly inched her way over to the next stack that was closer to Marina and Ellis. Once behind this stack, she positioned herself to where she could see Ellis and Marina. At this angle, she was able to see Ellis even closer and was once again shocked at the resemblance to her father. Then, she heard Ellis say, "So, yeh think yeh found someone better 'an me witch?"

Marina looked at him, smiled, and in a passive tone (as if she had not just been insulted) said, "Ellis, do not be daft. You know as well as I do that greed and power have consumed your heart. Your time has passed."

"What the hell do yeh mean passed." Ellis boomed. "Yeh found me a 'undred years ago, yeh crazy ol' bat, an' then, on'y allowed me to try a few times before yeh gave up on me!"

Evie was baffled. *One hundred years ago, that can't be true. This man cannot be any older than forty,* she thought. Then, Evie remembered Marina's story of how her bloodline lives longer than most. Evie was still having a hard time processing how their life span could be so long, but then realized she needed to not space out and focused her attention back on Ellis and Marina. Marina then said, "Ellis, I did not give up on you. You were just not able to figure out the scrolls. By the time I found you, I convinced myself that there was still purity in you, but you proved that wrong."

Ellis looked at Marina with burning eyes. "What the hell do yeh mean by wrong? Yeh told me that there was a treasure in a vault, an' that I was the on'y one who could help yeh find it."

Marina paused for a moment before calmly saying, "That is exactly the point. I never said it was a treasure. I said there was an item in a vault that could be very important to our family line, and you assumed it was a treasure, allowing your greed to consume you."

Ellis kept his burning gaze. "I don't care what yeh think. I'll be a part of this, an' once yeh find this so-called item, it WILL be mine."

Marina paused again before replying, "Ellis, if we do find what Magnus left for us, you have to realize it does not belong to us. The search was never about a treasure but about connecting us to our true past."

"Yeh said it belongs to the family." Ellis replied with more frustration in his voice, "I'm the on'y one left in this family besides yeh, an' yer time is almost up old woman, so it's mine. I don't care who yeh think yeh found that is better 'an me, damnit, but whoever it is will 'ave to answer to me, the true bloodline of Magnus."

Marina paused for so long, Ellis began to shift uncomfortably in his tiny chair. Evie then realized that Ellis may actually be intimidated by her. Even though he was a large, angry man, Evie knew he had been in this room before and seemed to react to Marina like a child waiting patiently for his teacher's response. Ellis didn't seem to be curious about the room as Evie had been when she first entered, and she also realized that there were several other chairs in the room that Ellis could have sat in that would have been more supportive of his frame, but chose the chair that seemed to be his. Marina then broke the silence and, in a tone a teacher would use, said, "Okay, Ellis. It is apparent to me that you will not be leaving this subject alone, and I think that you might be of some use on my new endeavor."

Marina then looked directly at the stack Evie was hiding behind and stated, "Come out, Evie, I want you to meet someone."

Evie was hesitant at first, but then Ellis's enormous body shifted in the tiny chair, making a cracking noise so he was looking in the exact direction that Marina was looking. Evie slowly gathered up her courage, and with great trepidation stood up and stepped to the side of the large stack so she was in view of both Ellis and Marina. Evie was still looking down to avert their gaze, now intently focused on her. She took a small step forward, still avoiding their stare and slowly raised her head to meet Ellis's fixed gaze burning into her soul. At first, Ellis's anger from before seemed to be the only expression on his face and Evie wanted desperately to look away, but she stood up even taller and matched his intense gaze. For a moment, the pair were like two storm clouds drifting towards each other, and Evie braced herself for the thunder. In this moment, Ellis's angry expression began to soften as she stood staring back into his face with all her might. Ellis then broke into a roaring laugh and bellowed, "This scrawny little thing is yer so-called hero that'll save our family? How ol' are yeh girl?"

"I'm almost seventeen, and I'm not scrawny," Evie shouted while still maintaining her might in confronting this man.

"Oh, geez Marina. She's just a child," Ellis stood up to examine Evie like a dog at a dog show. He then began to pace around Evie as if he were examining a microorganism through a microscope. Evie decided she had enough of this man, defiantly stared back at him, and yelled out, "That's enough you big beast. Now sit back down!"

This made Ellis bellow out in laughter even harder. The bellow was so loud, it sounded like a mountain laughing, and she could feel it cascade through her body. However, he wasn't laughing in a mocking way as he'd done before. It actually reminded Evie of the laugh her dad would let out when she was little and would get frustrated with something. It was a laugh that seemed to ease some of the tension that was previously there. After Ellis's booming laugh, he proceeded to sit down in his tiny chair while still chuckling and looked over at Marina. "Okay, yer right. I'm not the on'y one left in this cursed bloodline." He then turned his head and looked at Evie, almost lovingly now, and shook his head before saying, "I'm Ellis Ó Murchadha, or Murphy. Welcome to the family kid—yer doomed," as he chuckled a bit more.

Marina then gestured her hand over to another chair between herself and Ellis, so Evie sat down. Before anyone started talking again, Marina slowly got up from her chair, grabbed a glass sitting on the table with the scrolls, and brought it over to Evie. "This will help your head girl."

Evie looked down at the glass expecting water. However, what she saw was a green fluid that, at closer look, became iridescent and changed from green to blue to white and back to green again. Evie was hesitant to drink it because she never tried anything green that tasted good to her, so she held her nose and took a big swig. At first, it had a bitter taste but then changed to a sweet taste, almost like drinking rose water. As soon as she decided she liked it, it changed again, tasting like she had just drank sewer water and she spat out what remained in her mouth. This made Ellis bellow again while Marina chuckled a bit and said, "It is a family recipe called Virdis. It is used for healing and will help with the headaches, so drink up."

Evie looked at Marina with disgust but decided it was best not to argue with her nor Ellis, and she plugged her nose once again to chug down the drink as fast as possible. When she was done, Ellis said, "Don't worry kid. Yeh'll get used to it." And he chuckled some more.

As Evie sat there trying to regain her composure after her awful drink, Marina excused herself for a minute and walked behind another stack of books, leaving Ellis and Evie alone. Evie looked nervously around the room trying not to make eye contact with Ellis. Even though he was in a much better mood than before, he still made her uneasy. After nervously looking around the room at no particular thing, Evie could feel Ellis's gaze on her once more, to the point where Evie forced herself to look at him again. When she matched Ellis's gaze, there was a different expression on his face, almost one of pain. Not of physical pain but rather of emotional pain, as if he were longing or searching for something he lost. She sat there and stared back at him for a minute, and even though he was looking directly at her, he seemed to be lost in his own thoughts. Evie then built up the courage to interrupt the silence and asked, "Are we related?"

This question snapped Ellis out of his deep trance; he took a big sigh and shifted again in his chair. "If yer truly Magnus's heir, 'en I guess we are somehow, but I'm not exactly sure how closely related we are kid." He paused and took a deep breath before saying, "However, I 'ave a feelin' we'll figure it out."

Ellis again looked at Evie in silence and, as soon as he opened his mouth to say something, Marina walked back around the stack she had previously disappeared behind with a few books and another scroll in her hands. She gently pushed the two closed scrolls on the table to the side, carefully rolled up the open scroll, and set down the new items on the table. She fumbled through a few pages of a book until she stopped on a page and pointed at something in the center.

"Here it is!" Marina exclaimed, "I believe this might help figure out those maps we could not understand before."

Ellis got up and leaned over Marina's shoulder to examine the page she was pointing at. After looking intently at it for a bit, he motioned at Evie. "Come over 'ere girl an' give this a look."

Evie got up and tried to look at what they were pointing at, but Ellis was so large Evie couldn't see much until he grabbed the book from Marina and handed it to Evie. Evie looked at the page, which reminded her of constellations, but not the types one would see from Earth. Yet, she knew she had seen them somewhere before. She sat there for a minute looking at the page and searching through her memories. Then, all of a sudden, it clicked. She had seen them in the clearing on the walls when she was exploring earlier. She looked at Marina and said, "I've seen these before. They're on a wall in the back somewhere in this clearing that's guarded by dog statues."

Marina and Ellis both looked at each other and then back at Evie. They sat staring at her for a minute when Marina finally asked, "Could you read the map?"

Evie looked at both of them to try and read their faces, but both of their expressions seemed blank. After a brief moment of trying to read their faces and not getting anywhere, she answered, "Kind of, but my head was hurting."

Marina once again looked at Ellis with an "I told you so" expression on her face. Evie waited for Marina to wag her finger at him too, but she didn't. Instead, she turned her gaze back to Evie, waved her hand, and stated, "Well, let us go take a look at them again, shall we?"

Evie couldn't remember what direction the clearing was and looked around the room to gauge her surroundings to find where she had run out from when the boom happened. Luckily, she didn't have to search for long because Ellis and Marina both started walking past Evie, so she turned and followed them.

It seemed to take longer to get to the dog statues than it did the first time, but Evie then remembered she was wandering around for a while before she came across the guarded aisle. As they reached the aisle, Marina and Ellis proceeded to go forward, not even aware, like Evie, that the dogs were watching them. However, the dogs seemed to follow her again, so Evie just assumed that Marina and Ellis were used to it. Evie was about ten steps down the aisle when once again she heard the whispers along the stacks. Evie asked, "Do you guys hear that?"

Both Marina and Ellis, who were a few feet in front of her, turned around, and Marina asked, "What dear?"

Ellis and Marina looked at Evie slightly confused, so Evie decided it was best not to mention the whispers and shook her head. "Nothing, never mind."

As they got closer to the clearing, the whispers got louder and Evie began to feel light-headed but not as light-headed as before. Evie assumed that maybe the disgusting drink was working. Marina and Ellis were both standing in the clearing as Evie reached the end of the aisle. As before, the whispers stopped once she stepped into the clearing, but then something new happened. The clearing began to swirl so rapidly that Evie felt she was on a carnival ride. All the maps and drawings started to not only shift on their own pages, but seemed to switch places with each other from their places on the wall. The clearing became a swirl of symbols, drawings, maps, and colors, making Evie feel sick. Just as the swirling seemed it wouldn't stop and Evie felt that she would pass out again, the spinning room finally came to an abrupt halt, and a small, cloud-like object appeared over the map that was on the table. Evie, still feeling nauseous, focused her attention on the map when a cloud with a man's face began to appear. She could tell the man was saying something, but she couldn't make it out. Evie tried to focus harder, when suddenly, she clearly heard the man say, "I am Callais Baldais."

Then Ellis put his hand on Evie's shoulder, and the cloud disappeared. Ellis, in a concerned voice, asked, "Yeh alright girl?"

"Did you see that?" Evie asked, still feeling very dizzy.

Marina looked at Evie with concern as well and asked, "What Evie? What did you see?"

Evie realized that Ellis and Marina hadn't seen what she had seen and hadn't heard the whispers either. She thought for a moment about not telling them because she didn't want them to worry about her, but then she realized she was here to help them see what they couldn't find. Evie decided that it was safe to tell them. "When I walked into the room, everything was spinning around like the symbols and drawings on the scroll I read earlier, but this time a man appeared in a cloud over the map on the table."

"Do yeh know who this man is?" Ellis asked.

"No," Evie answered and then went on, "but he spoke, and he said his name was Callais Baldais. But that's not all. When I was in here earlier, I saw the map, and it began to swirl like it did just now, and just before I thought I would pass out from watching it, the words Callais and Antillis appeared in the corner."

Marina and Ellis stared at Evie for a bit and then at each other. Marina then asked, "What did you hear in the aisle on the way to this room?"

"I'm not sure, it was just whispers." Evie paused and shook her head. "I couldn't make them out. What does this mean?"

Marina and Ellis stood there for a minute in silence, each of them with looks of deep thought on their faces. Marina turned back to Evie and answered, "I am not sure. I have never seen this before. Maybe you should look at the other scrolls first."

Ellis nodded in agreement and headed back down the aisle, which Evie assumed was to retrieve the scrolls Marina had left on the table up front.

Marina then sat down in an armchair in the corner of the clearing, which Evie hadn't even noticed before. Once Marina was seated, a far-off look came across her face and she seemed to become lost in her thoughts. Evie decided to let her think and not ask any questions until Ellis came back. So, she scanned the room for a place to sit but noticed the symbols and drawings were moving, though not as rapidly as before. Evie thought they were trying to organize themselves since she began to notice some patterns in the swirls. Looking at the stuff on the walls began to make Evie feel light-headed again, so she scanned the room for somewhere to sit again and found a small stool on the far side of the room right under a drawing of a massive ship with sails that also seemed to be moving. Again, the ship looked familiar, but she couldn't remember why, so she pushed the thought aside. Evie patiently sat there while Marina was deep in thought when Ellis entered the room with the scrolls and some more of the green slop juice, Virdis, which made Evie cringe a bit. Ellis placed the scrolls down on the map table and walked over to Evie with the drink. "Sorry kid, but yeh need yer energy to keep this up."

Evie took the drink, looked at it with disgust, and plugged her nose again to drink it. As she took a big gulp expecting the worst, to her surprise, Ellis was right, it wasn't as bad this time—still gross, but not as bad as the first time. Evie then turned to look at Marina, but she looked different: she no longer looked like she was in deep thought, rather in a trance that reminded Evie of zombies in horror movies she hated so much. Marina's eyes were rolled back into her head so Evie could only see the white parts of her eyes, and her head was titled back with her mouth open. Her body was ridged and seemed to be tremoring. Evie thought Marina was having a stroke. As soon as Evie jumped off her stool to go running over to Marina, Ellis grabbed her arm and shook his head in a manner that indicated this was supposed to be happening. Evie gave Ellis a desperate pleading look and was ready to say that they need to help Marina when he just shook his head. "She's in the dream world now," Ellis reassuringly stated, then nodded at Marina before adding, "We 'ave to wait."

Evie gave Ellis a frantic look once more, but he gave her another reassuring nod and began to maneuver his huge frame to sit on the floor.

Evie stood there for a minute, looking at Marina and then back at Ellis, wanting to protest again, but she shrugged her shoulders, decided Ellis was right, followed suit, and sat down next to him. After a brief moment of staring at Marina again, Evie decided she couldn't look anymore and turned her back towards Marina, now facing Ellis. When she looked at this big man on the floor, she couldn't help but remember her father sitting on the floor next to her, showing her how to tie her shoes. Her father was a big man too, though not as big as Ellis. She remembered it was ridiculous seeing such a huge man sit on the floor helping her tie her shoes, just as ridiculous as Ellis looked now trying to cross his legs to find a comfortable sitting position. This image and memory made Evie giggle when Ellis turned and glared at her. "What the hell's so funny girl?"

Evie stifled her giggle a bit and shook her head like it was nothing, while Ellis scoffed and continued to position his legs one over the other. His continued struggle made Evie giggle again and Ellis shot her a look of warning. He finally found himself in a comfortable position, which still looked ridiculous to Evie. Once settled into his spot, Ellis turned to Evie and asked, "Who are yer parents?"

Evie realized she hadn't talked about her parents much and felt a sadness wash over her again. Ellis noticed the look on Evie's face, gave her a sorrowful look, and shook his head saying, "I'm sorry. I didn't mean to bring up anythin' painful. I was just wonderin' why yeh were 'ere an' not with yer parents."

Evie decided that if she was going to be on this journey with this old woman and giant man, that it might be good for her to tell them her story. She looked up at Ellis, cleared the frog in her throat, and told Ellis who her parents were, how they died, her time in foster and residential homes, and about

David and Ruby. Ellis listened intently to Evie and paused for a long while after she told her story. Just as Ellis began to open his mouth to say something, Marina came out of her trance and stated, "I think we can start now."

Evie felt relieved that Ellis was right and Marina was okay. As Evie watched Marina get up from her chair and slowly move to the table in the center of the clearing, Evie analyzed her slow movements and wondered how old Marina might be. Marina told Evie she had found Ellis a hundred years ago and she thought, *If they do really live long lives, Marina must be very, very old.* Evie got distracted from her thoughts as Ellis attempted to get up from his cross-legged position. He wasn't graceful and grunted the whole time as he brought himself up to his full-towering stance. Evie again giggled, followed suit, and stood up—with much more ease and grace than Ellis.

Evie walked up to the table and started to look down at the map, which was partially covered by the scrolls Ellis had just laid down. Although the map was still moving, it seemed to Evie to be organizing itself and establishing a pattern like the rest of the stuff in the room. Ellis noticed that Evie was looking at the map, so he cleared the books to the edges of the table so the map was uncovered and gently moved Evie over so she was positioned looking down at the map. He then asked, "Where d'yeh see the words?"

Evie pointed to the top right corner, where she saw the words appear before, but they weren't there this time. Marina shook her head and asked, "Do you see them now?"

Evie looked a little harder. "No, I don't, but the map keeps moving like it's trying to be right."

"What d'yeh mean, 'it's tryin' to be right'?" Ellis asked, sounding confused.

Evie looked again and began pointing at the map to show Ellis and Marina what she could see. "Well, everything keeps changing places like it doesn't belong where it's at and trying to find the place on the map where it belongs."

"Is it movin' now?" Ellis asked, sounding even more confused.

Evie looked up at him and she could see he was trying his hardest to see the map moving. The intense look on his face mixed in with confusion made Evie chuckle a bit inside. She then switched her focus back to the map and started pointing out what Ellis was so desperately trying to see.

"You see this symbol here?" she asked the both of them while pointing at a symbol on the map. "It keeps moving from this position, back to this position, but it's like it can't decide where it belongs. And this drawing right here," as Evie pointed to another area on the map, "the drawing keeps shifting from holding what looks like a sword at his side to it being raised above his head, but it wasn't there before, it was over here," she then pointed to the far side of the map.

Evie then looked up at Marina and Ellis to gauge their responses and both looked even more astonished than they had before. Marina then rubbed her head, as if she felt weary, before saying, "Evie, we do not see the drawing you are talking about."

Evie looked at them with questioning eyes, pointed back at the map, and asked, "You don't see this guy?"

As soon as she finished her sentence, the map began to swirl rapidly again and Evie was unable to see clearly what she was pointing at anymore. She once again tried to refocus her attention to make the map steady, but the map began to swirl even more. Evie was feeling light-headed again and this time her heart began to pound so hard in her chest she thought it would burst out. Evie looked back up from the map hoping she would regain her focus, but the room itself was spinning out of control. Evie felt an unearthly twist in her body, like her spirit was being ripped from her, had flown away, and then re-entered in scattered pieces before she finally felt herself whole once more. Evie, not knowing where to look or what to do, tilted her head down so she wouldn't have to see anything spinning. Right before her gaze reached the floor, she saw the map stop and, in the corner, once again, was not only the names *Callias and Antillis*, but a small cloud began to appear with the same man's face from before. As Evie tried to focus, she heard the man say once again, "I am Callais Baldais. I have been looking for you for a long time."

The next thing Evie remembered was hitting the ground and being picked up in Ellis's huge arms before she passed out.

Chapter 13

THE SCROLLS

◆•————————●————————•◆

Evie woke up to find herself in the same room she had been in before. Once again, she could faintly smell biscuits and tea coming from downstairs. Evie assumed it was morning the next day and began to rise from her bed. As she sat up, her head was throbbing and she remembered that she had hit it the day before. She rubbed her head for bit before she slowly got out of bed and went to the window to look out. The landscape was the same as it was before, with the dew on the ground and window panes. This time, she happened to notice the small flower bed with the color-changing flowers beneath her window and admired the flowers for a few minutes. She took another bath, got dressed, and headed back downstairs into the kitchen, where Marina and Ellis were both already sitting at the table eating their meals. Evie sat down in the open chair closest to the woodburning stove when Ellis got up and brought her a plate of biscuits and the green Virdis drink again. Evie took a bite of her biscuit in silence and drank the green drink with much more ease; she didn't even gag afterwards this time. After a few more bites and the Virdis was gone, Marina began to talk. "I feel that, before we get started today, I should explain to you how I found you."

"Yes," Evie eagerly replied before stating, "I remember you told me you found me through your dreams and mine, but how?"

Marina then went on to explain that one of the scrolls she had found (that Evie hadn't looked at yet) had some symbols, words, and drawings on it that Marina couldn't decipher at first. It took her a while to figure out because she also had dizzy spells while focusing on it. She then told Evie she happened to come across an old family cookbook that had a drink made from a rare flower that would help with what her family had called "dream faints." Marina continued to explain, "I found the flowers in the garden and the book also provided information that Magnus, my father, had brought this flower with him from a planet in a galaxy called Devas—the galaxy where Magnus claimed he was from. The book also described in great detail how to plant a garden so that it would not only maximize the growth of the plants but so the plants could grow year-round."

Marina took a moment to drink some Virdis herself and then went on, "As a child, I always thought it was unusual that the garden was always in bloom. However, when I read the book, I discovered that Magnus had placed a spell of some kind over the castle grounds that acted as a mini biodome, allowing the garden to grow continuously."

She continued to explain that the book also contained spells and recipes for healing. Marina then told Evie, "The flower itself was special to people Magnus had called keepers, and used by keepers to restore their powers and energy. Once I was able to figure out how to use the rare flower, I started making a healing concoction called Virdis, which helped with controlling dizziness when reading the scrolls."

Marina then continued to describe that she couldn't decipher the whole scroll that told of how to enter the dream state. However, what she did understand was that there was a way to connect with others in this world, as well as with those on other worlds, through the dream state. Marina then went on, "Over time, I was able to figure out how to go into a trance, while not asleep, and find those like myself…those in Magnus's bloodline. Yet, I still could not decipher how to find others located on other worlds, just those here on Earth."

Marina told them she figured this was because she wasn't true of heart, and that was the main reason why she could only find those in Magnus's bloodline on Earth but not on other worlds. Marina then explained, "I discovered there were many people on Earth from Magnus's bloodline," she paused and then added, "but the people I found, like Ellis, could not go any further than myself in understanding the scrolls and drawings."

Marina took a long pause as Ellis shifted in his seat before she continued, "I had almost given up, until I started dreaming of you, Evie, and I tried for years to reach out to you. However, it did not work until recently."

Marina then added that the previous day, when Evie had mentioned that she was seeing and hearing things after looking at the maps and scrolls, she once again went into a trance, hoping she could reach beyond this world. However, she wasn't able to do so. At the end of the story, Marina looked intently at Evie before saying, "I think you reached someone not on this world, Evie. I could not find anyone on Earth named Callais, or why he would be looking for you."

Evie and Ellis both sat there for a while, processing everything Marina had just told them. Ellis then chimed in, "As much as I hate to say this, I 'ave never 'eard of this man either, an' I 'ave been searchin' fer years, too."

Evie, still processing all of this information, shook her head and finally asked, "Well, how do I enter this dream state you are talking about to find this Callais?"

"I think before we go back into the guarded room, today we will have you look at the scrolls," Marina gently responded.

Both Evie and Ellis nodded in agreement and then helped Marina clean up a bit before they headed back down the long hallway to the giant tower room.

As they walked towards the hallway, Evie felt as if this wasn't the same direction she went before, and once again, everything seemed out of place. It was like the whole castle kept switching positions, like the maps and the drawings had done. She ignored this idea, thinking it would be crazy that a castle could move around, and picked up her pace to follow Ellis and Marina. They all eventually got to the long hallway, which also seemed longer to Evie than before, and finally reached the door to what Evie decided to call "the stacks," like they do at libraries.

Once in the room, the glowing orb seemed dull at first but began spinning faster and brightened the room. Evie thought about asking what the orb was but chose to focus on the weird thing they were already doing. Ellis proceeded to walk back in the direction of the guarded aisle while Marina pulled up a few chairs around the center table. After a few moments, Ellis was back with the three scrolls and books. He then stated, "I think it might be best to look at the scrolls out 'ere an' not in the back room, to help Evie focus on one thin' at a time."

Both Evie and Marina nodded in agreement as Ellis sat in the remaining chair. Evie thought, *This chair is much more suited to Ellis's large stature, but he still makes the normal-sized chair look tiny under his massive body.* Marina then began to carefully unroll the first scroll and proceeded to do the same with the other two. The table wasn't large enough for all three scrolls to be seen, so Marina gently spread them out so a portion of each scroll was showing. Once again, the scrolls seemed to be in gibberish, but they began to swirl again, this time much more slowly than before. Marina then said, "Just take your time. There is no need to rush. We have been doing this for hundreds of years, so find your own pace."

Evie looked down at the scrolls and started to focus really hard. She then decided to try not to look at them too hard and wait for them to finish finding their positions. She figured that maybe they were moving because they were really trying to organize themselves. Evie sat and watched for a while as the scrolls continued to swirl, symbols switched places with other symbols, drawings would appear and then disappear, only to show up in another spot. Some of the words that seemed foreign at first started to become clearer, and Evie was able to actually read most of them. At times, it almost seemed that what was on one scroll would jump the page and appear on another scroll. At one point, one of the scrolls even seemed to flash with a bright light in the center of it. After a while longer of watching the scrolls move around, they finally came to a complete stop, so Evie switched her attention from a curious gaze back to a deep focus on the scrolls.

As she looked at the scrolls, even though there were parts that were crystal clear, there were still parts that Evie couldn't understand, so she turned her attention to what she could actually comprehend. In the middle scroll, on the bottom left side, Evie noticed words that looked like English to her. So, she moved the scroll that was covering the rest of the blocked scroll and began to read out loud.

"Only in my dreams can I find the love I once lost. She is patiently waiting for me as she softly calls my name. I cannot find where she is in the mist of the dream, but I need only to follow my heart. Where my heart is, I do not know. Where my heart can be found can only be found in my soul. My soul aches for my love so far away, as she calls out…I am Etidorhpa, come find me."

As soon as Evie stopped reading, a light shone on the center of the scroll around a drawing of a large dog. She stared at the dog for a minute and then looked back up at Ellis and Marina. Both were looking at Evie as though they had seen a ghost, and before Evie could ask anything, Marina said, "That is the first time I have seen or heard that passage. I need to think about this."

Marina grabbed a book that was on the table and made her way to another part of the room, pacing while reading it. Evie looked back at Ellis and he seemed to still be in shock. He then said, "I don't know kid, this is also all new to me. By the way, how yeh feelin'?"

Evie realized that her head didn't hurt and she felt fine, which was a new experience for her since every time she looked at the scrolls, she felt sick and dizzy. She told Ellis she felt fine and decided to return her focus back to the scrolls, which now seemed to be moving again. Just as Evie decided to try and figure out the scrolls one more time, Ellis yelled out in excitement, "Who'd Magnus love the most?"

Ellis's yell startled Marina from her reading and Evie from looking at the scrolls. Evie looked at Marina and could tell she was processing what Ellis had just boomed. After a brief pause, Marina stated, "I am not sure. He had so many wives and children that I could not say whom he loved the most. From what I can remember of my father, he was very distant and did not seem to show much interest in his family and seemed even disappointed in them."

Evie, Marina, and Ellis all sat there in silence. Evie could tell that Marina and Ellis were both deep in thought trying to remember if Magnus ever loved anybody. Both were now pacing the room back and forth. Then, it hit Evie: the scroll lit up a dog after she read the passage, and there were also dogs that guarded the aisle to the room with all the maps and drawings. Before Evie even knew what she was thinking, she blurted out, "Did Magnus have a dog?"

Both Ellis and Marina stopped dead in their tracks from pacing the room and stared at each other. Marina then disappeared behind some stacks and, within a few seconds, she came scurrying out from behind another set of stacks holding an old piece of paper. She excitedly made her way back over to the table with Ellis at her heels, following like a giddy little schoolboy. Marina put the paper down and Evie saw it was an old drawing of a giant old man and his giant dog. Marina then began to explain, "My father never talked much, but I remember when I was little, he would always be in his room studying with his dog. I cannot remember her name. As a matter of fact, I do not think he even told me her name. I remember one day she was no longer with him, and he would tell me how sad he was because he had to leave her behind. I would ask him why he left her, and he would become sadder and only say, '*Sometimes we all have to make sacrifices for what needs to be done.*'"

Ellis then chimed in. "Well, obviously this must be 'bout his dog. Is there anythin' else in these godforsaken books that would tell us 'bout his dog?"

Marina sat there for a while then shook her head before answering, "I do not think there is anything but this drawing," she paused and then added, "I think it is best we call it a day, think about the information we learned today, and start with new eyes tomorrow."

Ellis reluctantly agreed and Evie could see that stubborn little boy he must've been when Marina first found him. Ellis then grunted a bit and headed out of the room. Evie began to follow Ellis when she heard Marina say, "You did good today, love. Remember to sleep well."

Evie gave Marina a small smile and then made her way back to the kitchen where she grabbed an apple and some cheese on the counter before she went up to her room. She noticed a big jar of green fluid on the counter and willingly went over and poured herself a glass of the Virdis and drank it with no problem or aftertaste at all this time. When Evie got to her bedroom, she pulled open the curtains and once again looked at the flower garden below her until it became too dark to see anything. She then made a phone call to David and Ruby but only got their voicemail, so she made her way over to the bed, changed into her pajamas, and crawled into bed, way more exhausted than she thought she was. As she closed her eyes and started to drift away, she felt herself begin to fall into a dream.

Chapter 14
THE LARGE WOMAN

❖•————————●————————•❖

The dream started the usual way with bright flickering lights and thick swirling fog. As the fog finally lifted, Evie found herself in one of the places she visited often in her good dreams, and everything was familiar to her (at one point, she even noted to herself that this was the first time she had dreamt since meeting Marina). As she wandered about her dream, she noticed she was in a small town she had been to a few times and began to navigate through this town like she had been living there her whole life. She was doing the usual things she did in this dream when she heard a sound coming from a cottage she hadn't seen before. So, she moved closer to the cottage, and soon, she heard the sound clearly—it was a woman singing. Evie was curious, so she walked up to the door and knocked. The singing instantly stopped. Evie felt a little nervous and was going to walk away when she heard a woman holler out, "Enter, dear."

Evie thought this was weird, almost as if the woman were expecting her. She shrugged her shoulders, shook off her nerves, and walked into the room where a heavy-set woman was bustling around a tiny kitchen that she took up half of. Like she had done with Ellis, Evie giggled at the sight of a large woman in such a tiny space. The woman kept going about her business for a while then finally turned to Evie and motioned to a nearby chair. "Sit dear, it will only be a moment."

Evie complied and sat in the chair. Although she felt nervous before, something about this woman made her feel comfortable and safe. She watched as the woman scurried about some more, gathering items from random shelves, and mumbling to herself. The woman paused for a moment and examined a shelf before saying, "Oh, there you are, trying to hide from me."

The woman grabbed one last item before she plopped her large body in the chair across from Evie. The woman's face was as round as her behind, with big rosy cheeks that rested into large jowls upon her neck. She also had a huge toothy smile and deep sparkling brown eyes. The large woman then proceeded to drop all the items she had in her pudgy arms on the table as she began to pick through them, mumbling under her jowls, "Let me see, let me see. What is it that we need," as she continued to pick through the pile on the table.

As the woman continued to mumble to herself, Evie was looking at the items she was picking through. Evie didn't even know what some of them were, while others seemed rather odd. One item was a large leg bone or arm bone—Evie wasn't sure. Another was an old watch that was cracked, but Evie could see a shimmering purplish glow emit from it. The item Evie thought was the oddest was a tennis ball. Normally, a tennis ball wouldn't throw Evie off, but this town was one you might find in an old fairy tale with straw roofs and cobblestone roads, so a modern-day tennis ball seemed out of place.

As the woman continued her search, Evie's gaze turned from the table to the surrounding room. She saw many more odd knickknacks as well as some weird plants in pots. There were a few pictures of ships on the wall that Evie thought looked familiar and a stack of old books in the corner. As Evie began to look harder at what the books were, the woman shouted out, "Here it is, love!"

Evie turned her attention back to the woman and the table. The woman almost seemed to be wagging her butt she was so happy. Evie instantly felt cheerful as well, since the woman's excitement was so contagious. Evie thought the woman was going to pull out something really amazing when the woman dropped an old shoe on the table and looked up at Evie with that huge jowly, toothy smile, beaming with pride. Evie gave a confused look at the woman before asking, "What's this?"

The woman looked down at the shoe and then back at Evie before answering, "This is what you are looking for; not here, but there."

Evie looked at the excited woman, who could barely even contain herself now. Evie was still confused and stated, "I don't understand. Why am I looking for this?"

The woman looked at Evie slightly disappointed for a minute and then jumped up quickly saying, "Oh my, I almost forgot."

She maneuvered her large body once again to the back of the kitchen and grabbed something from the stack of books in the corner. She turned back around (almost knocking over her chair), plopped back in her seat, and dropped the book next to the shoe, making a loud thud. Evie glanced at the book title, but it was all jumbled and it didn't make sense—just like everything else so far. Evie again gave an inquisitive, confused look at the overly happy woman and was about to ask her why she needed these things. The woman seemed to sense Evie's thoughts and said, "Things are not always what they seem. What was forwards is backwards. What is complicated is simple, and where you think it is, it is not."

Evie, feeling very flustered and confused, began to ask this woman again what she meant. Then suddenly, a loud knocking sound echoed in the room that seemed to come from outside of Evie's head. The noise began to wake Evie from her dream, but before she left the dream completely, she could hear the large woman say, "See you soon, Evie."

Another loud knocking noise vibrated around her again and woke Evie completely out of her dream. She sat up, still muddled and flustered from her dream, and realized the sound was coming from someone knocking on her bedroom door. She then hollered she was coming and made her way to the door to see Ellis in his pajamas, trying to catch his breath. Evie was about ready to laugh at the sight of Ellis in his pajamas as Ellis enthusiastically said, "I 'ad a dream, did yeh?"

Evie saw how excited Ellis was and figured he, too, must not have dreamt in a long time. Evie calmed Ellis down a bit and told him to go to the kitchen, where they could talk. She then grabbed the robe hanging on the door and followed Ellis.

Once in the kitchen, Ellis began to explain his dream. He told her he was on a ship that had been at sea for a really long time. He went on to say that every time he thought he would get off this ship, something would happen that would force him back to sea again. He then explained, "What was weird was that I wasn't me-self in this dream." Ellis then rubbed his head as if he was overwhelmed before he went on, "Methinks I was an ancient king an' from the past, an' the weirdest part was, I was given a shoe by some large woman right before I woke up."

Evie thought about this for a while, trying to recall her own strange dream. She knew that the large woman in her dream had also given her a shoe and a book that was gibberish, but Evie didn't know what any of it meant. Evie gave Ellis an exasperated look before saying, "I think Marina was right. We need to sit on this tonight and look at everything tomorrow with a fresh pair of eyes."

Ellis then mumbled and grunted under his breath like a little boy who was told he couldn't keep the frog in his pocket, nodded at Evie, and stomped back to his room. Evie sat in silence a little longer, trying to think of the meanings behind the dreams and began to feel exhausted once again, so she also made her way back to her room, hoping tomorrow would bring more answers.

Chapter 15
THE COBBLER

◆•———————●———————•◆

The next morning started just like all the other mornings. After Evie finished getting ready in her room, she looked out the window for a while and then made her way to the kitchen. Ellis and Marina were already there, but instead of eating in silence like before, Ellis was bouncing around the room, narrating his dream with gusto to Marina, who was sitting in her chair looking at Ellis like she must have when he was a child. Evie sat down in her chair, and Ellis acknowledged her but continued his story. After he was finished, he sat down next to Evie panting because he was out of breath from telling his elaborate dream. Ellis then blurted out, "Evie 'ad a dream, too!"

Marina, still chuckling from Ellis's animated tale, turned her gaze towards Evie and asked, "Do you care to share your dream?"

Evie went on to tell Marina her dream as well. After she finished telling about her own dream, Ellis seemed excited because of the similarities with the shoe and the large woman, while Marina sat there quietly. Evie assumed Marina was trying to find the connections as well. Marina sat there for a bit longer, then stood up and waved her hands. "Well, no use dillydallying around the kitchen. Let us go see if we can make sense of all this."

The three of them got up and made the long trek around the castle, down the long hallway, to the orb-lit stacks. Once in the room, Marina looked at Evie and said, "I think before we get started, you should wander around the room a bit and see if anything triggers your thoughts on the dream you had."

Evie was a bit reluctant to follow Marina's instructions because she thought they would be going over the scrolls again, but she figured Marina might be right and took off in the direction she thought the guarded aisle was.

Evie wasn't even sure if she was headed in the right direction because she still felt that things shifted in the castle, but once again, she pushed that silly notion out of her head and continued her hunt. Just when Evie thought she was lost, she found the guard dogs in front of the long aisle again. Evie looked up at the dogs' gaze before she headed down the aisle when she thought she saw one of the dogs move its head up and back down, like it was giving her directions with his head. She thought it was silly to believe that a statue could move and continued down the aisle. As she entered the aisle, the whispers became louder than they had been before, and this time there seemed to be a multitude of whispers at once. Evie started to become overwhelmed by the whispers, when suddenly the whispers stopped and she heard clear as day the voice of the large woman from her dream say, "Go back."

Evie froze for a minute and wiggled her finger in her ear, not believing what she just heard. She then heard the woman's voice again, even louder this time, telling her to go back. Evie quickly bolted back down the way she came and found herself standing in front of the guard dogs again. She was confused. She didn't understand where the voice was coming from and looked around her but didn't see anybody, so she decided to head back down the aisle. Just as she was heading back down the aisle, she saw for sure this time one of the guard dogs nod his head again, as if giving directions. Evie shook her head, took a giant step back to where she had both dogs in her view, and just as she stood there thinking to herself that it was absolutely ridiculous that a statue could move, both dogs bowed their heads and raised their paws, pointing to the aisle directly behind her. Evie froze as she tried to process the fact that two statues had just moved. She shouldn't have been surprised. After all, everything else had been weird up to that point, why not pointing dog statues. So, she shrugged her shoulders and turned to walk in the direction they had pointed out.

As Evie began to walk down this new aisle, she anticipated that she would begin to hear whispers again, but this new aisle remained silent. Evie also had no strange feeling like she did before, so she proceeded to look at the titles of the books like she would in a normal library. She realized the aisle was filled with books about many different mythologies and lost civilizations. There were books on mythology—Roman, Chinese, Mayan, Egyptian, and so on. As she came to a section that seemed to be dedicated to Greek mythology, she noticed a book hanging out of the shelves slightly and grabbed it. It was a book about a cobbler. Evie had no idea what a cobbler was but opened the book anyway to find out a cobbler was a shoemaker. She thought it was odd there was a book about a cobbler among all the books of mythology and lost civilizations when, all of a sudden, Evie felt a rush of excitement, took the book, and ran back to find Marina and Ellis.

After running around the stacks in circles trying to find her way back, she eventually found Marina and Ellis sitting by the table where the scrolls were, quietly talking. Evie ran up to them out of breath. "I think...I may have...found something," she said through gasps.

Both Marina and Ellis looked up at her as she showed them the book. Just as they both looked like they might laugh, Evie excitedly stated, "It's about shoes!"

Ellis stopped and realized this might be something worth investigating, while Marina still looked a little wary of what Evie thought she found. Evie ignored Marina's response, placed the book on top of the table, and opened it. The book itself wasn't much, but once they started flipping through the pages, they noticed that there was writing in the margins and certain words or sections had been underlined. Marina bent down to get a closer look and gasped. "This is Magnus's handwriting. I recognize it from when I was younger!"

Everyone was excited, thinking that there would be something huge that Magnus would reveal somehow, but as they kept looking, it was just more notes he had written about making shoes, and everything underlined was also about making shoes. When they came to the end of the book, all of them felt a little disappointed, thinking they would get some answers, but to no avail. They just felt more lost and confused. Ellis then went to shut the book, but his big bumbling hands knocked it to the floor. Evie bent down to grab it and, as she turned it over to close it, the words on the margins began to move. Evie paused and looked at it. The words stopped moving, but still, the words seemed jumbled and didn't make any sense. Then Evie realized that the jumbled words were exactly the same as the jumbled words on the book the large woman gave her in the dream. Evie thought for a second and then shouted out, "Grab me a pen and paper."

Marina rushed to a nearby file cabinet–looking thing and grabbed a piece of paper and pen. Evie wrote down the words that came out looking like a jumble still, reading,

sremoh diali dna yessydo

All three stood there looking at the words, trying to figure it out. Evie then jumped up and, without a word, ran back towards where she had gotten the cobbler book. Marina and Ellis stood there still looking at the jumbled words, when soon, Evie came back carrying two large books. She dropped the books down, titles faced up: Homer's *Iliad* and *Odyssey*. Evie then stated, "It was just written backwards. It wasn't even encrypted or confusing like all the other stuff so far."

Evie beamed with joy because this seemed to be the first clue that had come to light in their long three-day hunt so far. Evie then said, "Ellis, I think in your dream you were Odysseus, the ancient King of Ithaca, and your dream was leading us to find this book."

Just as Evie was reveling in her excitement, Marina said, "There is so much in these pieces, where do we even start?"

Evie's excitement went down. Ellis was thumbing through one of the books when he stated, "There's tons o' writin' on each page, just like the cobbler book, but this is even more detailed. This may take a while."

Evie's excitement completely deflated as she fell into the closest chair. She sat there for a while as she watched Marina and Ellis look over the books some more, trying to find anything that stood out. Evie was going to look at the books again (hoping that maybe she would get lucky) when she remembered the passage from the scroll from the day before. She thought about it for a minute, and then once again, it clicked. She immediately grabbed the same piece of paper and pen and wrote down,

Etidorhpa…Aphrodite

"That's it!" she yelled out loud, "It has to be something about Aphrodite!"

Both Marina and Ellis looked at her slightly relieved, but then Marina said, "There is so much about Aphrodite, not just in the Homer pieces but in all of Greek mythology. Where do we even begin to look?"

They all began to search again, but no one could come up with anything else. It was getting late, so they decided to call it a day.

* * *

As they all went off in their separate directions, Evie noticed it was still light outside and decided to go out the kitchen door to explore the grounds a bit and clear her head. Once outside, she saw the flowers she had been looking at from out her window and decided to head in that direction. She admired the flowers for a bit and then decided to explore the rest of the garden and headed in the direction of the forest where she, David, Ruby, and Steven had first entered. She looked wistfully at the path where they had arrived and thought about watching David, Ruby, and Steven leave. She then felt a pang of sadness and reminded herself that when she got back, she would call them. Evie had her cell phone so she could stay in contact with them, but the last few days, when she would call, she only got their voicemail. Evie thought, *I hope they're okay*, before she continued to walk through the garden.

Evie still didn't recognize many of the plants and flowers and thought about Marina's story about Magnus bringing rare flowers from a distant galaxy. Before she could think about the crazy idea of a distant galaxy, she came across a small trail of roses leading up the far side of the hill around the edges of the garden. They smelled so wonderful she decided to follow the trail for a while. At one point, she sat down among the roses to take in their sweet smell and enjoy the view. After sitting for a while, she remembered something she read once, which said that one of Aphrodite's symbols was a rose. She thought this was just a coincidence and continued to sit and enjoy the landscape around her. As she looked back up the far side of the hill, she saw something small and white sticking up out of the trail of roses. Evie got up and started making her way to this new curiosity.

Once she reached the object, she noticed it was a small statue of a dove. Again, Evie didn't think much of it—many people have statues in their gardens. But again, Evie remembered that another symbol for Aphrodite was a dove. This piqued her interest even more, and Evie began searching the trail for more things when, all of a sudden, the dove statue moved and took to the air. Evie was just as frozen as she was when the dog statues moved and watched the white marble bird circle above her. She then realized the bird was hovering directly above her, so Evie started to walk when the bird seemed to follow her. Evie and the bird went back and forth for a bit, each following one another when Evie realized the bird wanted her to follow it somewhere.

Evie then allowed the bird to lead her further along the trail of roses, which moved up the hill and back down over the other side to the edge of an older part of the forest. She stopped and looked back towards Marina's castle, which she could still see the top of, and she said to herself, *As long as I can see the castle, it can't hurt to follow the bird.* The dove hovered over the edge of the forest line, waiting for Evie to catch up.

Once Evie reached the edge of the forest, the dove swooped down from high into the forest, all the while chirping at Evie, as if inviting her to follow again. Evie once again stopped, looked back, and could still see the tops of Marina's castle, so she decided to venture in a bit through brush, bramble, and trees that were as ancient as the world. She looked back once more to make sure she could see the castle and followed the bird a bit farther into the trees. Just as Evie decided she had gone far enough, the bird swooped by her head and flew to the left of her, chirping at her again, but the gleeful twittering sound was consumed by the intervening trees. Evie followed the bird with her eyes (since the bird's chirps were hard to follow), and to her amazement, she saw a small cottage among the crooked branches of the trees that the bird had landed on. As Evie approached the cottage, she felt like she had seen it before but couldn't place her finger on where. It reminded her of the fairy tale with Hansel and Gretel. She chuckled to herself a bit thinking it was a funny idea that this was the house of a witch who would eat her.

As she approached the cottage, she realized instantly that this was the same cottage she saw in her dream where she met the large jowl-faced woman. Evie stood for a moment, bewildered that this could be the same cottage and, just before she reached for the doorknob to explore further, she heard a rustling in the bushes right next to her. The noise surprised Evie so much, she jumped back and was ready to run back to the castle. However, before she could turn and run, she saw a small nose poke through the bush, followed by a long furry snout. Evie realized the dog was more scared than she was, so she bent down and gently cooed to the dog so it would know she wasn't a threat. The little dog played peekaboo with Evie for a bit but then eventually came out of the bush, wagging its tail, and approached Evie with curiosity. Evie and the dog played for a while, when Evie realized it was now getting dark. She thought about going into the cottage but then decided it would be best to investigate it further tomorrow.

Evie started to head back to the castle with the dog in tow. She figured the dog was a stray, so she decided it could spend the night and get some food while she figured out what to do. Evie and the new companion found their way back to Marina's, stopped in the kitchen for a quick snack, and made it back up to Evie's room. Evie called David and Ruby again but got their voicemail, so she left another message and decided that she would ask Marina tomorrow if she knew how to get in contact with them. As Evie laid down, her new furry companion jumped next to her. Evie realized it was a female dog as she made a small circle and snuggled up to Evie's chest. She slowly drifted away to sleep thinking how wonderful it was to have her new friend.

Chapter 16
BELLA

Evie, once again, found herself dreaming in the same little town she was in the previous night. She began searching for the little cottage and the large woman, hoping that there would be other clues or answers, but she couldn't find either and continued to wander her usual path. She soon found herself in front of a large body of water and couldn't remember if she had ever seen this body of water before in this dream but decided to go explore it anyway. She walked over to the dock at the water's edge and saw there was a large ship sitting in the bay; however, the ship seemed to be shimmering and flickering with vague light and Evie thought it almost matched the water it was sitting on. Evie realized the ship was similar to the drawing she had seen at the large woman's home as well as the one that was hanging down the guarded aisle. Evie shrugged, not knowing why the ship was there, and scanned her surroundings. The dock was fairly empty except for a few men walking around with barrels and ropes, doing fishermen stuff, Evie assumed. When she looked back over the water, she saw a small boat moving towards the dock, leaving the ship. There were two figures in the boat, both wearing hooded cloaks. The two figures finally docked, got off the boat, and started walking towards her. Evie felt as if she should run, but she couldn't bring herself to do so. As the two figures—one large and one small—got closer, the urge to run got more intense, yet Evie's body wasn't moving. Just as she was ready to cave and walk away, the large figure took off his hood and there stood Ellis, who loudly boomed, "Aha, I knew she'd be 'ere!"

The other figure took off her hood and there was Marina. Evie, absolutely stunned, shouted out, "How are you here? Is this real or am I still dreaming?"

Marina then explained that for some reason, she and Ellis both had dreamt of this place, but they had never been to it before. So, when Evie went off to bed, they decided to go in a dream state together to see if they could find this place again and hopefully find Evie. Marina mentioned that it took some time because Evie was covered in a haze when they first entered the dream state, and they found themselves on a strange ship; however, as soon as Evie made her way to the water's edge, they were able to finally see her. Evie couldn't believe this was happening; she always thought that her dreams were more real than others thought they were, but this was unreal even to her. After standing there for a few minutes while Ellis struggled out of his cloak, he asked, "Where to, girl?"

Evie thought for a minute. "I've been here many times, but I never thought much about it, and I can't seem to find the large woman or her house again. So, I'm not sure where to go."

At that point, all three looked around as if trying to see if something would guide them, when Marina suddenly turned to Evie and said, "You are not alone."

Evie looked at Marina confused and then began to scan the surroundings again, worried someone followed her. Then, Marina clarified, "No. You are not alone while you are sleeping."

This shocked Evie and made her realize that there was someone in her room at Marina's while she slept. It scared her so much, Evie jolted up from her sleep, scaring her new friend onto the floor. Moments later, both Ellis and Marina were at Evie's bedroom door as Ellis kicked it open, thinking the same thing Evie did. Evie's furry friend scattered under the bed and began to whimper. Evie got down on the floor and began to gently coo at the scared dog while Ellis searched her room for Marina's mystery person. After searching and flipping everything over, Ellis determined the room was safe and accused Marina of being a crazy old witch. Marina looked at Ellis like she was going to slap him when her face went blank for a second and then lit up with excitement. "It was the dog! I felt the dog in your room!"

Evie and Ellis both let out a sigh of relief. Ellis then turned accusingly towards Marina. "Yeh called us outta the dream state, where we've never been, an' found Evie, fer a damn dog?"

"Yes, but I think this is important," Marina said. "Just as Magnus had his beloved dog. It reminds me of a story he told me."

Marina went on to explain. "Magnus told me when I was younger that where he comes from, everyone with powers has a companion. The companion, or dog, has a more important role to Magnus's bloodline and keepers than what most people think a dog's purpose is."

Marina then explained that Evie's having found this dog and Marina's feeling its presence were signs that shouldn't be ignored. They all sat in silence, lost in their own thoughts. Marina then said her now-famous line, "I need to think on this. We will revisit what this all means tomorrow."

Both Evie and Ellis shrugged as Ellis and Marina walked back down the hall, and Evie and her new friend positioned themselves back in bed. As Evie was beginning to drift off, she looked at the fuzzy little dog, cozied up to her chest, and said, "I'm going to call you Bella."

Evie kissed Bella on the head and fell asleep, this time with no dreams.

Chapter 17
The Cottage

Evie woke the next morning to Bella pushing her nose against her neck and nuzzling her ear. She sat up and rubbed Bella's belly while calling her fuzzy friend her new name, to which Bella seemed to respond by bouncing around the room. Evie watched her for a while and noticed that, although Bella looked black at first, her coat was actually striped brown and black with a few random white spots on her nose and paws. Bella's hair was short and felt like soft wire, and although she was small, most people would consider her a medium-sized dog. Bella reminded her of a Jack Russell terrier she once knew, mixed with something else. Bella was also a little ball of energy, so Evie decided it would be best to take her out before breakfast.

As Evie got downstairs to the kitchen, Ellis was already there, but not Marina. Evie introduced Ellis to Bella and proceeded to let Bella out, when Ellis stated that he could use some fresh air himself. As Bella frolicked around playfully outside the garden's edge, Ellis and Evie just stood there watching her and laughing. Bella would leap up to catch a fly, miss it, and tumble awkwardly back to the ground. After a few minutes of watching the happy dog, Evie turned to Ellis and asked, "How exactly did you find me in the dream last night?"

"It was mostly Marina's doin'," Ellis explained, "but what I do know is that when one enters a dream state, everythin' can be really fuzzy an' hard to navigate, like tryin' to find a way through thick fog."

He then told Evie that he had never been able to navigate the fog very well on his own, but it helps to have another person, so things can become clearer. He then said, "When two or more people are in the dream state together, well, they start to see what the others see."

He rubbed his bearded chin and went on, "I 'ave gone into the dream state a few times on me own, but I was never very successful." He then added, "Last night, when she asked me to join 'er, after a few minutes in the dream state, the fog lifted instantly. That's when we found yeh."

After a long pause, Ellis turned to Evie and said, "I think yer the reason the fog disappeared so quickly, an' why it was so easy fer Marina to find yeh. I've never seen anythin' like it, an' I don't think Marina 'as either."

Evie thought about this for a while and then turned her attention back to playful Bella, who was intent on trying to catch a butterfly this time. Suddenly, Bella froze. Evie noticed Bella was staring in the same direction that the dove had led her the previous evening. In an instant, Bella took off as Ellis and Evie both jumped to action and followed her while yelling her name.

They chased Bella to the edge of the forest, when Bella stopped, turned back around, playfully made a circle, and made a little jump for Ellis and Evie to follow her in. At that same moment, the dove from the night before whizzed past Evie's head, and the dog gleefully followed the dove into the forest. Evie took a step forward to follow when Ellis grabbed her and looked at her with a bit of fear in his eyes. Just as Ellis was about to say something, Bella barked and Evie said, "Don't worry. This is where I found Bella. Maybe she actually belongs to someone here."

Evie took hold of Ellis's grasp on her arm to lead him deeper into the forest. After walking in a bit more, they found themselves in front of the cottage. Evie then explained that this was the same cottage that had appeared in her dream, but she hadn't looked in yet. Ellis scrunched up his nose, which looked hilarious on his big bearded face, looked back at Evie, and said, "Methinks I might know this place."

Evie waited for Ellis to say more, but he didn't, so she proceeded to the front door.

As Evie did the night before, she went to grab the handle, but then thought that someone might be in there, so she decided to knock instead. Just as she was about to lift her hand to knock, a strong wind blew the door open. They stood in the doorway looking in. There wasn't much light, but it was apparent, with all the cobwebs and the scurry of small rodent feet running unseen across the wooden floors, that no one had been here in a long time. After a few more minutes of cautiously looking through the open door, they finally entered the small cottage and began looking around.

Once they were farther inside, Evie went to the right while Ellis went to the left. Evie was investigating a shelf that had several small vials of something in them when she heard a banging noise from the far side of the room. She turned to see Ellis standing there with broken shards of glass at his feet as he looked up at Evie with a guilty grin on his face. Evie laughed and walked over to Ellis to help him pick up the broken pieces. After they cleaned up the mess, Evie stood up and looked back in the direction where she was before she came to Ellis's rescue. At that moment, she saw a drawing of a large man and his large dog next to the small vials. Evie jumped across the room, grabbed the drawing, and unlike the drawing Marina had shown her, there was some faint writing at the bottom. Evie strained her eyes, but the light in the cottage wasn't bright enough for her to see. She made her way back out the front door and found some light leaking down through the cracks of the old trees. As she looked again with the new light, she read out loud, "Magnus and Aphrodite, 1014."

Evie shrieked with excitement as Ellis moved over to where she stood. By the time Ellis reached her, she was jumping up and down yelling, "Aphrodite is the dog, Aphrodite is the dog. That's the love he lost!"

Ellis began to jump up and down with Evie, and the two must have been a sight to see, jumping around like giddy schoolgirls who just found out their crush liked them back. After a few moments of joy, Evie realized, "This cottage must've been Magnus's at some point, and the large woman in my dream was leading me here all along."

Evie then remembered the riddle the large woman told her: "*Things are not always what they seem. What was forwards is backwards. What is complicated is simple, and where you think it is, it is not.*"

Evie felt elated that it wasn't as complicated as she thought it would be, but as soon as she came to this conclusion, she remembered that the only thing she actually knew was the name of Magnus's dog and nothing else. She had also found the place where Magnus himself must have lived, so she thought, *There must be something here!* Evie turned to Ellis and said that they should go back in the cottage when Ellis pointed out that Marina should be up by now and that it might be best to go see her and at least tell her what they found. This disappointed Evie as she sighed, shrugged, hollered at Bella, and then followed Ellis back to the castle.

Once they reached the forest's edge, Evie thought she heard whispers, so she turned her head to look back. She thought she saw something moving in the forest, and as she turned back around to tell Ellis, she saw he was already a hundred yards in front of her, bouncing around the rose trail, frolicking with Bella. Evie took a mental note and told herself she would mention this to both Marina and Ellis once they got back.

Once they reached the house and entered the kitchen, there was still no Marina, so they decided to go search for her in the stacks. They made their way back down the hallway while Evie thought, *Nothing ever seems to be in the same place as it was before*, but Ellis seemed to know his way, so Evie just kept pace with him.

Once they reached the long doorless hallway, Evie started feeling a little light-headed and said to Ellis, "It might be best for us to have some of the green drink before we start."

Ellis looked back at her as they reached the doorway to the stacks, shrugged, and headed back down the long hall to get her the Virdis. Evie and Bella entered the room, but still no Marina in sight. As Evie looked around for her, Bella bounded off towards the guarded aisle. Evie decided to chase after her dog, who was patiently waiting for Evie right in front of the guarded aisle. She looked up at the guard dogs, seeing if they would move, but they didn't so she headed down the aisle with Bella at her heels. Once again, Evie heard whispers coming from the aisle but chose to ignore them since she still couldn't make out what they were saying.

As she reached the clearing, she expected the maps, drawings, or even the room to start spinning as it had done every other time, but nothing spun around as it had before. She made her way to the center table with the map on it and began to examine it. This time, it didn't swirl or move either, but there was something different about the map. In the far left corner, there seemed to be an arrow pointing in a direction off the map. Evie watched it for a minute to see if the arrow would move, but it didn't. She looked up following the direction of the arrow and saw a small glowing object hanging almost out of view behind the drawing of the ship. As she crossed the room, Evie realized the glowing object was a small broach with a sparkling gem in it. She then grabbed it. However, as soon as she touched the broach, a barrage of images started to flood her head and swirl around just as rapidly as everything else had the last few days. Evie tried her hardest to focus, but the harder she focused, the more everything spun around. She decided to sit on the stool she had before, hoping that eventually everything would stop. Bella perched herself right at her feet. As soon as Evie touched Bella's head, all the images stopped, and there stood the man Callais, clear as day. Evie had no idea what to say or how this was happening, so she kept her hand on Bella's head as Callais began to speak. "Hello, Evie. I see that you have found your companion. This will make it easier for us to communicate and for you to figure out how to find me."

Evie sat dumbfounded for a minute and thought to herself, *How could a dog be helpful?* She then remembered Marina saying that dogs were more than just pets to Magnus's bloodline, so Evie continued to touch Bella while Callais continued to talk. "Magnus left a couple sacred relics and texts for you to find on Terran so that you may find me and help the Devas galaxy finally defeat Camulos. Magnus traveled several times after leaving the Devas galaxy to ensure that you would find us, and we could find you and help you. Although I am not sure what relics or texts Magnus left for you or how you can find them, I do know you need to find Aphrodite. She is the key."

Evie thought of the drawing she had found of Magnus and Aphrodite that was done in the year 1014, and thought, *How could Aphrodite still be alive?!* She then thought, *It is the twenty-first century. That means Marina and the others have lived a really, really long time!* She then reminded herself that perhaps the dog also lived longer, since everyone else had longer life spans. Evie pushed this thought aside and once again focused on Callais when he said, "You also need to figure out how to navigate the dream state. This will be the only way to find me once you find what you need on Terran. Be sure to use this broach to unlock how to find Aphrodite."

Just as Evie was about to ask Callais a question, Bella moved from under her hand, making Callais a blur. He then disappeared.

Evie opened her eyes to see that Marina and Ellis were already in the room, looking at her in complete shock. Marina asked her, "How did you go into a dream state all by yourself?"

She looked a Marina and then at the confused Ellis before answering, "When I touched this broach

I found, my mind began to spin, so I sat down and Bella came to me. When I touched Bella's head, everything stopped, and that man Callais appeared before me and spoke."

Marina and Ellis were still in shock as Ellis asked, "What'd 'e say?"

Evie told Marina and Ellis what Callais had told her. Evie also went on to say, "I believe that there might be more answers in the cottage Ellis and I found, and I think that it might be best if we all go explore there today."

Marina looked a little confused when Evie mentioned the cottage. Ellis apologized and explained, "We found a cottage this mornin', an' it's where Evie also found Bella the other day."

Marina shook her head in disbelief. "I have lived here for many years and have explored the forest many times, but I never came across a cottage in the forest."

Evie and Ellis reassured Marina that it was there, and then all three concluded that it would be a good idea to go to the cottage and check it out. They all stopped in the kitchen to pack up some food, as well as some Vidris—just in case—before heading out.

The threesome and Bella headed back to the forest again, this time a little slower so Marina could keep up. Once they reached the edge, Evie thought she heard whispers but still couldn't make them out. She scanned her surroundings to see if she could detect the movement she thought she had seen previously, but nothing moved—just the light breeze flowing in and out of the tree branches.

They finally found themselves in front of the small cottage when Evie turned to see a baffled look in Marina's eyes. Marina shook her head in disbelief again. "I swear, this was never here before. I have been to this part of the forest several times, and this was just an area covered in thick trees."

With a baffled look still on Marina's face, they all proceeded to enter the cottage and explore some more. Once inside, they all went in different directions, not really sure what to look for, and after a while of searching, they decided to take a break and go outside for lunch. They ate quietly, pondering different thoughts and ideas, as Bella periodically came over for a treat then playfully bounced some more.

Once they finished their lunch and were ready to head back in, Bella bolted and then bounced out of sight behind the cottage. Evie hollered for her, but she didn't come. Marina and Ellis continued to go inside as Evie went in search for Bella. She made her way around the back side of the cottage to find Bella hadn't gone far and was playfully rolling in a pile of leaves. As soon as Bella saw Evie, she got up and barked at the back of the cottage. Evie tried to get Bella to follow her back inside, but the dog stayed where she was and barked once again at the back of the cottage. Evie started to get a little frustrated because she wanted to go back in and continue searching when she remembered, *Every time I get stuck in my search, the dogs—whether statues or real—always guide me in the right direction.* Therefore, Evie decided to go investigate what Bella was barking at.

Evie approached Bella, who barked, jumped up, spun around, and pointed her head in the direction of the back of the cottage. Evie followed Bella's gaze and found a small door, which stuck out of the back of the cottage. The door seemed to be an entry not back into the cottage, but to a small room attached to the back side. Evie took a closer look and realized that there was no handle or keyhole to get in. Instead, there was a strange shape where a doorknob and keyhole should be. Evie looked at it even harder and then almost completely lost herself in excitement. She jumped back and told Bella to stay as she ran back into the cottage to get Marina and Ellis.

When she saw Marina and Ellis, she shouted, "I think I found something!" And began shuffling through the bag of supplies they brought for the day.

When Evie found what she was looking for, she shouted once more at Ellis and Marina to follow her. The three of them made their way back behind the cottage, where Bella was patiently waiting for them. Once they got to the door, Evie grabbed the item she had, the broach, and stuck it in the weird shape on the door. It was a perfect fit. Evie took a step back and waited for something to happen, but it didn't.

They all stood there for a few minutes. There was still nothing when Ellis said, "Maybe there's a password o' somethin'?"

They all sat for a minute thinking of what it could be. Evie turned her head to see Bella patiently waiting at the door when Evie got up, went to the door, and said, "Aphrodite."

At that moment, the broach fell farther into the shape on the door, the gem inside lit up, emanating a purplish glow, and started spinning rapidly. After a few seconds, the door made a loud cracking noise and slowly creaked open.

Evie, Marina, and Ellis stood there in shock for a minute when Ellis then gently pushed the door the rest of the way open to reveal a small room covered in cobwebs with a spiral staircase leading down into the ground. The staircase was dark and, as they looked down, it became darker. Ellis pardoned himself and, within a few minutes, he came back with some candles from the cottage and lit them. He handed each of them a candle as they made their way down the staircase, which seemed to wind downwards forever. There were times Evie thought she heard voices again but pushed them aside and continued downward. The dim candlelight would sometimes shine on an area on the surrounding walls where there seemed to be ancient runes and markings etched on the sides, which Evie couldn't make out. When they finally reached the bottom of the staircase, they found themselves in front of another large door, covered in the same runes and markings that they had seen on the walls. Again, there was no doorknob or keyhole, just another weird shape in the door. They all bent down to get a closer look when Ellis asked, "Well, hell. Is it the same shape as yer broach?"

They all looked harder and saw it wasn't the same shape, then each of them took a big sigh of defeat as Marina said, "It is getting late. We should head back to the house and see if we can find the item that fits here tomorrow."

With their venture stopped in its tracks, they all headed back up the staircase. Once they reached the top of the staircase, Evie made sure to grab the broach out of the door, and when she did it shut so loudly the ground shook. It startled them, but they shook it off and proceeded to head back to the castle.

Once they were in front of the cottage, Evie thought she heard a voice again and turned to look back. Bella followed Evie's gaze as well, when Evie thought she saw something move in the cottage. Bella bolted back into the cottage as if she had also seen the movement, with Evie following right on Bella's heels this time. Back inside the cottage, Evie was expecting to see someone, but instead, in the far corner where she had found the drawing of Magnus and Aphrodite, there was a small opaque cloud hovering in the corner. She approached the cloud and saw the large jowly woman smiling her big toothy grin. Evie leaned in even farther because the woman began to move her lips. As she leaned in, she heard the woman say, "Find the watch." Then, the cloud disappeared, leaving Evie to question what watch she was supposed to find.

As Evie made her way back out of the old cottage, Ellis and Marina were no longer in sight. She walked for while through the forest when she finally found Marina and Ellis, slowly making their way back across the garden to the castle, so Evie and Bella ran to catch up with them. When Evie caught up with them, she was out of breath, panting, and tried reporting what had just happened when Ellis laughed a bit and said, "Catch yer breath girl."

After a few minutes, Evie finally caught her breath and told them about what the woman said about the watch. They all went into deep thought about what watch the large woman could be talking about, but by the time they reached the castle, none of them could figure it out and, since it was late, they headed off to their rooms. As Evie was getting ready for bed, still thinking about the day, she remembered that the large woman had placed a cracked watch down on the table when they first met. Evie tried to remember if she had seen the watch anywhere in the waking world but couldn't figure it out, so she climbed into bed, hoping that maybe she would be able to remember tomorrow.

Chapter 18

NEWS FROM DAVID AND RUBY

◆•————————●————————•◆

The next morning, Evie went downstairs and saw that Marina was looking over a letter. When Marina saw Evie, she gave her a big smile. "I have received word from David and Ruby."

Evie bolted over to the table, began jumping up and down, and shouted, "What do they say? Are they okay? Have they found anything? Are they coming back?"

Marina laughed and held up her hand. "One thing at a time, dear."

Marina held up the letter again and said, "They found a man in Egypt who was part of The Order. It seems that he also has very little information but is willing to help them on their endeavor to restore The Order."

Evie smiled as Marina continued to tell her that David and Ruby had also found another woman located in Russia who they believe will be helpful. Marina told Evie that they were leaving for Russia in a few days and were most likely already on their way. Marina then said, "David said he has received your voicemails and he is sorry that they have not returned your calls. Apparently, the man they found was in an area of Egypt with no service." Marina paused and finished, "David said they will call once they get to Russia, so hopefully you will hear from them soon."

Evie smiled and ran upstairs to get her phone. She had been leaving it in her room during her time here, but she didn't want to miss David and Ruby's call, so she placed it in her pocket.

* * *

David dropped the letter he wrote to Evie at the post office in Cairo and made his way over to Steven,

Ruby, and Amam, who were waiting in a taxi to go to the airport. Amam Kalb was the member of The Order David and Steven had found and was going with them on their trip to Russia to find another member who Amam believed could help them. David and Ruby had tried several times to call Evie while they were in Egypt, but David's phone couldn't get through, so he decided he would write a letter to let her know they were okay and would call once they landed in Russia.

When David called Amam before they left Ireland, he seemed very nervous about David and the others coming to see him, but Amam told David he would be willing to help however he could. When David, Ruby, and Steven reached Cairo, they were met by a young man at the airport who took them several hours out of the city to where Amam lived. It was a very desolate place, but David had the feeling that Amam had chosen to live in this isolated area.

Amam was taller than David and Steven. He had brown skin, curly jet-black hair, and deep brown eyes. David also noticed that even though Amam was

Egyptian, he had a very clear English accent when he spoke. He wondered if Amam had received some form of education in English institutions or was well traveled; however, he never asked. David could also see some kind of sadness or pain behind Amam's eyes, and his face was often a cold blank mask. David wondered why but pushed the thought aside, hoping that Amam would reveal someday the cause of his pain and sorrow. Amam was also very private and didn't seem to answer David's or Steven's questions about who he was, what he did, or how he came to be part of The Keeper's Order. However, over several days during their stay, Amam disclosed several things he knew, but David still felt like he was holding information back or possibly was too scared to talk about certain subjects.

During one late-night conversation David and Steven had with Amam, he mentioned a ring that Magnus left with one of his ancestors, passed down through several generations in his family. Amam then told them, "The ring is one key to unlocking a forgotten city, where most of the lost knowledge on Earth can be found. However, my ring has been lost, or was possibly stolen a very long time ago, and I could never find any information about where it could be."

Amam also told them that there were other rings given to different families around the world, but again, he was unsure whether these rings still existed. He then told them of a woman in Russia who had helped him search for his lost ring. "She might know more than I do about the rings or other Order members." Amam then sighed. "I gave up my own search several year ago, so I'm in the dark in regards to what The Order is doing."

After a few more days of sifting through the texts Amam had held on to, they decided that the best thing to do was go and talk to this woman in Russia to find out what she knew.

As soon as they landed in Russia, David decided to call Evie, just in case this woman also lived in isolated area with no service. He pulled Ruby and Steven aside and made the call.

* * *

Evie, Ellis, and Marina were back in the stacks before they decided to go search the cottage again. They were hoping they might find something useful when Evie's pocket began to buzz. Evie jumped up quickly and grabbed her phone. She was so excited she almost dropped it before she answered, "Hello!"

Evie heard Ruby say, "Hello, sweetheart. It's Ruby."

Before Evie could say anything, she began to cry uncontrollably, and she realized just how much she missed her family. Ruby began to talk, trying to calm Evie down; she put Evie on speakerphone, and Evie then heard David and Steven talking. Evie began to cry even harder, trying to tell them through her cracking voice how much she missed them and loved them all.

After a few more minutes, Evie finally calmed down enough to tell them everything that she was doing. Evie could tell that all of them were absolutely shocked by all that she had learned and all that she,

Marina, and Ellis were doing while they were away. David and Ruby then told her about their own mission and what they were trying to accomplish and told her that hopefully they would be back soon. Before Evie hung up, Ruby got back on the phone by herself and said, "I love you so much, my brave girl. I can't wait to squeeze you in my arms again."

Evie began to cry again, and through her shaking voice she pushed out the words, "I love you so very much, Ruby."

After she hung up, Evie didn't feel like hunting for lost secrets, and she and Bella went to her room. Eventually Evie fell asleep, tears still rolling down her cheeks.

Chapter 19

CALLAIS

That night, Evie began to dream more vividly than she ever had before. She dreamt of many different places, each of which appeared for a brief moment before she was whisked away to another place. It was as if her mind was trying to find something. At times, Evie had a bird's-eye view. She could see she was on a glistening ship, one that resembled the ships in the drawings. The ship was floating on trails of sparkling stars, leading her from one location to the next. She then remembered her dream on the plane to Ireland and realized this was the same ship from that dream and these were the same star trails. The soaring and floating from place to place on the starship went on for a while when Evie finally settled over the bay as the ship gently landed in the water below. Then, Evie saw a smaller boat heading towards the ship with two cloaked figures on it, and she shouted out, assuming it was Marina and Ellis. However, there was no response from the boat's occupants. As the small boat reached the ship, the two figures made their way up the side and over to Evie. They then both removed their hoods and there stood the large woman and Callais. Evie took a step back and was shocked. Before she could say anything, the large woman gently reached for her with an open palm and said, "Come."

Evie, although extremely nervous, followed Callais and the large woman off the ship and back into the small boat as they made their way in silence across the bay to the dock. She thought about asking them questions, but she got the feeling there was a reason for the silence.

Once at the docks, they made their way along a dirt trail behind the back side of a small town. Evie recognized the town immediately: it was the town where she had first met the large woman. She assumed they would head back to the woman's cottage, but instead, she followed them into the forest outside of the town. They came to a small clearing where once again, there was another cottage. Evie was shocked again because the cottage was the same in appearance as the one in the forest by Marina's house. The threesome then made their way in when two dogs came bounding out from the back room. To Evie's surprise, one of them was Bella. Evie bent down to greet her faithful companion as the large woman and Callais took off their cloaks and sat down at a table. Callais then said, "Your companion helped us find you tonight."

Bella gleefully wagged her tail and continued to play with her new friend. Evie noticed that this new dog was a little larger than Bella but had a similar coat that was much softer. Evie then remembered that this new dog looked a lot like a pit bull dog she had helped find a home for when she worked at the veterinarian clinic's adopt-a-dog day. Callais smiled and added, "Well, both Bella and Apollo helped find you tonight!" as he nodded his head at Apollo.

Evie joined the woman and Callais at the table waiting again for someone to talk when there was a knock at the door. The woman jumped up a little and wagged her behind as Callais went to answer the door. Two more cloaked figures entered. Evie was a little worried at first, but relief flooded her body when they removed their hoods and she saw it was Marina and Ellis. Although Marina kept her composure, Ellis seemed to bounce around with excitement until he settled down in the seat next to the large woman. It made Evie giggle to see these two large people, giddy with excitement, sitting in chairs almost too small to hold them or to contain their joy. Callais and Marina remained silent for a few minutes until it was almost an uncomfortable silence. Callais then finally spoke. "I am Callais Baldais. It is good to meet all of you." He paused and then said, "It took me a long time to find all of you and I know we still have a lot of work to do, but this is a great start."

Marina introduced herself and Ellis before saying to Callais, "We have made some headway in our search, but we may be further behind than you would like."

Callais listened as Marina explained everything that they had been doing on their end. After Marina finished her story, the large woman got up and began to search for something. Both Marina and Callais were in deep thought when the large woman returned with a book and opened it to a page with a drawing on it. Everyone leaned over to see a picture of a cracked watch—the same one the woman had presented to Evie the first night they met. Evie asked her, "Don't you have the watch?"

Callais chuckled a bit. "In a way she does, but not here. She can only show you what you need to find on Terran. She can reveal but not give. That is for you to find."

Evie was slightly confused by this, and it seemed like another riddle when Callais chimed in and explained, "Before Magnus passed away on Terran, he left his companion, Aphrodite, to guard what he had hidden until the right person in his bloodline could find it. Before he left Aphrodite, he placed a spell on her so that she could connect with myself and others in human form. Although the spell allowed for this to happen, Aphrodite can only communicate in small sentences and by showing us what she has found to help us. Evie, may I introduce you to Aphrodite." Callais then gestured his hand in the direction of the large woman as she turned around gleefully, knocking over her chair and almost bouncing Ellis out of his chair.

Evie sat there dumbfounded as she watched the large woman, Aphrodite, go back to looking at the book and then looking back at Evie with her big jowls, toothy grin, and sparkling brown eyes. Evie started to laugh and realized that this large, happy woman was yet another dog somewhere waiting for her as she thought, *Dogs really do mean more to our bloodline than just pets!*

After introducing them to Aphrodite and pondering what Marina had explained about their search, Callais began to explain more about Magnus and the Devas galaxy history. "Magnus was a powerful keeper and one of the first ever known to exist in the universe." Callais paused before continuing, "There are several galaxies in the universe that were created by two powerful beings, known only as the mother and father. The mother and father had many children, whom they called keepers, and each keeper had great powers beyond those of other beings."

Everyone sat there in silence and Evie could tell this was new information to Marina and Ellis as Callais then continued explaining. "The father provided the gift of memory to his beloved creations. With memory, the beings in the universe would always remember where they came from, knowledge of those before them, and most importantly, that they were loved." He took a deep breath and added, "Like any good father, he wanted the memories to be passed down to each being from those who came before them. These beings who passed down the memories were selected by the father and had the qualities of patience, courage, and deep wisdom, like himself; this is why the father chose to call them keepers."

Everyone was still quiet, listening intently to Callais, so he went on, "The keepers also live much longer than other beings and have powers beyond other normal beings. They are also gifted with the ability to control the elements of their galaxies and worlds. A head keeper was either an original keeper that the mother and father created or came from one of the original keepers' bloodlines. A head keeper can control all the elements for the entirety of their life span and did not need any training, for they were born with the gifts."

Callais then told them that there were also lower keepers and that he was a lower keeper. "The lower keepers could also control the elements of the world they were assigned to and only that world. Lower keepers were either far decedents of the original bloodline or had the power and knowledge passed down to them from an original keeper who did not have a bloodline through procreation."

Evie had no idea what to say, and Ellis and Marina remained silent as well. Callais looked around the room but hearing no response from anyone, he continued. "The very first keepers were the father and mother's children and born with powers of the father and mother and trained by the father himself. There is belief that Magnus was one of their first children."

Callais then went on to say that each keeper was placed in their own galaxy, was in charge of the galaxy, and Magnus was the head keeper of the Devas galaxy. Callais then said, "Magnus had a brother named Camulos, who was in charge of his own galaxy called the Camulus galaxy. He is also very powerful, but a very long time ago, he became evil and corrupt and began an intergalactic war across the universe."

Before Callais could say anything more, a loud noise, almost like an explosion, interrupted him. The booming sound came from the direction of the town and immediately, Aphrodite, Apollo, and Bella jumped up and ran to the back room. Callais quickly turned to Ellis, Marina, and Evie and in a hurried voice said, "You have to go now. I will find you later, but we cannot stay here. The Camulus Pack has invaded again."

Callais then quickly made his way to the back room where Aphrodite, Bella, and Apollo had disappeared. Evie turned around to see Marina and

Ellis slowly fading away. Evie was soon left in the room, alone and terrified, and didn't know what to do. Just as she heard more explosions and yelling outside of the forest edge, she sensed a warmth on her right cheek and then what felt like a bite. This jolted her, and the next thing she knew she was back in her room at Marina's home, with Bella nibbling at her face. As soon as Bella realized Evie was awake, she stopped and bounded towards the door, where soon after Ellis was knocking with a loud thud.

Chapter 20
THE WATCH

Evie opened the door to see Ellis's relieved face. "Good, I wasn't sure if yeh knew how to get out o' the dream on yer own, so I figured I'd come wake yeh," Ellis said as he gave Evie a quick hug.

Evie was glad to see Ellis but still terrified of what had happened in the dream and wondered what would have happened to her if she hadn't woken up. This thought frightened Evie even more when she realized that she really needed to work on navigating the dream state, as Callais had mentioned before. The last thing she wanted was to be left alone in this crazy new world of dreams. Evie then felt Bella rub up on her leg, as if to console her, and she realized just how important Bella was to her. Evie then leaned over and gave Bella a quick kiss. When she looked up, it was still dark out. Ellis noticed this too and said, "Get some sleep kid. We'll figure out everythin' we need tomorrow." He then went back to his room.

Evie was left in her room to her own thoughts and couldn't fall back asleep, mostly because she didn't want to dream again and find herself back in the town that was under attack. She then began to wonder why it was under attack. Callais had mentioned briefly who Magnus was and the wars his brother started, but Evie had been so concentrated on everything that had been happening since she met Marina, she didn't even think to ask why they were searching for all this stuff and why they were trying to save a whole galaxy. *I'll ask them in the morning,* she thought.

Evie still couldn't sleep, so she decided to go down to the kitchen with Bella in tow to look for something to eat. Once in the kitchen, before Evie could grab something to eat, Bella barked and then ran down a hallway. Evie didn't even hesitate and ran after her, following Bella down an endless path of more hallways and doors. When they finally stopped, she found herself in front of a new door she had never seen before. Bella sat there waiting for Evie to do something and then impatiently barked, looking at the door. Evie trusted Bella, so she opened this new door and walked into a giant room that was filled to the ceiling with what looked like junk. The room reminded her of when she went to the scrapyard with David to find car parts for her car when she first started driving. It was filled with metal and all kinds of odds and ends. Evie slowly navigated around a few piles; everything looked like it had been stacked in there haphazardly, and at any moment, a tower of junk would come crumbling down on top of her. Bella stayed by her side, although Evie hoped Bella would show her the reason why she was brought to this room.

As Evie continued her search, she could see a streak of light coming through what was most likely a hidden window behind all this junk and figured it was morning. Just as Evie was about to give up and head to the kitchen to find Marina and Ellis, Bella barked and leaped behind another tower of junk. Evie followed Bella around the pile when she saw Bella pawing at an old armchair that was falling apart. Evie went to go get a closer look and found that the chair was empty; it was just a chair, nothing else. Evie plopped heavily into the chair to take a break before heading back to the kitchen. Evie sunk farther into the chair when she felt a lump under her right cheek. She moved her body over slightly to investigate what the bump was and saw that whatever it was, was under the cushion. Evie got off the chair and pulled the cushion off, and there it was…the cracked watch.

Evie was shocked, mostly because she found the watch and also because she found what seemed to be such an important part of the puzzle in an old armchair—in a junk room. She thought, *Surely Magnus would not hide something so important in such an obscure place, but then again, nothing really makes too much sense anymore!* She grabbed the watch, and when she did it let off a glistening purple glow, but instead of analyzing it she quickly headed back to the kitchen just as Marina was entering as well.

"Good morning, girl," Marina greeted her as Evie quickly made her way over to Marina's side and handed her the watch with pride. Evie almost felt as giddy as Aphrodite. Marina examined the watch and looked at Evie with curiosity. Evie then said, "I found it in a room full of junk."

Marina started to laugh and then let out a sigh. "Oh my, you found Magnus's old hoarding room!"

Evie gave Marina a confused look as Marina continued to explain. "This castle was once Magnus's own, and it is the home I grew up in as a child. My father was a bit of a collector of stuff. Some things he collected were important and other things were just things he seemed to collect for no reason. Either way, I am surprised he would leave such an important item in the junk room."

"I thought that was weird too," Evie said right as Ellis walked into the room and asked, "What's weird, besides every damned crazy thin' so far?" He chuckled a bit.

Evie realized that this whole journey has been just as crazy and weird for Ellis. She then explained to Ellis that she had found the watch they were looking for in a room filled with junk. Ellis laughed and said, "That's me favorite room. I remember as a kid I loved to go explorin' in that room. So much neat stuff."

Marina and Evie both laughed a bit and realized Magnus may have not been the only one in the family interested in junk as Marina handed Ellis the watch. When Ellis looked down at the watch, it began to sparkle and shimmer even brighter. He froze and said, "I knew I'd seen this watch before when they showed us the picture of it in the dream, but couldn't remember where I saw it before."

He sat and turned the watch over in his giant palm and looked at it like he had found a lost treasure from his childhood. "I found this when I was a kid, but I completely forgot 'bout it 'til last night. When I saw the picture, me thought 'bout the watch last night after the dream meetin', but couldn't remember what I did with it. Now that yeh told me where yeh found it, it makes perfect sense. Always hid me treasures as a boy in that room. Let me guess, yeh found it in the chair."

Evie smiled and said yes. Marina then asked him, "Where did you find it before you hid it?"

Ellis told them he couldn't remember and then loudly boomed. "Hey, we 'ave the watch now an' that broach. Maybe the watch is the piece that fits in the door at the bottom of the stairway?"

Both Evie and Marina nodded their heads in agreement. They all quickly finished their meal, packed a bag, and walked back to the cottage in the forest.

On their way there, Ellis was turning the watch over and over again in his hands as if trying to remember something. Before Evie could ask him any questions about his thoughts, they found themselves in front of the cottage and made their way to the back door. Evie decided she would ask him later then grabbed the broach, placed it in the space on the door, and said, "Aphrodite." The broach then began to light up, spin again, and the door opened.

They slowly made their way down the staircase again; this time, they had packed flashlights so

Evie was able to see the walls better. The runes and markings on the wall began to swirl around like the maps, drawings, and scrolls. Evie again decided not to focus on the walls. She didn't want to get light-headed and pass out while going down a staircase. Instead, she turned her focus to Ellis's enormous back until they finally reached the bottom.

This time, Ellis approached the door and tried to place the watch in the space on the door but it didn't fit. He looked up at Evie and Marina as if disappointed and confused at the same time when the watch suddenly began to shimmer and glow even brighter then floated out of Ellis's hand and began spinning. The watch then moved around the entire doorframe, and as it passed the markings on the door, they also lit up. After the watch spun and glided around the doorway three times, it finally stopped in the center of the door and remained floating, flickering with a purple-yellowish light. Everyone held their breaths for a minute, thinking the door would open, but it didn't. After a few more minutes, Marina started digging in the bag, pulled out a scroll, made her way over to Evie, unrolling the scroll. "Evie, see if you can read the scroll again or see if what is on the scroll or the door makes any sense."

Evie looked down at the scroll expecting it to swirl too, but as she glanced down, it was holding steady this time, with images lit up on it that matched the markings on the door. Evie told Marina, "The scroll markings and the door markings are the same, but I don't know what they mean."

They all sat there trying to think of answers while Evie looked at the scroll and back at the door trying to see if she could figure it out.

After a long period of time, Evie was ready to call it quits when she realized that these markings were also the same on the map in the clearing down the guarded aisle. She understood that the markings on the scroll, the door, and the map were constellations. She then said, "I believe these markings on the door and scroll are constellations, but they're not constellations I'm familiar with."

Both Marina and Ellis looked at her with questioning eyes before Ellis finally asked, "Yeh think they are Devas galaxy constellations?" all the while looking at Marina.

Marina realized this was a direct question for her, looked at both of them, and with an apologetic tone said, "I am sorry, but I do not know anything about the Devas system constellations."

"Well, how did you know this scroll was the right one to bring?" Evie asked.

Marina told them she brought all three and just pulled this one out on a feeling, hoping it would work. They all stood there for a while when Evie stated, "Maybe we can go into a dream state to see if there is something we are missing. Callais said I'd have to work on that anyway."

Marina and Ellis agreed and as they were getting ready to pack up, Evie turned and looked back at the door when one of the markings on the door began to shimmer, and then another across from the first. After it dimmed, another began to shimmer, and so on with each marking. Evie suddenly shouted out, "It's a pattern!"

Both Marina and Ellis turned around and looked at Evie as she was making her way back to the door.

She stood there and watched the twinkling pattern for a while. The marking she first saw shimmer lit up again as Evie placed her hand on it. Then, the door made a noise, as if it was unlocking. Evie kept her hand on the mark until the next marking began to shimmer. She moved her hand across the door to the next shimmering mark when the door made another unlocking noise. Evie continued to do this with each mark until she reached the last one. As she placed her hand on the last shimmering mark, the door began to shake and tremble along with the whole room. Evie thought the room would cave down on them because the shaking became increasingly violent. All of a sudden, the shaking stopped, the floating watch crashed into the center of the door creating a blinding light, and when the light faded, the door flew wide open as a blast of air came sweeping into the room that knocked them all on the ground. After the dust from the blast of air settled and they got themselves back up, they stood in front of the doorway that opened to a long cavernous walkway.

With much trepidation and a bit of excitement, Ellis grabbed the watch that was floating in the air again, and they began their way down the dark path. Again, Evie was glad they brought flashlights to light up the way because the path was pitch black. Evie also noticed the path had areas that looked as though they had been man-made and dug out, while other areas of the path looked like they were part of a natural cave that had been around since the beginning of time. The smell was damp and mossy and there were cobwebs and giant spiders everywhere, making it harder to navigate the dark path. They continued to walk for a couple hours before they finally came to a clearing and, at the end of it, found themselves in front of two paths. Ellis immediately let out an exasperated grunt. "Oh hell. Which one do we take?"

They all sat for a while and stared at the two paths before deciding it was a good time to take a break. As Ellis and Evie ate some food and drank some of the Virdis, Marina was poring over some books she had also brought. Bella was gleefully bouncing around the clearing and every once in a while would make her way to Ellis or Evie, who offered her some of their food. Evie kept a close eye on Bella, thinking she might know which path to take, but Bella seemed content where she was. After they finished eating, Marina looked up from her book and wearily said, "I do not know, and it is getting late. So, I guess it would be best to head back and try again tomorrow."

At this point, both Ellis and Evie let out grunts because they were tired of getting close to finding something and then having to start all over the next day. They both reluctantly agreed with Marina and began to pack up their stuff.

As they made their way back to the path that led them there, a loud eerie noise echoed around them and, in an instant, the trail in front of them disappeared. They were now trapped in the clearing, with only the two other paths behind them. Ellis shouted so loud that Bella came running to Evie and hid between her legs while Marina turned around with an infuriated look on her face. They all stood in complete silence for a long time when Ellis finally broke the silence and waved his arms in the air saying, "What'd hell do we do now?"

Marina looked around the clearing once more and shrugged. "Well, I guess we try and figure out how to get out of here and make do until then."

Evie sat there for a while, still staring at both paths in front of them, hoping something would happen that would show them the way. She thought for a while and then realized that before she figured how to open the door with all the markings, they were going to go back to the castle and help Evie with the dream state. Evie thought about this for a minute and remembered Marina also had all three scrolls with her, so Evie suggested again, "Let's go into a dream state and see if we can find the answers we need."

Both Ellis and Marina agreed that this would be best since there was really nothing else they could do. Marina then directed all of them to sit in a circle on the floor as she began to explain to Evie how to purposely enter the dream state. Marina continued to explain that she felt it would be best if they all had one single focus on where to go or who to find. Both Ellis and Evie thought for a while who would be best to find or where would be best to go. After a short period of silence, Evie said, "Why don't we try and reach out to Aphrodite, the large woman or dog, since she seems to be the key."

Marina and Ellis nodded in agreement while Marina went on to explain the process of entering the dream state. "When just one person enters a dream state, it can often be more challenging. This is why it is wise to do it with others, not only to bring clarity to the search, but also to ensure there are others if a person gets lost or finds themselves in an unwanted situation. Having other people with you can hopefully help prevent that."

Evie thought of the last time they were all in a dream together and everybody's panic when they heard the explosions. This gave Evie the chills, which Bella sensed. She crawled in Evie's lap. As soon as Marina saw Bella in Evie's lap, she said, "It is also a good thing that Bella is here. So, be sure to hold on to her during the trance since she has seemed to be helpful in the past."

Evie looked at Bella and rubbed her head, also glad she had her faithful companion by her side since it was Bella who woke her up the last time things got dicey. Bella gave her a quick kiss on the nose and repositioned herself back in Evie's lap as Marina continued to explain. "Once we enter the dream state, it might be a little confusing at first since oftentimes things can become foggy and unclear."

She then told them that once all three enter the dream state, it might take some time for all three of them to find each other and to be patient while Marina searches for both Evie and Ellis. Evie then asked, "How do we enter? I'm not sleepy and don't know if I'll even dream."

Marina gave a reassuring nod before answering, "To purposely enter the dream state while not actually dreaming requires deep concentration. Once you close your eyes, the best thing to do is focus solely on the thing you want to find. In this case, only think of Aphrodite."

Marina told them that even though they had seen a picture of Aphrodite as a dog, the best thing to do would be to concentrate on the woman, not the dog, since they had all seen and interacted with her.

Ellis and Evie looked at each other and then nodded again.

Marina then reached out her hands so that they were extended to both Ellis and Evie and told them, "Holding hands will make it easier for me to find both of you in the dream state."

They all then held hands and closed their eyes. Evie tried to concentrate on Aphrodite, but nothing was happening. At one point, she opened her eyes a sliver to look at Marina and Ellis, and not only were both their eyes partially closed, but like before, their eyes were rolled back into their heads, with only a small bit of white showing. Evie immediately closed her eyes again, and this time, instead of focusing on Aphrodite, she focused on Marina.

At first, Evie felt like nothing was happening. She felt Bella wiggle on her lap and, just as she felt like giving up, a small cloud appeared and then moved around. Evie then followed the cloud in her mind. It seemed to be racing past different things, pause for a minute over something, and then race around again. Evie kept following the cloud and then remembered to concentrate on Marina. She began to picture Marina's face while still trying to follow the cloud. After a few minutes, the cloud seemed to stop over something, or someone, and Evie caught up to it in her mind. Once the cloud stopped moving and Evie reached it, everything around her was still a little fuzzy and she couldn't see anything clearly. She concentrated even harder on Marina's face when she heard a voice say, "There you are."

She looked around once again and saw a figure moving towards her in the haze. Soon after the figure moved out of the haze, there stood Marina, but no Ellis. Evie looked around, but Marina seemed to read her thoughts and said, "Ellis is on his way. I can feel him."

A few seconds later, a large cloud appeared and Ellis came bulldozing out of it when he exclaimed, "Damnit woman. Yer 'ard to keep up with!"

Both Marina and Evie chuckled a little as he walked over to them. Once he was standing next to them, Marina stated that it was time to find Aphrodite. Evie looked around her, but there was really nothing there; the surroundings were all just kind of a swampy haze, like morning over the water before the fog lifts. Evie looked back at Marina with questioning eyes as Marina answered her thoughts again, "Just like before, everyone concentrate on Aphrodite."

Evie reached out her hands in either direction to hold Marina's and Ellis's hands, but they didn't reach back. Evie looked at them as Marina told her, "Once inside the dream state, it is not necessary to hold hands but to just concentrate."

So, Evie closed her eyes and began to concentrate on Aphrodite. After a few minutes, Evie felt herself floating in the air. She opened her eyes and when she got a bird's-eye view, she was on a ship that was floating on trails of stars. She floated around for a few more minutes when the ship stopped and hovered next to a mountain. However, this time it didn't land. She looked around trying to figure out what to do when Marina and Ellis appeared instantly on the deck of the ship next to her. Marina smiled and said, "Good job, Evie. We just followed you!"

Evie didn't have time to process how they just appeared out of thin air before the three of them began to look around and down at the mountain, trying to figure out what to do. The ship seemed to be hovering right next to a small cave-like opening, leading inside the mountain. Evie assumed they needed to go into the cave, but she was unsure how. Just as the three of them began looking around for a way off the ship again, it made a cracking noise, and off its side, a ramp began to extend out towards the cave opening. Ellis shrugged his shoulders and motioned for them to follow as they climbed over the side and made their way across the ramp. Evie looked down and was instantly terrified. They were up so high she couldn't even see the ground below. Looking down, Evie's head began to spin, so she quickly shot her head back up and just concentrated on Ellis's large back in front of her. Ellis's arms were extended out as he balanced his large frame on the ramp, and Evie thought, *He's probably just as scared as I am.*

They finally reached the entrance to the cave and, as all three stepped into the opening, the ramp began to move back. They turned their heads and watched as the ramp receded and the ship drifted away. Evie turned back to look at Marina and Ellis, who both looked as frantic as she felt. Ellis just shrugged again, "Well hell, there goes our ride. Hopefully, there's another way back."

Marina gave a nervous smile and shrugged as well, so Evie also shrugged and turned towards the opening to the cave. It was a long dark walkway, and she realized they didn't have anything to light it up. Just as she was about to mention this, Marina moved both hands in a circular motion. She then moved her top hand away from her bottom hand and a small glowing orb appeared. Evie gasped as Marina looked at her and smiled. "I have learned that there are many things you can do in a dream state that you cannot do in the waking world. Do not worry. When we have spent more time in the dream state, I can show you some tricks. But for now, let us go find Aphrodite!"

All three began to make their way down the cave. As the cave became darker, the orb seemed to light up even more, making the cave walls glisten.

Evie examined the walls of the cave and they seemed to be filled with some kind of shiny metal that changed color. She thought to herself, *It looks like the sides of the ship that brought us here, as well as the ones in the drawings I've seen.* Evie pushed this out of her head (again, she didn't have time to process any new mysteries) and continued to follow Marina and Ellis when they finally came to a clearing with two different paths. Ellis then bellowed out in frustration again, "Damnit, two paths again. What'd we do now?"

Both Evie and Marina looked at each other and Evie could tell all three were thinking the same thing—when will this search ever end? Marina began to pace, Ellis followed suit, spewing profanities in front of each opening while raising his fist in the air as if to curse some unseen power. Evie just stood there until she decided that if she thought of Aphrodite again, something would happen. So, Evie closed her eyes and began to focus on Aphrodite. She thought of her jowly, toothy smile and how she would wiggle in excitement when she found something. Evie was beginning to enjoy her thoughts of the large woman, whose mannerisms did resemble a dog's, when Aphrodite's face became clear and Evie then heard, "Open your eyes, Evie."

Evie shot her eyes open and there was Aphrodite, standing in the clearing. Marina and Ellis looked shocked. To them, it seemed that she had just miraculously appeared from thin air. Marina looked at Evie with questioning eyes as Evie exclaimed, "I just was thinking of her. She must've found us!"

Aphrodite then smiled her goofy grin, did a little jump, spun around, and turned her face back to Evie. Evie burst out laughing because it reminded her of Bella playing around and trying to get Evie to notice her when she did something good. Evie walked up to Aphrodite and placed her hand on her arm. Aphrodite smiled even larger and embraced Evie in a big, bear-like hug while bouncing up and down. Evie began to laugh even harder as Aphrodite finally stopped and released Evie. As soon as Aphrodite let go, she bounded down the path to the left and all three followed her. As they walked down the dark cave pathway, every once in a while, Aphrodite would stop, look back at all three, and then happily jump up, turn around, and keep walking.

After walking for a while, they finally reached a large door, similar to the one they had entered before they got stuck. Aphrodite approached the door, but instead of pulling out an item to open it, she seemed to whisper something. A few moments later, the door made a creaking noise and she wiggled her way through the cracked opening. Ellis followed, also having to wiggle his large frame through the crack, while Evie and Marina entered without trouble.

The room had a glowing orb circling above, like the one in the stacks back at Marina's castle. This orb was not as yellow as the one at Marina's castle, but blueish-white. Evie looked around and saw towards the back of the room that there was another cave opening leading somewhere else in the mountain. The room was also similar to the stacks because it had drawings and maps on the walls; however, there was only one scroll on the table in the middle and no books. There were also a few artifacts, such as a sword in the far corner that Evie had seen in some of the other drawings. After a minute of looking around, Callais walked in from the back of the other cave opening and entered the room. Evie smiled because she hoped that, since Callais was there, they might get some answers. Callais made his way over to the table in the center of the room with the scroll on it, Aphrodite following at his heels. Callais then said, "It is good to see all of you again. I am glad you were able to find Aphrodite."

Callais then gestured his hand towards Aphrodite, who returned a large smile and ran off as Callais began to unroll the scroll. Aphrodite disappeared down the cave pathway towards the back of the room as Marina explained their predicament to Callais. As they talked, Evie analyzed Callais. He was short in stature but thick and sturdy with a muscular and athletic build. He had light blond hair with a reddish tint to it, braided in rows across the top of his head (which reminded Evie of how Vikings wore their hair), and a thick curly red beard. He also had bright, fun, sparkling blue eyes. Evie's thoughts were interrupted when Callais unrolled a scroll, placing it gently on the table. He looked at Marina intently and said, "Oftentimes, the path in front of us is not the one we are supposed to be on. Is there nothing else in the clearing with you besides those two paths?"

Ellis, Marina, and Evie thought about it, but without being able to look around the cave they were in outside of the dream state, they couldn't remember anything in particular that stood out. Marina then shook her head and answered, "No, I do not think there is anything in the cave. Is there something we should be looking for?"

Callais looked up as if trying to figure something out but then shook his head and told them he didn't know either. In that moment, Aphrodite entered the room again carrying something in her arms. At first, Evie couldn't see what she was carrying due to her large, pudgy arms. Aphrodite made her way between Ellis and Evie and dropped a large rock with purple flecks in it on the ground in front of them as she bounced around and wiggled her butt proudly. Evie looked at the rock, then at Ellis, and back at the rock again. Evie then looked at Aphrodite and asked, "Why do we need a rock?"

She bounced around in a circle a few more times before saying, "Move the rock, move the rock, find the key, find the path!"

Callais, Marina, Ellis, and Evie looked at each other and then at Aphrodite as she continued to bounce about happily when Callais asked, "Is there a rock in the clearing where you are?"

Ellis bellowed again and threw his hands up in the air. "There are tons o' damn rocks. We're in a cave!"

"Well, Aphrodite is never wrong," Callais said while rubbing his head. "She may be hard to understand, but she is never wrong." He then began rubbing his chin and added, "When you leave here, search for the rock she has presented here back on Terran, but before you go, I would like to show Evie something on this scroll."

Callais then gestured his head towards Evie as if to come closer, so she moved over to the table where Callais had spread out the scroll. He looked intently at her and then motioned to the table and scroll. "Go ahead, take a look."

Evie looked down at the open scroll and, like before, it began to spin with markings and symbols switching places. This time, she didn't feel light-headed while watching the scroll swirl about; she figured that maybe in the dream state it's easier to understand things.

After a few minutes, the scroll seemed to settle down as each marking and symbol found their home. Evie still couldn't make out much of the scroll, but things were clearer to her this time than any other time. There were three drawings that would light up, and down the left side were a few words that at first Evie didn't understand. After a few moments, however, she was able to make out what they meant. She read out loud, "*The search for love is kept in the purest of souls. Once love is found, evil cannot hold.*"

Everyone in the room was silent for a minute, thinking about what the passage meant, as Evie looked at the drawings that were lit up on the scroll. One drawing was of a large dog, which was apparently Aphrodite; the second one was a box that looked like a treasure box; and the third was of a small rotating planet that Evie had never seen before. Evie didn't know how these drawings were connected to the words she just read, so she said, "I think we need to go back and find the rock with the key. We have to find Aphrodite. She's still the only way to help us move forward with what we need to do." Evie pointed to the scroll where the dog was lit up.

Marina, Ellis, and Callais looked down to see what Evie was pointing out, but they all looked back up at Evie, confused. Marina then explained to Callais. "Evie has been able to see things on the scrolls that neither myself nor Ellis can see."

Callais squinted and then nodded. "There are many of us here that can partially read the scrolls. There are also many stories that told us about how the person in Magnus's bloodline will be able to see what we cannot." He then looked almost lovingly at Evie and said, "This is a good thing, Evie."

After a few minutes of looking at the scroll and talking, they all decided that it would be best to leave the dream state and figure out what they were supposed to do. Once again, Evie was unsure of how to leave the dream state as she watched Ellis and Marina disappear. Just as she was about to ask Callais how to leave, he said, "Evie, I know this may seem hard, but I believe in you. Just have patience."

Evie gave him a nervous smile and just as she was about to ask him what she needed to do, she felt a sharp pain on her left ear as everything became foggy. She found herself back in the cave clearing, with Bella nibbling on her ear.

Chapter 21

APHRODITE

It took Evie a few minutes to orient herself as she felt very light-headed. Ellis walked over with the Virdis as Evie gratefully took it and drank it up. After a few minutes, Evie began feeling much better and went on to help Ellis, who was already searching for the rock. As Ellis had pointed out in the dream state, there were a lot of rocks scattered throughout the clearing. While Evie watched Ellis pick up a rock and then curse as he tossed it back down, she tried to remember what the rock looked like in the dream state. Evie slowly scanned the room, but nothing stood out to her. Just when she was about to join Ellis in his endeavor of picking up rocks and cursing at them, Marina asked, "Ellis, can you come here?"

Ellis looked at Marina, shrugged, and made his way over to her. Marina pointed at a very large rock and asked him if he could move it. Ellis gave her a cocky look, like it would be no problem, and bent down to lift it. The rock was obviously a lot heavier than Ellis anticipated, and as he struggled to lift it, his face turned a bright red while he scrunched his nose. This made Evie laugh as she made her way over to help him. Just as she reached Ellis, he yelled out the biggest grunt Evie had ever heard, then he raised the rock to knee level and dropped it only a few inches to the side as he gasped for air. Evie looked at Marina and back down, and there, right under where the large rock had been, was a smaller rock with purple flecks in it. Evie looked at Marina shocked and asked, "How did you know it was under there?"

"I did not know." Marina answered, "It was just the only large rock in the room. So, where better to hide a key than under a large rock?" She gave Evie a wink.

Ellis bent down after catching his breath and picked up the smaller rock. While turning it over in both of his hands, he said, "Well, there's no damn key 'ere. What'd we do?"

Evie and Marina both looked at the rock as Ellis was still turning it over in his giant hands. Evie thought about the rocks people use to hide their house keys, in case they get locked out. Evie thought that was a ridiculous idea since when this rock was hidden, there was no such thing as rocks that hide keys. Before Evie could think any further and make another suggestion, Ellis accidently dropped the purple-flecked rock in frustration, and when the rock hit the ground, it made a loud booming noise that shook the room. Evie then saw the cracked watch that was still in Ellis's possession fly out of his pocket and connect with the fallen rock. Soon, the rock and watch began to merge, light up, and hover in the air. Suddenly, a flash of purple light came out of the spinning rock and a key appeared in the purplish glow, floating and spinning in the air. After a few spins, the key whizzed between the two paths and crashed into the cave wall. As soon as the key hit the cave wall between the two visible paths, another path miraculously appeared that wasn't there before. Before anyone could say a word, Bella ran down the new dark path, chasing after the key that was still spinning and glowing as it moved farther into the new opening.

Evie, Marina, and Ellis all immediately jumped forward and began running down the path as well. The path made several twists and turns, and soon, they were standing in front of another large door. The key began to circle the door as the watch had done, and when the key had made a complete lap around the doorframe, it floated to the center of the door and violently crashed into it, making a thunderous noise. The door then slowly opened and, before they could even enter the room, the largest dog Evie had ever seen came leaping and bouncing out the door. The massive dog jumped on Evie, knocking her to the ground, and began kissing and licking Evie as long strings of slobber covered her face, arms, and neck. Evie could hear Ellis and Marina laughing, and after a few more slobbery kisses from the giant beast, the dog got off Evie and sat towering over her body with a big jowly, toothy grin and sparkling brown eyes. Evie smiled from ear to ear because she immediately recognized the dog as Aphrodite. After admiring the size of Aphrodite and giving the joyous dog a tight squeeze around her massive neck, Evie picked herself up and followed the others into the room behind the door.

Inside, there was another small orb floating above them that was the same color as the one in the stacks. The room definitely looked like it belonged to a dog, with many chewed-up bones, sticks, and tennis balls scattered about. Evie wondered again how a tennis ball got in the room but again decided to just focus on the task at hand and ask questions later.

Evie also noticed Aphrodite must have slept in the far corner because there was a pile of straw, sticks, and chewed-up blankets. It looked like a nest you would find in a bear's den. On the opposite side of the room, there was another small door, where the key was already hovering, as if it was patiently waiting for instructions. Evie saw that Bella and Aphrodite were also sitting below the floating key, both of their heads raised, looking patiently at the key and door and then back at Evie. Evie glanced at Marina and Ellis as they both nodded. Evie took this as an indication that she was to be the one to use the key. Evie then made her way over to the key and grabbed it, and just as her hand touched the warm metal of the glowing key, the unopened door lit up and a small keyhole appeared. She took the key and stuck it slowly in the hole, scared that it might make a violent explosion like it did before. The key didn't do anything, so Evie slowly turned the key and the door opened.

Behind the door was the treasure box that Evie had seen on the scroll back in the cave with Callais. She approached the box as the key followed her. It moved so it was in front of Evie, hovering right above the box. Evie then saw another keyhole appear, so she grabbed the key, slowly placed it in the box, and turned it.

Evie then felt the box begin to shake and tremble. Bella started to bark and Aphrodite wagged her tail in excitement. Then, with a loud thud, the top of the box opened and air came whizzing out so fast it made Evie have to turn her head because it stung her eyes. Once the whizzing effect was over, she looked inside and she saw two items and some loose pieces of parchment. The first item was a chain that glistened and shimmered, like the stars she had seen while traveling on the ship in her dreams. The other item was a shiny piece of fabric that had been gently folded up with a string tied around it. Evie looked up at Ellis and Marina as they once again stood silent and nodded for Evie to take them. Evie slowly and carefully grabbed the two items and the loose parchment, placed them gently in the traveling bag they had packed, and asked, "Now what?"

They all stood there for a minute and realized they had what they came for, but they couldn't go back the way they came because the pathway was gone. Evie looked around the room a bit and realized that Bella and Aphrodite were no longer there. She made her way back to Aphrodite's room, hoping that's where the dogs had gone, with Ellis and Marina right behind her.

As they entered Aphrodite's room, the two dogs were waiting on the far side of the room, where a new opening to a new pathway had appeared. Bella and Aphrodite began to make their way down the new path as they turned their heads back to make sure that the other three were following them. The group of humans and dogs followed another long, dark path with many twists and turns; Ellis again took out the flashlight they had packed, which made Evie happy. There were a few tree roots sticking up from the cave floor, which she nearly tripped over, even with the light.

Eventually, the group came to another clearing as Evie watched both Bella and Aphrodite crawl through a hole in the dirt wall on the far side of the clearing. Fortunately, the hole was fairly large because of Aphrodite's size. If it had been any smaller, there would've been no way Ellis would've been able to get out. Evie bent down and crawled through the hole. Soon, she reached the end of the tunnel, crawled out, and fell out onto a pile of wet leaves under a large tree. Evie got up, brushed the leaves and burrs off, moved away from the opening and watched Marina and then Ellis both fall out of the tree hole too. As soon as they were all out and had brushed themselves off, they looked around and saw that they were on top of the hill looking over Marina's garden.

Evie watched Bella and Aphrodite frolic though the garden and thought, *How wonderful it must be for Aphrodite to be free after all these years of guarding the treasure box!* She then thought about how loyal Aphrodite must have been to Magnus to stay on guard for so many years and thought again, *No wonder Magnus loved her and trusted her so much. It was a tremendous and patient task to take on, even for a dog.*

Evie, Marina, and Ellis made their way slowly down the hill and through the garden back to the castle when Evie also began to wonder how long they'd been gone and what day or time it was. Evie decided not to focus on this too long and took a mental note to try and call David and Ruby again. She then remembered the broach back in the door and mentioned this to Ellis, who grunted and headed back to the cottage. After a few minutes of waiting, Ellis returned with the broach and handed it to Marina, and the group again made their way back to the castle.

As they were almost to the kitchen door, Evie also remembered that she wanted to ask about why she was doing all this and thought, *I know I have to save a galaxy, but why?* She pushed this thought aside because Evie realized how tired she was and, as she looked at Ellis and Marina, she could see they were exhausted too. So she decided to wait to ask questions for another day. Marina then said, "Get something to eat. I think it is also best if we all get some rest and start tomorrow."

Evie and Ellis didn't protest since they were so drained. They grabbed some Clonakilty black pudding from the table that Marina had made before they left and went to their rooms. Evie assumed that Aphrodite would follow her and Bella, but instead, she followed Ellis to his room. Evie shrugged and then pictured the large man and large dog in Ellis's bed—something that made her crack up as she entered her own room and flopped down on her bed, fully dressed. Bella then snuggled up to her chest, and they both drifted to sleep.

Chapter 22

KALI

As soon as Evie fell asleep, she was floating across the star trails she had been on before in the dream state. She could tell she was on the same ship. However, this time the ship seemed to match the star trails even more than before and was almost invisible. Evie watched as the star trails and ship led her to a small blueish planet that she recognized from the scroll she had seen in Callais's cave. As the ship approached the planet, she saw that parts of it were covered by swampy areas. She saw people, but it was almost like they were shadows or spirits. As the ship made its way around the planet, she saw several small establishments with people who didn't look like shadows or spirits. However, their faces were hollow, full of sadness, and strife filled their eyes. The sight of the people made her insides twist with sorrow and longing. Evie wondered why they all seemed so sad, but pushed the thought aside as the ship continued to circumnavigate the planet. The ship then lifted away, and Evie found herself taken back into the dark night, floating though the starry trails.

The speed of the ship seemed fast yet slow at the same time. It felt weird to her to be moving at such an unearthly pace. Before she could think on it any further, another planet, colored in vivid and dazzling greens, came into view. As the ship approached the green planet, she saw it was covered mostly with thick forests, making it hard to see anything below the trees. Evie thought she could make out a few houses or buildings in the forest, but it was so dense that she couldn't tell for sure. As the ship reached the opposite side of the green planet, Evie was shocked to find it was completely barren. She also saw that a massive military base had been set up in the middle of the wasteland, with multitudes of soldiers and large, scary-looking weapons. The sight of the enormous base made Evie nervous, and she hoped she wouldn't be noticed by anybody down below. Before she could think any longer about who might see her, the ship shot rapidly into the sky and Evie was soon back on the star trails.

Soon enough, the ship took her across the stars to another planet that was a massive shimmering white ball in the dark night sky. She instantly remembered it as the one from her dream when she was on her way to Ireland. As the ship got closer to this planet, she could tell it was a highly populated one, as there were several buildings and cities that rose high into the air; some buildings even looked like they were floating in the surrounding clouds.

Evie noticed that the city was vibrant and beautiful in some areas, while other areas looked like they had gone through wars with bombings. As Evie watched, the ship began to slow down over an area of the city that was damaged and decrepit. It then suddenly stopped next to a window on the side of a very broken-down building. A ramp appeared from the ship, connecting it to an open window in the building. Evie made her way over the side of the ramp and slowly entered the room. It looked like a typical living room, but all the furniture and items, like the buildings, were old and broken down. She looked around some more when she heard hushed whispers coming from a room off to the right side. Evie was hesitant at first but then decided it was probably Callais and said, "Hello, is anyone here?"

The whispers stopped.

Then, she heard a scurry of shuffling noises and soon after, a tall beautiful woman appeared in the doorway. The woman had long blond hair with sparkling blue-gray eyes, light skin, and was at least three inches taller than Evie. The woman looked at her intently, but Evie could also see fear in her eyes. The woman then asked, "Who are you and why are you here, child?"

Evie took a moment to find the right answer but then realized she had no idea why she was there because the dream ship just took her. She looked at the woman and admitted, "The ship brought me here," while pointing at the window.

The woman rushed to the window and looked outside. When she turned back around, Evie saw a look of complete shock in her eyes. Suddenly, the woman rushed back to her and said, "Wait here, please."

After a few minutes of waiting, the woman reappeared with an elderly man who was shorter than Evie and had a wisp of crazy gray hair on his head, with whiskers on his face to match. His face was so wrinkled, it looked like a road map. He walked slowly over to Evie and reached out to touch her arm. Evie jumped back a bit as he chuckled and said, "My name is Newton Evander and this is Clara Bellatrias." As the old man motioned to the woman next to him, he asked, "Tell me, young one, how did you find this ship?"

Evie looked at him and was again unsure how to explain it, so she decided—since she had no reason not to trust them—to give him a brief history of how she got here. She explained about finding Marina and Ellis, how she found Callais and Aphrodite, how she traveled in her dreams on the starships that often took her to places she didn't know. After she finished telling her story, Newton and Clara stood there completely baffled. Clara then turned to Newton and said, "So, it is true. Magnus did figure out a way to save us."

Just as Evie was about to ask the odd couple some more questions, a loud trumpeting noise came from the streets below, followed by an explosion like the one she heard in the cottage a few nights before. Newton and Clara ran to the window and Evie, terrified, ran behind them to look out.

On the streets below, about five hundred yards away, was a horde of soldiers marching down the street with weapons in tow. They were the same soldiers and weapons Evie had seen on the forest planet's barren side, and the soldiers were making their way over to the building where Evie, Clara, and Newton were. Evie, feeling even more frightened, wanted to pull away, but she couldn't take her eyes off the soldiers. She watched as some of them would break rank and kick down doors, while others were shooting people down the streets. It quickly became a massacre as

Evie watched in horror. The soldiers were killing women, children, and the elderly with no mercy, and Evie could hear screaming and crying coming from all directions as the soldiers continued their raid. Evie watched as a few brave men tried to stand up to the soldiers, but the bold men were quickly beaten down or shot. Evie was horrified and wanted to yell out but was stopped when she saw a section of the soldiers in the center of the formation marching with a large cannon-like weapon. Evie realized that this was the weapon that created the explosions. The soldiers positioned the cannon, fired it, and a massive blast hit a building next to Evie, Newton, and Clara. Before Evie could do anything more, Clara frantically pulled Evie away from the window, shouting, "They have found you. You cannot go back the way you came. You need to leave!"

Clara grabbed Evie away from the window then scrambled to grab a bag and began rushing around the room, putting items and pieces of loose parchment in it as she turned to Newton and fanatically said, "We need to leave as well."

Evie rapidly followed Newton and Clara out of the room and across the hall into another room. They walked farther into the dingy apartment as Newton and Clara made their way to the far window when Clara opened the window and jumped out of it, followed quickly by Newton. Evie screamed in horror, knowing they were at least ten stories up and this leap would kill them. She ran quickly over to the window, hoping there was a ledge below where she would find Clara and Newton, but as Evie looked out she saw no ledge below. Clara then said, "Come on, girl."

Evie looked up and, to her amazement, Newton and Clara were just floating there. Evie looked at them and asked, "How? I don't know how to float!"

Newton then floated back in Evie's direction and reached for her arm just as another explosion hit the building Evie was in, knocking her off her feet and to the ground. Evie jumped up quickly, ran back to the window, and leaped. Just as Evie began to fall to the ground, she felt a strong hand on her arm and looked to see Newton holding on to her. It was a very strong grip for such a frail old man. However, Evie reached up, grabbed his arm with both of her hands as he lifted her up to his position and floated away with her.

Evie looked back at the building as they drifted farther away and realized that her floating ship was the target. Even though the ship was still slightly invisible, Evie could see its outline, which she figured was enough for the soldiers below to see as well. Evie then watched the ship burning, as thick black smoke began rising in the air. It then slowly sank behind the building, out of Evie's view.

Evie turned her attention back to Clara and Newton and although they were floating, she noticed every once in a while Clara and Newton would make contact with another building and push off again to regain momentum. They continued gliding and vaulting off of buildings for a while when Evie saw a small river below them nestled in between several partially fallen buildings. She then heard Newton say something under his breath as a small boat came up from the bottom of the river. Clara, Newton, and

Evie landed gently on it. As soon as they were settled in the boat, it began to move, making its way down the river, which was covered on either side with old buildings.

Evie noticed some of the buildings had obviously been burned or bombed, and some were just falling apart due to lack of care. Evie then felt the river swiftly dip down as they moved along a smaller trench and began to enter an underground tunnel. Evie became a little nervous, but Newton gently touched the top of her hand as if to console her. She looked at Newton as they entered the tunnel, and he smiled an almost toothless grin at her, which instantly comforted Evie.

The tunnel was dark for a while when dim lights started to shine and Evie could see that there were small stone buildings and homes stacked closely together, winding and weaving along the sides of the river and across the tops of the tunnel. The buildings and homes looked ancient when Evie thought, *This must be a long-forgotten older part of the massive cities above.*

As she looked harder, she saw that the lights were small orbs, similar to the one Marina conjured up in the cave pathways. Evie also began to notice that there were people, most of them in their homes or buildings, but she saw a few walking down by the riverside. As she looked at them, she could tell by their hollow faces and sad eyes that something bad had happened to them to push them underground. Evie noticed that some of the people had scars or badly burned areas on their body. At one point, she saw a group of children, and as they came closer, she saw that many of them were missing an arm or were badly scarred as well. The sights made Evie's hairs rise on the back of her neck as she teared up thinking of the poor souls in this awful place and what must have happened to them. However, she kept silent and decided again to ask questions later.

Evie watched her surroundings in silence as the boat finally made its way around another small bend in the river when Clara pulled out an oar and slowly navigated towards a small dock in what seemed to be the center of this underground city. The threesome got off the boat and started to make their way down an old cobblestone path. Evie examined the buildings around her and noticed how carefully built and detailed they were. There were many intricate and delicate carvings on the sides of the buildings that looked like they naturally grew into the stone. Evie could tell that these old buildings must have been white at some point but were now all dirty and dusty from years of being underground. She thought about what this city must have looked like in its prime, and she imagined it must have been majestic.

Evie followed Newton and Clara into an opening in the middle of the underground city that Evie thought must be the town square. It reminded her of a picture she saw once of town squares Italians call borghi. There was a small fountain in the center of this city with a statue of a large man. As Evie took a closer examination of the statue, she recognized it as Magnus. Evie gasped in amazement as Newton turned to look at her and smiled his toothless grin again. Evie smiled back and continued to follow Clara and Newton down another cobblestone path to the right of the Magnus statue.

They followed the path until they came to a row of tall skinny buildings that looked like they might tumble down. Clara entered a door in the center as Newton and Evie followed. It was dark at first, then Evie watched as both Clara and Newton maneuvered their hands together and made a circular gesture, just like Marina had, and a small blueish-white orb appeared in both of their hands. Evie looked around and realized she was in a typical entryway with jackets hanging on hooks, boots and shoes scattered underneath, and a small table covered with miscellaneous items across from the coats. There was a long narrow staircase leading to the upper levels and a path behind the stairway where Evie could smell something cooking.

She followed Newton and Clara to a large doorway to the right, past the hanging coats and jackets, and entered a large room with a large fireplace crackling merrily in the hearth. There were many places to sit, as the room was filled with comfy chairs, loveseats, and couches. There were also drawings and maps on the walls and a table in the front of the room overlooking the cobblestone street they were just on.

As Evie turned her gaze back to the fireplace, she saw two dogs sleeping peacefully nearby. Evie made her way over to the fireplace, hoping to see Bella, but as she got closer it was clear that Bella wasn't one of the dogs. She wondered why Bella wasn't there, but again she decided not to try and figure anything else out for the moment; she had enough on her plate already. Evie bent down to rub the dog's head closest to her as the other dog got up and moved next to Evie's other hand. She got the clue and began to rub this dog's head as well. Newton sat down on the couch closest to Evie and the dogs as he seemed to lovingly watch her caress them. "These are Delila and Darwin," as Newton pointed at each dog.

Evie bent down, smiled at each dog, and introduced herself. Evie then watched as Clara made her way over to the table and begin to pull items out of the bag that she had hurriedly packed back at the apartment building where they first met. Evie was enjoying the moment for a bit, trying her hardest not to think of all the horrible things she had just witnessed or the thousands of questions she had, when she heard a clatter come from the kitchen followed by loud cursing. Evie darted a questioning look at Newton. "Do not worry. Declan is just trying to be helpful!" he chuckled and continued to look lovingly at Evie.

Clara was continuing to shuffle around with the bag, placing items on the table while mumbling under her breath, when the door in the back of the room swung open and a young man about Evie's age came stumbling out, carrying a tray of food and drinks. He was tall and lanky and probably about the same height as Clara, if not a little taller. He had light blond hair, deep blue-gray eyes, and light skin. Evie made the assumption that this must be Clara's son because of the striking resemblance. As he made his way over to a small coffee table in front of Newton and the fireplace, he clumsily set everything down and looked up at Newton with a beautiful smile. Evie was struck by how attractive he was as he turned his head for the first time and noticed her. He stood there stunned for a minute then awkwardly made his way over to her and reached for her arm. Evie figured it was something like a handshake here since Newton had tried to reach for her arm back at the apartment as well. The young man then introduced himself. "I'm Declan Bellatrias, Clara's son. Why are you here?"

Clara turned her head and barked at her son. "Do not be rude, Declan. That is not how you welcome someone."

Declan hung his head low, mumbled an apology under his breath, straitened back up, looked at Evie, and said, "Sorry. Welcome to our home and welcome to the ancient city of Kali on planet Canopiuis."

Evie smiled back and thought, *I have never heard of a planet called Canopiuis*, but dismissed the thought, stood up, reached her hand out to Declan's arm like he had done and said, "I'm Evie MacDunleavy. Nice to meet you. I'm from Earth, from the city of Denver, Colorado."

Declan looked confused for a minute, but then extended his arm, grabbed her arm in the center, and squeezed. She raised her head to match Declan's gaze and saw he was intently looking at her, something that made Evie blush a bit, so she pulled her arm quickly back and turned to sit on the ground next to the dogs. Declan gave her an awkward smile and sat down on the couch next to Newton, both stealing quick glances at each other every once in a while.

Clara then seemed to be done with whatever she was fussing over and made her way to an armchair across from Newton and Declan and asked, "So, you are really from Terran and you really are a descendant of Magnus?"

Evie looked around at them as they all seemed to be waiting in anticipation for her answer. Since she didn't know what to say, she decided to respond with a simple yes. Newton gleefully clapped both his hands together as he rubbed them back and forth in excitement, his eyes glistening with joy. This made Evie smile just as Newton asked, "Are you dreaming or are you here on purpose?"

Evie looked around the room as they, once again, waited on the edges of their seats for her answer. She went on to explain that she was actually sleeping and that she had only gone into the dream state on purpose once. Evie then told them of Marina and Ellis—also Magnus's descendants—how she met

Callais and Aphrodite, and how they were all teaching her how to navigate the dream state consciously.

After she finished telling her story, both Newton and Declan were wiggling in their seats with excitement and Clara seemed to be deep in thought over what Evie just told them. Clara then moved, breaking her meditative state, and said, "I do not know how long you have here, but I will be sure to reach out to Callais so that we can maintain contact once you have figured out how to navigate the dream state. I am afraid you have much to learn and a short period of time to do so. When you get back to Terran, be sure to tell Marina and Ellis that they need to focus on training you as well."

Clara paused for a minute and then asked, "Do you have any questions before you wake from this place?"

Evie thought for a minute and then decided to ask about the ship, soldiers, weapons, and why the soldiers would attack them. Clara, Newton, and Declan all exchanged hesitant glances. The excitement that once filled the room was now a deafening silence. Evie started feeling uncomfortable when Newton began to speak and told Evie about Camulos, an evil man who was bent on destroying all. "Camulos's powers, his evil wars, his rule over several other galaxies, and his creation of the Camulus Pack, which were the soldiers you saw attacking your ship, are the reason we are all hiding."

He went on to explain in detail about the wars Camulos started and how many keepers—including Magnus, Clara, himself, and many others—tried to fight Camulos's growing power and evil. "Camulos conquered every known galaxy with living beings, and he vowed to destroy Magnus and the Devas galaxy last." Newton took a deep sigh and went on, "There is the belief that Camulos and Magnus were the first keepers created by two powerful beings known only as the mother and father; however, no one knows for sure if this is true or if the mother and father still exist, and no one knows for sure what happened between Magnus and Camulos or why Camulos would turn on all of us."

Newton looked intently at Evie and then continued his story. "The Devas galaxy belonged to

Magnus, and he decided it would be best to protect Devas by separating it from the rest of the universe and Camulos's evil power. Many head keepers were performing a great ceremony to hide and separate Devas when the Camulus Pack invaded, disrupted the ceremony, and left everything in complete chaos."

Newton told her how he and Clara were able to escape, along with a few other keepers, and hide from Camulos and his forces. Newton then said, "I had learned of Callais's escape and his continued effort to train protectors, so I reached out to him for his help."

"What are protectors?" Evie asked.

"The protectors are a force created by Magnus to help protect Devas," Newton answered and then paused again before saying, "Callais is the leader of the protectors; that is why it was so important for me to reach out to Callais, knowing he could help all of us who were left." He then sighed before saying, "The ship that brought you here…well, it was one of the protector ships, something we all thought were destroyed a long time ago. It's a very curious thing that you came here on one."

Evie gave him a questioning look, but Newton didn't explain any further. Evie was already overwhelmed by all she was hearing, so she kept listening as Newton explained that it was unclear if Magnus had survived, and there were only stories from a few people who claimed they saw him and spoke with him in the early years after Camulos's invasion. "It was so long ago that these stories were told that no one was certain if there was any truth to them. Still, it never stopped our search." Newton shook his head and said, "Once we found Callais, he confirmed that Magnus had been in contact with him, which renewed our efforts to fight against Camulos and continue searching for what Magnus left us to save the Devas galaxy."

Newton then described the torture, pain, and destruction that Camulos and his forces had been creating for over a thousand years. He took another long pause and sighed before saying, "There were many who still resisted and held out hope that Magnus had left us a savior after we lost contact with him." He paused for so long, Evie could see tears begin to fill his eyes. He wiped them away and said, "I had almost given up hope, Evie, until you. I am so glad you are here."

Just as Evie was about to ask some more questions, she felt a sharp familiar pain on her ear, followed by a distant rumbling noise. Just as she was about to say wait, the room, as well as Clara, Newton, and Declan became fuzzy. Evie soon found herself sitting up in her bed back at Marina's. Her hands were extended out, as if reaching for something, when she heard Ellis pounding on her door to get up with Bella still nibbling at her neck.

Chapter 23
THE FABRIC AND CHAIN

◆•————————●————————•◆

vie felt slightly disappointed; she didn't want to wake from that dream. She had so many questions left to ask. She sat in silence for a minute trying to process everything when finally she slowly got out of her bed and made her way to the door to answer Ellis's relentless knocking. She opened the door as Ellis said, "Geez girl. Yeh must've been tired. We've been waitin' all mornin' fer yeh to join us before Marina made me come up 'ere an' get yeh."

Evie smiled a sleepy grin at Ellis and said, "Oh boy, do I have a lot to share with you guys today."

Ellis looked at her when he realized Evie was still in the same clothes as the day before and said, "Get yerself freshened up girl an' come meet us downstairs in yer stacks." He then headed back down the hall.

Evie got cleaned up and realized she only brought a few clothes with her and she had nothing fresh. So, she put on some clothes she felt were less dirty than the others and headed downstairs. She stopped in the kitchen, grabbed some food, and drank a huge glass of the green juice before heading in the direction of the stacks. Evie felt she could navigate Marina's castle somewhat successfully now because, unlike when she first got to Marina's, the castle didn't seem to be moving and shifting as much anymore. She thought, *either because I'm finally used to all the weirdness, or because I'm actually getting better with whatever power I have.*

Evie entered the stacks to find Marina and Ellis waiting for her, while Bella bounced over to Aphrodite, who was lying at Ellis's feet. They looked like they already had an agenda in mind when she thought, *Instead of just following whatever they say this time, I'll take charge.* Evie then approached the table, but before Marina or Ellis could say anything, she began to talk first.

Evie told Marina and Ellis about her dream, traveling to a few planets on the ship, and meeting Clara, Newton, and Declan. She felt her cheeks turn a dark red thinking of Declan and how handsome he was. She pushed away her thoughts of Declan and continued to tell them how she witnessed soldiers tormenting people, shooting the ship down, and about how Clara and Newton floated out of a window with her. She went on to tell them about the boat, the river, the underground city she was taken to, and how she revealed Marina's and Ellis's existence to Clara, Newton, and Declan. Evie paused, looked at Marina and Ellis, and saw their faces switch from disbelief to amazement as she told her story. They didn't say anything, so Evie then told them what Newton had said about Camulos, Magnus, Callais, the wars and destruction, and how Magnus and other keepers had tried to save the Devas galaxy.

After Evie finished telling them all she had seen and learned, both Ellis and Marina sat for a while in silence. She watched them again as their faces shifted back and forth between wonderment and confusion.

Marina then got up and began pacing, and soon Ellis was up pacing around as well. Evie then said, "Clara told me to tell you that I need to figure out how the dream state works and how to navigate it. She said I have a lot to learn and little time to do so. I'm not sure what you were planning today, but I think it might be a good idea to work on that."

As soon as Evie finished her sentence, Aphrodite and Bella came over to her and stood on either side of Evie, almost as if they were showing support of her decision. Ellis stopped his pacing and turned to look at Evie and the two dogs, then laughed. "Well, Marina. It looks like it's three against two. What'd yeh think?"

Marina turned around and Evie could see that she was distraught but then gently nodded in agreement as she made her way to the table and began to unroll the scrolls. She then placed the chain, fabric, and loose piece of parchment out on the table next to the scrolls.

Evie almost forgot about the items they struggled so hard to find and made her way over to the table to investigate them. She glanced back at the table with everything on it, then she looked down at the top scroll that was most visible. It was spinning slightly, but far from being annoyed Evie thought, *They seem to show me what I need to see or need to know.* She waited patiently while the top scroll organized itself and eventually settled down so Evie could see it clearly. To Evie's amazement, this time she was able to see and understand much more of what was on the scroll. As she began to read the scroll to herself, Ellis said, "Read it out loud this time an' show us where an' what yeh see." Evie nodded and looked back down.

At the top of the scroll, there was some writing, so she began to read it out loud as she pointed to the words for Ellis and Marina. "*The mother left trails of stars for her children to find each other when she could no longer be reached. The trails connect each sibling, comprised of seven, to ensure they would never be lost. There are many groups of seven spread throughout the universe, and each group of seven has trails of stars so that, if any of the seven became lost, the stars would light the path back to their home...back to their siblings.*"

Once she finished reading the passage, a drawing on the scroll lit up, so Evie turned her head to look at it and pointed out the drawing to Marina and Ellis. There, in the corner of the scroll, was a drawing of a shimmering chain that was exactly like the one sitting on the table next to the open scroll. Evie gasped, took a step back, and turned her head to match Marina's and Ellis's gaze. Marina's earlier distraught look had turned to a smile, while Ellis began jumping up and down in excitement as the two dogs playfully joined. Then Evie remembered that when she was floating in the ships that carried her in her dream state, there were vague star trails that the ship seemed to be sailing on. Evie shouted, "This chain may be a way we can navigate the dream state on the star trails to make it easier to find people in Devas!"

Evie then joined Ellis and the dogs jumping around while Marina plopped in the chair next to her, looking like a heavy weight had just been taken off her shoulders. After a few minutes of relief and excitement, Marina made her way back over to the table and asked Evie to join. As Evie approached the table, Marina asked, "How is your head feeling?"

To Evie's surprise, it didn't hurt at all, and she happily said, "Just fine!"

Marina then asked politely if Evie would look at the other two scrolls before they got too excited, so Evie looked down at the scroll she had already read to see if there was anything else, but it remained the same. Evie mentioned the scroll was the same, so Marina moved the top scroll to the side and laid out the next one in front of her. Evie watched the new scroll move around again, so she waited for it to settle and find its place.

When the scroll finally stopped, there was a drawing of a galaxy with seven planets and a small square in the middle. The square seemed to shimmer and move a bit in its spot when Evie saw a crack of white light come from the center of the scroll and slowly cover up each planet in the galaxy. Soon, the whole scroll was blank with only a shimmering glow on it. The scroll surface then started moving again and it looked as though the square was refolding itself as each planet and the whole galaxy slowly came into view again. Once the whole galaxy was back in view, the square cracked open with white light once again and disappeared. Ellis was impatiently bouncing behind Evie and asked her, "What is it yeh see?"

Evie looked down and explained to Marina and Ellis what she saw. They all stood there for a minute when Marina reached across the table and pulled over the small piece of tied-up fabric that had been in Aphrodite's guarded den. She slowly began to untie it as the fabric started shimmering. As Marina untied it, she held a small square of shimmering fabric and looked at Evie with questioning eyes. Evie looked at Marina and then back down at the scroll just as the scroll had words appearing at the bottom. Evie read out loud again, "*To stay hidden, it is not too hard. Just wish the place whether close or far. To move forward, think of time. In an instant, time and space will divide.*"

Marina then looked at the tiny fabric square in her hands, closed her eyes, and whispered, "I wish to be..."

Evie and Ellis didn't hear the rest of her sentence as Marina took the fabric and whipped it over her head. The fabric then expanded and gently landed over her. In an instant and with a crack of white light, Marina was gone. Seconds later, across the room, another crack of white light appeared along with Marina. Marina looked at Evie with the biggest grin she had ever seen. Ellis and Evie stood there in shock for a minute and Ellis boomed in joyful laughter. "By god girl. We're gettin' somewhere!"

After a few moments of Marina's disappearing act, she slowly took the dangling fabric and said, "Back to the pocket you go."

The fabric made a whooshing noise and was instantly back to the small square. Marina made her way back over to the table, tied the string back on it, placed it in her chest pocket, and stated, "How about we try and go find someone?"

The threesome plus the two happy dogs excitedly made their way back to the guarded aisle after Marina's suggestion the aisle might be the best place to go into the dream state since it seemed to be a place to which Evie was sensitive. Marina also stated that since Evie had gone into an unguided trance in the guarded aisle, it might also be a good place to start exploring what they could do with their newfound items.

Once they reached the guarded aisle and made their way down to the clearing, Evie heard the whispers again and decided to look around for where it was coming from. She realized it was actually coming from the books and scrolls that were stacked on either side, so she took a closer look this time when she found a book that had the name "Clara" on it. Evie found the book title to be strange and wondered if it was about the same Clara she had met. She thought, *It would be weird if it was about Clara, but there are so many weird things happening already. After all, Marina just disappeared under a small piece of fabric.* She made a note to herself to grab the book on her way out and continued to follow Marina, Ellis, Bella, and Aphrodite.

Once in the clearing, Evie half expected the room to swirl again. She looked at Marina and Ellis and she could tell they, too, expected her to pass out or get light-headed. However, the room remained still as if it anticipated the reason they were all there.

Ellis then made his way over to the table in the center of the room with the galaxy map still on it and pushed it aside as they all sat in a circle again. Bella climbed into Evie's lap while Aphrodite plopped her big, slobbery head on Ellis's lap with a single strand of drool hanging out of her mouth, covering Ellis's knee. Evie laughed a little bit, but Ellis seemed not to be bothered by the monstrous dog's slobber. Marina then handed Evie the chain, but it was unclear what Evie was to do with it. Marina simply said, "Just hold it and see what happens."

Marina then extended her hands out towards Evie and Ellis and told them that they should try and find Callais. The other two agreed as Marina grabbed Ellis's hand and held on to the other end of the chain that was in Evie's extended hand. They closed their eyes and began.

As Evie started to slip into the fog thinking about Callais, she thought about the book she found on Clara and then thought of Declan. She tried her hardest to refocus on Callais but just couldn't get Declan out of her mind. Before long, Evie was surrounded by fog and soon found herself in the starry sky.

Chapter 24
TOGETHER IN KALI

⬦•————————•⬤•————————•⬦

Unlike before, Evie didn't find herself on a ship floating the star trails but seemed to be floating among the stars by herself, and it reminded her of how Newton and Clara floated from building to building. Even though Evie could see the star trails, she couldn't make out anything else, as if she was surrounded by the stars completely. After a few minutes of traveling through the stars, Evie began to make out something below. It was still unclear what was below her, but she found her body slowly making its way to the ground. Once on the ground, the fog and stars lifted, and she finally saw that Marina and Ellis were standing next to her. All three looked around, and while Marina and Ellis looked confused, Evie knew exactly where she was. They were standing next to a small river surrounded by old, broken-down, and burnt buildings. Ellis turned to Evie and asked, "Where the hell 're we girl?"

Evie looked at them and explained that they were on the planet Canopiuis, where she had met Clara, Newton, and Declan. Ellis flashed Evie a sheepish smile after she said Declan's name and then looked around. Ellis then said, "Okay, so no Callais. Where do yeh think we go then?"

Evie looked around for the small boat that took them to the underground city but then remembered it emerged from under the water. She couldn't remember what Newton said to bring it up. Evie looked around some more and told them that they would have to follow the river by foot.

Just as they were headed in the direction Evie pointed, a rustling sound came from a small alleyway between two buildings. Evie's heart stumbled and stopped with fright as she remembered the last time she was there. Marina sensed Evie's fear and quickly reached in her pocket and pulled out the fabric. Just as she was untying the knot over the fabric to hide the three of them, Bella and Aphrodite came bounding out of the alleyway playing chase with each other. Everyone let out a huge gasp of relief and continued down the river's edge while Aphrodite and Bella took turns chasing each other.

It took a lot longer on foot to reach the tunnel. When they finally reached the tunnel entrance, Marina made a movement with her hands and a small orb appeared. Marina held the orb up and proceeded to walk carefully along the side of the tunnel with the others close behind. Once in the tunnel, they found the path by the river was very narrow and unstable. There were a few times Ellis and Evie almost fell in when a rock or a piece of ground would collapse under their feet. To Evie's amazement, Aphrodite gracefully navigated the small path despite her large stature.

The group finally came to the end of the tunnel and began to walk through the ancient city called Kali. As they made their way through town, people saw them coming and scattered, running quickly back into their homes and into nearby buildings. The few people that remained outside gave Evie and the others deep stares that Evie took as a sign that they were unwanted guests. Evie was able to make out the scars and burns on many people's bodies more clearly. She wondered why so many people had the same injury. She also saw there were a few people who were wandering around in no particular direction, mumbling to themselves. One woman walked over to Evie. Her eyes were glazed over and she was missing her left hand and the lower part of her forearm. Before Evie could ask anything or offer any assistance, a man came rushing over to the woman and slowly escorted her back to a nearby house. He darted an accusing look at Evie before they entered the home.

Evie felt that it took much longer to reach the middle of the city when she noticed that they were on the wrong side of the river. She looked around but couldn't see a way to get across and started thinking of another plan when she felt a tiny tap on her arm.

She turned around and saw a small boy—he had to be no older than six—staring back up at her. Like the others in that town, his face was hollow, and his green-yellow eyes were filled with sadness. He had a long scar that started in his dirty blond hair, passed across his face, and made its way down his neck and under his shirt. Evie realized that he, too, was missing a left hand and lower forearm. She bent down at eye level with the small child as he said, "Come...Clara knows you're here and sent me."

Evie gave the little boy a smile, reached her free hand out, since she was still holding the chain in the other, when she saw him hesitate for a minute. Then he gave her a small smile and extended his only hand out to Evie, which she happily took and followed him.

They went back through the town for a few yards when they came to a small door in the back of an alley. The boy pushed the door open and headed down a set of dark stairs with Evie in tow as Marina lit up her orb and Ellis and the dogs followed. Behind the door and down the stairs was another tunnel, and although it wasn't very well lit, it was still bright enough that Marina put her orb away. At one point, Evie felt a drip of water on her head and looked up to see water leaking from the tunnel roof when the boy pointed up and said, "The river."

After a few minutes of following the boy, they came to a stairway and slowly climbed up. They walked slowly because the stairs looked to be a million years old, and Evie thought they would crack under their weight at any second. They soon came to a door at the top of the stairs. The boy knocked and mumbled something under his breath. The door then swung wide open and they all found themselves standing in a kitchen where Evie saw that Declan was cooking. His back was to the door, completely oblivious to the strangers who had just entered. The boy cleared his throat to get Declan's attention, making Declan jump. Declan spun around and seemed shocked for a minute, but then he saw Evie, smiled, and scurried over to the group. "Hi, welcome back Evie. I see you brought friends! My mother is waiting for you. She sensed your arrival."

Declan then spun on his heels, headed for the door on the far side of the kitchen, and held it open for his guests. Marina, Evie, Ellis, and the two dog companions made their way through the door into the adjacent room. Evie then turned around and went back into the kitchen where they had left the little boy. Evie saw the small boy was patiently waiting for Declan to give him a reward for bringing Evie and her friends to Clara's house. Evie bent down to eye level with the child and asked, "What's your name?"

The boy hung his head down and shyly whispered, "Collin Junaius."

Evie felt a pang of sadness for a minute as she remembered her father, because that was his name too. She pushed her hurt aside and said to Collin, "I would very much like for you to join us."

He looked back into Evie's eyes and, instead of sadness, she thought she saw a glimmer of hope. Collin then asked, "Can I have cookies too?"

Evie laughed and said, "I'm sure Declan can figure out how to get you some."

Evie looked up scanning the kitchen and, to her surprise, Declan had followed her back in and was standing there with a goofy smile directed towards her as he handed her a plate full of cookies. Collin jumped up with joy, grabbed the plate, and began stuffing his face as Evie tried to stifle her blushing. Declan and Evie watched him for a bit, smiling and laughing as Declan gently placed his hands on the boy's shoulder and guided him to the door as the three of them made their way into the room with the others.

Once they entered the room, the first thing Evie saw was a whirlwind of fur and tails as dogs ran about chasing each other. Evie realized that Bella and Aphrodite must have enlisted Delila, Darwin, and, to Evie's surprise, Apollo, in their game of chase. Evie then scanned the room and saw Clara and Newton were there with Callais. Evie gave Callais a quick smile. She was glad to see him there. Before Evie could say anything to him, she saw Clara shoot Declan a mom look (one that Evie assumed only he could interpret). Declan immediately understood his mother's hard look. So he quickly began to round up the rowdy bunch of dogs and escort them into an adjacent room across the hall where Evie could still hear them barking and roughhousing.

After the dogs were out of the room, it was much calmer, so everyone began to find a seat. Evie and Collin sat down next to the fireplace where Delila, Darwin, and Apollo had probably been enjoying the warmth before Bella and Aphrodite disrupted their peaceful perch.

Once everyone was seated, Callais noticed Collin and gave a questioning look, which Collin caught; his head sunk. Evie saw the exchange and chimed in that she wanted Collin to be there. Collin looked up at her again, smiled a big grin with his two front teeth missing, hugged Evie's arm, and then returned to his plate of cookies. Callais just nodded, smiled a bit, and began talking.

Callais started the conversation by asking Marina about Terran, Magnus, and how she found Evie as Marina explained. "I am one of Magnus's many children on Terran. He procreated with several people for many years in the hopes that someone in his bloodline would be pure enough to help him." She paused and sighed. "Many children in Magnus's bloodline lost their purity to greed, vanity, corruption, and deception. Not only that, but Earth itself has also become corrupt and it was a struggle for Magnus to maintain purity among his children, so he created The Keeper's Order to try and preserve lost knowledge."

She also explained that David and Ruby, Evie's adoptive parents, were trying to restore The Keeper's Order even now. Marina then admitted that even she had lost her purity like others in Magnus's bloodline, and she talked about finding Ellis. Ellis shifted uncomfortably in his chair as she told his story and how he, too, had become corrupt in his own way. Marina explained she had almost lost hope when she started dreaming of Evie, who she was able to find after many years searching. Callais turned his head to Ellis, Marina, and then to Evie and asked, "So, you are all Magnus's descendants?"

Before Evie could answer, Marina replied, "Yes, but Evie seems to be the only one who can read the scrolls and has been able to navigate the dream state with very little help. She was the one who actually brought us here today."

Callais returned his gaze to Evie, who was shocked by what Marina said. She thought she had randomly got there following the star trails. Callais was still looking at Evie, who was wondering whether she really meant to go there or whether she just happened to get there because she couldn't stop thinking about Declan. She blushed and looked down to avert the eyes of anyone who might be looking at her. When Evie collected herself a bit, she looked up to see that everyone, even Collin, was looking at her. Evie shifted on the floor and then said, "I didn't mean to purposely get here. To be honest, I still have no idea how I got here."

Clara then asked, "Last time you came by ship, what about this time?"

Evie then saw Clara and Callais give each other a glance she couldn't interpret but ignored it and explained that there was no ship this time and she just seemed to float on the star trails. She added that she had the chain in her hand this time and said,

"Callais, remember when you said that when we found Aphrodite, we would be able to figure out more?"

Callais nodded as Evie continued, "Well, we found her, as you can see," pointing into the direction of the dogs. "She was guarding a box with a chain in it, a piece of fabric, and some old pieces of parchment paper. Right now, I'm holding the chain in the dream state."

After Evie finished, Clara, Newton, and Callais all exchanged bewildered looks at each other. Callais then said, "Evie, if you have the chain, then you are really here this time. This is not a dream."

Evie looked at him slightly confused but remembered she was still holding onto the chain. She opened her hand and there is was: a shimmering, warm ball of light. She looked up at Callais and then the rest of the room, completely baffled. Callais then reiterated, "You are not in dream state anymore. You are actually here."

All of a sudden, Evie felt light-headed and dizzy, as if the room had started spinning. She felt like her body moved out from under her and she was tumbling down a dark abyss. Just as she was about to drop and hit the floor, she felt herself propped up by someone with really strong arms. Evie fell into them while she collected herself, all the while assuming it was Ellis who caught her. When she opened her eyes, she was staring right in to Declan's deep, baby-blue eyes as he slowly propped her into an upright position, smiling at her. As soon as Evie gathered herself, she pushed away from Declan's arms, avoiding his eyes and hiding her blushing cheeks. Declan got up and walked away, and when he sat back down, he had a hurt look on his face. Evie realized he just saved her from hitting her head and probably felt he had done something good. So, she looked at Declan and thanked him as he returned a smile and looked less hurt. Evie then turned her attention back to Callais and asked, "How can I actually be here and not dreaming this?"

Callais rubbed his head and said, "The chain can be used by Magnus's heir or other powerful keepers to travel the stars without the aid of dreaming. The chain and the fabric are two of the sacred relics the keepers used in the ceremony to separate and hide themselves from the rest of the universe and Camulos." Callais paused and then went on, "The chain and the fabric's purpose were not only to hide us but also bring us back into the rest of the universe once Magnus found a way to defeat Camulos. This is why Magnus's heir can use the chain to travel the stars. The chain is a way to bring us back together when the time is right."

Evie looked at Callais with amazement, not able to speak, when he continued to tell everyone, "During the ceremony, the Camulus Pack invaded. Everyone who was able to escape went into hiding. Most of the remaining keepers finally gathered to search for anything that could help, but no one could find the chain of reality, the fabric of space and time, or the other missing relic, the horn of infinity." Callais paused and added, "We also lost several of the ancient texts."

Callais continued to tell them after the invasion, Magnus eventually found Callais and told him that he had hidden the sacred relics and added that only one person in his bloodline could find them and use them to destroy Camulos. Leaving his heir this power would ensure that Camulos and his followers couldn't use the sacred relics. Callais then said, "Magnus did as much as he could to help us and others defeat Camulos after the invasion. However, we eventually lost contact with Magnus, and after many years without his help, hope was eventually lost." Callais took a deep breath and finished, "Myself and others never stopped fighting against Camulos even after we lost contact with Magnus, but the chain itself is one of the sacred relics that Magnus took and hid. As I already told you, Magnus left us a connection with Aphrodite so that his heir could make contact with us; however, after a thousand years with no contact from Magnus's heir, hope became thin again."

Callais took another deep breath before saying, "The chain, if used properly by someone from Magnus's bloodline, can connect his heir to the stars, making traveling the stars possible without aid. This is because the chain's light connects you to your heart; if you are unsure of where you need to go or who you need to be with, it searches your heart and finds where or who you want or need." Callais gave Evie a knowing look. "Obviously, the chain knew you needed or wanted to be here."

Evie looked around the room. She could tell that Marina and Ellis were processing the information while Clara stared intently at her. Declan smiled while Collin finished the last of his cookies, wiping his mouth off with his sleeve. When Evie looked over at Newton, she saw tears welling up in his eyes. She gave him a soft questioning look. Newton then said, "Oh child, I am so happy. I have been living on stories and myths for so long that I am just so glad there might be an end finally."

Newton got out of his seat and slowly made his way to the floor in front of Evie. He looked at her with his tear-filled eyes as he reached out, placed a hand on either cheek, and slowly leaned forward to kiss Evie on the forehead. He pulled back and looked at her for a bit longer when he turned to the rest of the group and said, "Well, enough stories for now. Since Evie is here and it is getting late, maybe we should all go to sleep and start again tomorrow." It reminded Evie of something Marina would say.

Everyone mumbled in agreement as the group started to slowly disperse, and just as they all started preparing for sleep, Callais asked Evie, "Marina mentioned your adoptive parents. Who are your real parents?"

Evie hung her head down, but before she could say anything, Marina interjected, "Unfortunately, Evie's parents have passed away and we do not know much about them. However, David and Ruby, besides trying to restore The Keeper's Order, are also trying to find out more about them."

Callais rubbed his chin and said to Evie, "I am sorry to hear about your loss, but hopefully David and Ruby will be able to find more about them for you."

Evie nodded, and as everyone began to get up again to head to bed, Evie suddenly shouted, "Wait… there are some things back on Earth that I think we should get if we intend to go forward."

Everyone stopped as Evie continued to explain that there were maps and scrolls there, as well as the pieces of parchment they found Aphrodite guarding. She didn't mention the book on Clara but thought to herself to grab that too. Callais stated that he would go to Terran with Evie while the others got some rest. He said he was interested to see if Evie could take him back to Terran. Evie then finally realized Terran was what the people from Devas called Earth.

The rest of the group agreed with Callais's plan to retrieve the items with Evie. Evie said goodnight to Marina and Ellis as she watched them head up the stairs, guided by Clara. Evie then saw Callais go to the room across the hall and holler at Apollo and Bella to follow him. The two dogs followed Callais, joined moments later by Aphrodite.

After everyone was upstairs, Callais made his way over to the fireplace and sat across from Evie. Bella climbed in Evie's lap as Aphrodite and Apollo rested on Callais. He asked Evie to take out the chain and then extended both hands towards her. Evie reached out her open hand to his and extended the chain. He grabbed it, and they both closed their eyes as Evie focused on Marina's castle. Evie soon felt herself drifting into the fog again and traveling the star trails. This time, when Evie opened her eyes and looked around into the starry fog, she was surprised to see Callais right next to her, holding her hand. The two smiled at each other and continued to float in the sparkling light.

After traveling for a while, Evie saw them approaching a swirling mass of stars, moving rapidly in a circle. She tensed up a bit since she hadn't seen this happen before, but she relaxed a little when Callais squeezed her hand as they flew towards the tunnel of stars. Soon, they were traveling so fast that everything became a blur, and just as everything was swirling about her, she heard a loud crack and everything instantly stopped. Evie could feel that she was standing on hard ground and no longer floating, but her surroundings where still dark and fuzzy. Evie then heard Callais say, "Give it a minute."

Evie waited a few more minutes as things slowly came into view. Soon, she realized she was standing in front of Marina's castle by the door that led to the kitchen. Evie looked over to Callais, who was looking around in awe. When he caught her gaze, he asked, "Is this Terran?"

"Yes. This is Marina's home," Evie replied.

Callais looked around some more and said, "I bet it was also Magnus's home. It looks exactly like his old home on Antillis."

Evie smiled and proceeded to go into the kitchen, wondering what was Antillis, but she figured she would ask later. When they entered the kitchen, they were met by Bella, Aphrodite, and Apollo, who somehow were already waiting inside Marina's home. Evie wondered to herself how they got there but decided it was best not to speculate too much. She was just happy they were there. Evie then made her way through the kitchen and towards the stacks with Callais and the dogs following closely behind. When they entered the stacks, Callais let out a chuckle as he was looking around and said, "Yes…This is Magnus's work."

Evie didn't ask any questions again and began to gather up the scrolls on the center table and the old pieces of parchment. She looked around for a bag and found the one they had been using, so she stuffed it with her collected items. She then made her way to the guarded aisle with Callais right behind her. Again, he chuckled and shook his head as he looked around and Evie wondered how long Callais had been alive for if he was old enough to know Magnus. He had a little bit of gray in his hair but looked no older than fifty. He definitely looked much younger than Marina, but not much older than Ellis. She shook the thought out of her head, realizing that Callais and Marina had already said that they had been searching or fighting for a thousand years. It was all so much to take in already, so she just continued to make her way down the aisle.

Evie heard the whispers again once in the aisle, but she ignored them and discretely grabbed the book about Clara off the shelf and stuffed it in the bag. She turned back to see if Callais had seen her do so, but he was looking around still. He also seemed unaware of the whispers, like Marina and Ellis. Evie shrugged, made her way into the clearing, and was glad to find that nothing was spinning around. She quickly grabbed the map of the galaxy and a few drawings on the wall. She looked around some more to see if there was anything else when she met Callais's intense stare. Evie ignored it, looked at him, and asked, "Do you see anything else that might be useful?"

Callais broke his gaze and looked around as he grabbed the drawing of the ship and rolled it up. He scanned the room a bit more and then shook his head. "I think this is a good start. We can always come back."

They packed up everything in the bag and hollered at the three dogs, who came bouncing into the clearing as Evie and Callais were taking a seat. They all assumed their normal positions as Evie and Callais closed their eyes and began their journey back.

Chapter 25

NADIA

David, Ruby, Amam, and Steven found themselves driving to a desolate area of Russia. Amam mentioned to them that most of The Order members had gone into hiding even before Dermot's death, and many more scattered after he died, afraid for their own lives. David felt a little guilty for recruiting Amam in their new effort to restore The Keeper's Order, but he also knew that this needed to be done to help Evie.

As they pulled up to a large stone and wood cabin, Amam leaned over and said, "Nadia is very knowledgeable, but she doesn't trust anyone. So, be very careful when you meet her."

David felt a little tingle of fear go up his spine, but he knew that he had to find out more. He shook off his fear as they got out of the car and knocked on the front door. They stood there for several minutes before they could hear footsteps come to the door and a voice firmly ask, "Who is it?"

David got worried again; he thought Amam had called her to tell them they were coming. He hoped Amam did call, and they were not catching this woman off guard. Before David could think anymore, Amam simply replied, "It's Amam. I bring the people I told you of."

The door slowly opened. David saw a tall, thin woman with dark black hair and golden eyes standing in the doorway. She nodded at the group and, with a thick Russian accent, said, "Come in."

David could feel Nadia's cold stare as they passed her. Once in the entryway, Nadia walked past them towards a large room off to the side and said, "Follow me, but do not touch."

They entered the room, and David was amazed to see that it was filled with books, scrolls, maps, and strange artifacts and objects neatly placed in display cases against the walls. Nadia pointed to a few seats as they all slowly sat down. After a few minutes of awkward silence, Nadia said, "I am Nadia Lebedev. I am told you found the girl."

Ruby began to fidget, so David reached out for her hand as Steven answered, "We believe we have, and we've been instructed to restore The Keeper's Order and gather information so we may help her."

Nadia sat for a while, which David assumed was because she was thinking about what Steven had said. The room remained quiet since no one wanted to break the silence as David analyzed Nadia's unusually beautiful face masked by her stony and lifeless stare. Nadia soon interrupted David's thoughts and said, "Dermot did not tell me much, but I was able to find out some things about this girl's parents before he died."

She paused and then went on, "It seems the girl's father was a direct descendent of The Order's founder, a man named Magnus. Dermot told me that once the girl's father learned of his true identity and true past, he became upset and did not want anything to do with it, so he asked Dermot to hide him and his young wife."

She paused again and then continued, "The girl's father was not upset because he was frightened, but he told Dermot he had watched all of the people he loved fall to the power that Magnus's bloodline conveyed, and he did not want that for himself."

Nadia cautiously looked around the room before saying, "Dermot promised to hide this man and his wife, with the proviso that this man would come out of hiding if Dermot was to ever discover the secrets of Earth's past and if he needed the girl's father to help him."

She took a deep breath and then went on, "The girl's father agreed and Dermot hid him and his wife. Dermot did not tell a soul about hiding them."

David looked confused and asked, "How do you know that he hid them if he never told anyone?"

Nadia's cold lifeless stare then changed as she smiled and said, "My ancestors were enlisted into The Order by Magnus himself because of my family's special gift. He called my family watchers. We can see into time and into other's visions. However, what we can see is limited and often vague. What I tell you is of the vision I had the last time I was with Dermot."

Nadia then explained more about being a watcher. She told them Magnus was from a distant galaxy where a group of people called Keepers enlisted others to help them protect their galaxy. She then went on, "There are head watchers and lower watchers, who had the special assignment of keeping an eye out for any approach of darkness and evil. These watchers had the special gift of sight into other's visions as well as sight through time but could only hold this power for temporary periods of time."

She revealed that Magnus found people who had this gift and trained them in how to use this sight to find and store knowledge as well. Nadia then explained, "Magnus had also given my ancestors a watcher glass to help them hold their sight. However, my glass was stolen from me long ago, but I can still use some of my powers to view others' visions. Although, I do not have sight through time without my glass."

She took another deep breath and said, "I felt Dermot was hiding something from me. I did not like this because I have always helped him, and my family has always been loyal to The Order. When I pressed him about what he hid, he said that he would share with me later but he could not at that time. I did not believe him, so I went into his mind and was able to see what I told you about the girl's parents. However, Dermot felt my presence in his mind and pushed me out before I could gather anything else."

Nadia paused again and sighed. "Because of my actions, Dermot secluded himself even more, hiding what he knew from others."

Everyone was in deep thought after Nadia told them how she came across this knowledge. Finally, Amam broke the silence and said, "I wasn't sure until now if I should tell you, but the girl's mother, although not a descendent of Magnus, comes from a family that was very powerful and whom Magnus trusted with information."

Amam paused before saying, "There is much thought among The Order members that this man's wife also knew much about the knowledge that we have lost and where to find it. However, all this is only rumor. Nothing is known for sure."

David, Steven, and Ruby sat in silence. After a few minutes, David asked, "What do we do now?"

Nadia shook her head and motioned to all the books and artifacts in the room. "We begin our search again. You will stay here for now until we figure out where to start."

Ruby started to protest, but before she could, Nadia interjected, "I am sorry. I do not mean to intrude, but your thoughts of love are so powerful. I can see them as if I am looking at a picture. I know you want to be with the girl, but if she is the heir, she needs to journey on her own for now. Do not worry, you will be with her soon enough."

Nadia smiled at Ruby, stood up, and held out her hand. "Come with me, I think I have something you will like." Nadia took Ruby to a table close by and began to show Ruby her collection of books on healing, easing some of the tension in the room.

Soon, the others joined and began talking and making plans.

* * *

Over the next few days, David, Steven, and Amam began looking over everything Nadia had in her collections. Nadia would help them often, but she took a liking to Ruby, and Ruby seemed to like Nadia as well. So Nadia spent much of her time with Ruby, teaching her about herbs, plants, and flowers, as well as a few lessons on reading the stars and celestial signs.

The following weeks were spent studying all the information they could gather. There were struggles and some misdirection in their search, but they finally arrived at what they thought would be a start. Soon, they all began to make their plans to restore The Order, restore knowledge, and save Evie.

Chapter 26

THE BLACK SHIP

vie and Callais left Marina's home and Earth, traveled through a rapidly moving tunnel of stars, and then slowed down to a much slower pace. Evie glanced over and saw Callais floating next to her, but this time he wasn't holding her hand. Evie decided she was getting better at this star traveling business. Soon, a white planet came into view, which Evie now recognized as Canopiuis, so they moved forward toward their destination. However, before they could reach the planet, a bright flash of red light streaked across the sky, almost blinding Evie and disrupting the star trail in front of them. For a minute everything was chaotic, but

Evie noticed the star trail seemed to begin to piece itself back together. Just as soon as Evie thought everything was okay, she glanced over at Callais to see him looking straight in front of them, and Evie saw a look of terror in his eyes. Evie followed his gaze to see a massive black ship floating a hundred yards away, surrounded by a plume of dark-colored smoke. Then, Evie heard a loud eerie voice echo through her head saying, "Ah, Callais. We have finally found you."

She realized with a ripple of terror that someone was looking for them when Callais immediately grabbed Evie's arm and shouted, "Hang on."

Evie was stunned and immediately grabbed on to Callais. As they began to move across the stars, she thought, *How can I hear Callais in space?* but then assumed the chain made it possible for her to hear those with her on the star trails. Before Evie could think any further on the ability to hear Callais, he grabbed her tighter and she soon felt herself twisting and turning rapidly along the star trails and into the darkness of space. She was spinning so fast, she had to reach out her other hand and grab on to Callais and held on as tight as she could. At one point, Evie felt as though they stopped somewhere, but it was so brief that she was unsure and all she could feel was her body twisting and turning as she desperately clung to Callais. It seemed to Evie the spinning would never end and she felt her body slowly giving away to an intense pain as her grasp began also to weaken. Evie then heard Callais shout, "Do not let go. It is almost over!"

Evie looked at Callais and, from his opposite side, she saw another bright flashing light fill the space around them. Evie then saw Callais extended his arm out when she saw a huge sword present itself, permeated with a white glow. Callais then yelled out something Evie couldn't understand as he charged forward, holding the sword straight in front of him. Evie looked in the direction of the charge and saw the massive black ship appear again right in front of them as Callais continued his advance. Evie began to yell "Stop!" but there was no time; Evie, Callais, and the sword went headfirst into the side of the ship, ripping it apart as they hit. When they came out the other side, Evie looked behind them and watched as the black ship exploded into a cloud of dark smoke.

After the ship exploded, it began to fall into the darkness below and then slowly disappeared. Evie found they were floating alone in the stars once again. She then looked over at Callais to ask him what happened, but when she did, Callais gave her a desperate look, lost his grasp, his body became limp, and he began to slowly fall into the darkness and out of Evie's reach. Evie instantly dove down into the nothingness and grabbed Callais's falling body, and when she had him back in her arms she looked around her but had no idea where to go. In the distance, she saw a small green planet and decided to head in that direction, pulling Callais's limp body behind her with all of her might.

Part Three

◆———————•———————◆

ANTILLIS

Chapter 27

ANTILLIS

＊• —————————— • —————————— •＊

Evie was unsure how long it would take to reach the green planet and if it was safe enough that she'd be able to help Callais. She continued to make her way to the planet anyway because she knew there was nothing she could do out in space and had no idea if or how long it would be before another black ship appeared out of nowhere. As she neared the green planet, she immediately recognized it as one of the planets she had hovered over before when she was on the ship that took her to Clara and Newton. She remembered that on the barren side of the planet, there was a large military base with soldiers, so she reminded herself not to go there. As she reached the planet, she also decided it would be best to hover as close to the ground as possible so that she wouldn't be seen too far out and be spotted by someone she didn't want to meet. However, the trees were so tall and thick, it was hard to stay close to the ground, so she hovered as close as she could to the tree line. She also remembered that the last time she was over this planet, she thought she could make out small establishments on the ground. Although she wasn't sure, she tried to look for them anyway.

Evie hovered for a long period of time, still not finding anything. She was about ready to land despite her empty search when she felt a sharp pain on her right side and saw that a rock had hit her from below. Evie spun around in the direction the rock came from and scanned the ground. She saw in a very tiny clearing was a young girl looking up right at Evie, frantically waving her hands, motioning Evie to come down. Evie thought this girl seemed harmless and she really had no other option, so she slowly made her way down to the tiny clearing where the girl stood.

As Evie landed, she realized how heavy Callais's body was and accidently dropped him on the ground with a thud. The girl ran over to Callais's limp body and made a hand gesture for Evie to stay, as if Evie were a dog, and the girl ran back into the thick of the forest. Evie stood there for a while and thought, *maybe this is not a good idea*, and went to drag Callais's body in the opposite direction from which the girl ran off. She once again realized how heavy Callais was and how exhausted she was and couldn't move him more than a few inches before she was too tired to advance any further. She felt a sudden flicker of madness and dropped to her knees as she frantically thought about what to do. Evie, feeling defeated and scared, decided to wait for the girl's return. After a few more minutes of waiting, the girl returned from the forest with a man. The man bent down over Callais's body and then, with a big grunt, heaved Callais over his shoulders and headed back the direction they came. The young girl again motioned her hand at Evie to follow, so Evie followed, too defeated to do anything else.

They walked through the forest for a long period of time. The forest was so thick that Evie got caught in several branches and tripped over some roots sticking out of the ground a few times and quietly cursed her clumsiness once again. After walking for what felt like five miles to Evie, they came to a large rock that had a small cave-like entrance going into the rock. The man had to duck to go into the entrance while Evie and the girl were able to walk in without having to bend down.

At first, the cave was dark and Evie expected one of them to make a hand orb, but after a few feet, she saw that there were several little orbs on each side of the wall, lighting up the rest of the path. They walked for a while when they came to a large underground opening that looked like it went downwards and upwards for miles. The three of them were standing on a ledge with steps leading down into giant tree roots. As Evie looked up, she saw massive tree roots above her, cascading their way down into the colossal cave below. She realized that the roots were so large, dwellings were built right into the roots and honeycombed mazes of bridges and pathways corkscrewed around and connected one set of root dwellings to other sets of root dwellings. Evie was absolutely astounded by this underground city.

As they made their way down the root steps, Evie saw that, unlike the underground city of Kali, this one was bustling with people who seemed much happier than the ones in Kali and, although there were a few people with battle scars and missing limbs, most of them looked healthy and unscathed. As they continued down the steps, they passed a few dwellings with people busily talking in them. One dwelling was quite large and there were several people around a large table having a discussion like they were planning something in a business meeting. One of the women in the big room, who looked to be the same age as the man that carried Callais, saw him, came running over to the man, and asked, "Otto, who's that?"

"It's Callais. He's weak and I'm taking him to Regina," Otto replied.

The woman looked worriedly at Callais strung over Otto's shoulders and followed them down the steps for a little while longer when Otto turned right into another tree root dwelling. As they entered, Otto had to duck again while the other three entered with ease. They entered a room that was much larger than Evie expected and was filled wall to wall with vials, herbs, and jars of stuff Evie didn't recognize. She thought to herself that it looked like an apothecary's home she had seen in a book. Across the room, another woman who looked to be about fifty or sixty rushed over and directed Otto to a table in the far corner. Otto laid Callais's limp body on the table as the two women, the girl, and Otto looked at Evie. The woman named Regina then asked, "What happened?"

Evie explained as much as she could to them. They all stood there for a minute, stunned by what Evie had told them, as Regina ran around the room collecting random items from the shelves and carrying them back over to Callais. Regina then began taking items out of jars and grinding them with a pestle and mortar as she directed the young girl to rub some kind of salve on Callais's head. After a few minutes, the woman began chanting as the others watched her rub more stuff on Callais and burned incense over his body. Otto then moved closer to Evie and said, "This will take a while. Why don't we go over there and talk for a bit as you fill me in on everything that is going on."

Evie was a little nervous because she was still not sure how much she could trust them, but they all seemed to know who Callais was and were helping him, so she followed Otto to the opposite side of the room where there were a few chairs and a small table that had bread, water, and what Evie believed to be Virdis. She realized how hungry and depleted she was as she looked eagerly at the table. Otto chuckled and gestured his hand for Evie to help herself. Evie greedily grabbed some bread and washed it down with the green juice. After stuffing her face, she wiped her mouth with the back of her hand and looked up at Otto and the young woman sitting across from her when Otto said, "I'm Otto Vegas. This here is Emmeline Freyas," he gestured towards the young woman, "and over there is my younger sister, Amelia, and that's Regina, who is our healer."

Evie nodded, introduced herself, and asked, "How did you see me through the thick trees?"

"We have scouts all over this side of the planet and Amelia happened to be in a scout post." Otto pointed at Amelia again and said, "I just assumed Amelia saw you and realized you weren't a threat before she came to get me."

Evie wondered what would have happened had Amelia seen her as a menace. She pushed the thought aside and was just thankful that Amelia rescued them. Otto then asked, "So, besides the battle with the ship, what were you and Callais doing out there anyway, and how did you even get to this planet?"

Evie felt she could trust them a little more now, so she told them as much of her story as she could think of. When she was done, she noticed Otto and Emmeline were taking it all in. Otto had a puzzling look, as if he didn't fully believe her. Then, he shrugged and said, "Well, I believe you are stuck here for a while, at least until Callais regains his strength. I'm not sure what to do next until he wakes. So, in the meantime, you'll stay with me and Amelia."

Emmeline shot him a dirty look of jealousy, which Evie caught but ignored. Otto then turned his head and told Amelia to head home once she was done helping Regina. Otto began walking out of the dwelling when he turned to Evie, who hadn't moved, and waved his hand. "Come on now."

Evie got up and followed Otto as Emmeline followed Evie. They made their way across a bridge to another tree root dwellings and entered. Otto didn't have to duck this time, so Evie assumed this was definitely where he lived since he probably picked a dwelling that he could enter easily. She followed Otto over the threshold and once inside, she was surprised to see that the dwelling was very much like a home. The center room had couches and side tables that held lamp-like stands with little orbs glowing on the tops. On the other side of the living room was a small kitchen area with a table and chairs, cabinets on the back wall, and what looked like a small stove. On either side of the kitchen were two openings, which most likely led into what Evie assumed were bedrooms. Otto gestured his hand towards the right opening. "You can stay in Amelia's room. . .Emmeline, why don't you help her get set up."

Evie and Emmeline walked into the bedroom and Evie noticed it was similar to a typical teenage girl's bedroom. There was a bunk bed in the far corner, a dresser on the opposite wall, and a small desk up against the center wall with an orb lamp on it. The room was scattered with items of clothing, drawings, and what Evie thought to be colored pencils. The room was fairly messy, but Evie felt comfortable in it because it reminded her of her room. *It's functional chaos*, Evie thought as she laughed to herself when she used that statement to justify to David and Ruby why she didn't clean her room. She felt a pang of sadness thinking of David and Ruby and remembered that she didn't call them and hoped they weren't too worried. She reminded herself that she needed to figure out how to contact them and let them know she was okay as soon as she got a chance.

Emmeline was bustling about the room picking items off the ground, trying to clean up a bit. As she held a pile of clothes in her arms, she looked around unsure where to put them, so she gently put them down in a pile next to the dresser and turned to Evie. "I'm sorry Amelia's room is such a mess," she said apologetically, scrunching up her nose. "I think Amelia usually sleeps on the top bed. If you would like to take the bottom, I don't think she'll mind."

Evie smiled at Emmeline, thanked her, and made her way to the bottom bed. It hit Evie just how tired she was as she laid down. Evie looked over at Emmeline and asked her, "Are you okay?"

Emmeline nervously smiled. "If you are who you say you are, I'm really happy and will do anything to help. But if you're Magnus's savior, you really have to be careful who you trust."

Evie looked at her with questioning eyes when Emmeline said, "It was no accident you and Callais were almost caught. Callais has been hiding successfully for years without ever getting close to being caught. We know there are many spies for Camulos. Someone who knows Callais and knows where he was must be a spy we aren't aware of and may have told them how to find you in the star trails."

Emmeline paused for a moment, then continued, "Please be careful. So much has happened to us already. We can't afford to lose any more hope."

Emmeline gave Evie a pleading look with slight sadness in her eyes as she turned around and made her way back into the other room. Evie couldn't even process anything anymore and she slowly drifted to sleep, completely exhausted from her encounter. She didn't dream that night, but at one point, Evie thought she heard Bella barking as she gently whispered into nothingness, *Don't worry sweet dog, I'm okay and will find you soon.*

Chapter 28

AMELIA

———●———

vie woke up the next morning to Amelia sitting at the edge of her bed staring at her. As soon as Amelia saw Evie's eyes open, she jumped up happily and motioned with her hands to follow her to the kitchen. Evie slowly got up and followed Amelia to the next room, where breakfast and Otto were already waiting. She pulled up a chair to the table and Amelia sat down next to her as both of them began loading up their plates. Otto was across from them eating and intently reading something when Amelia waved her hands back and forth in front of her face, trying to get Otto's attention. Otto didn't look up, so Amelia grabbed a biscuit and tossed it at

Otto's face. Evie let out a short burst of laughter as he looked up, grabbed the biscuit, and flung it back at Amelia shouting, "WHAT?"

Amelia picked up the biscuit, pointed at the paper Otto was reading, and opened her eyes really wide while looking directly at Otto as if to ask what was he reading. Then, it occurred to Evie she hadn't heard Amelia talk and wondered why she didn't. Otto satisfied Amelia's curiosity by explaining it was news about what was going on. Suddenly, it occurred to Evie she had no idea where she was, so she asked Otto, "Where am I?"

Otto gave Evie a curious look before answering, "You are on the planet Antillis, in the underground city of Mari. We are a city that Callais created many years ago to set up a central location for the resistance. Antillis was originally the planet were Callais would train the protectors before the Camulus Pack invaded. Many of us here have been trained by Callais to help defeat Camulos and his evil forces."

Evie looked around and thought, *This is definitely a great place to be since Callais was the one who built this city and trained people to fight.* Evie then looked at Amelia and asked her about the scout post and how she saw Evie. Amelia looked at Evie and then back at Otto when Otto said, "Amelia can't talk. She cut her tongue out when she was a child."

"Why?" Evie asked, looking at both in complete disbelief.

Otto shook his head and began to explain. "I had been recruited by Callais to train for the resistance. While I was gone, our home planet, Sirios, was invaded by Camulos's soldiers and by Camulos's right-hand man, Balor Kronius." He paused and then told Evie, "Balor had learned that many of the people recruited to be the Devas protectors came from Sirios. In an effort to learn who the protectors were and where the protector base was located, Balor and his Nox guard made it their personal mission to find anyone who would know any information about the protectors or their base."

Otto paused to see if Evie had questions, but she was curious about what he was saying (and thinking she would finally get some answers), so she just nodded as Otto continued, "Balor learned that I had been personally recruited by Callais to be a protector and that Callais was training me to be his right-hand man. Balor then learned who my family was and decided to bring them in for questioning." Otto sighed and then went on, "Fortunately, the individual Balor had captured and tortured for the information about my family and my location escaped and warned my family that Balor and the Nox guard were coming."

Otto then went on to explain that once Balor and the Nox guard approached Otto's family home, his mother and father were already prepared for the fight. Although his parents were outnumbered, they had procured a Devas protector staff that hadn't been destroyed and put up a ferocious fight, killing many of the Nox guard. Otto then said, "Balor apparently stood back for a while and watched my parents fight the Nox guard until he felt it was his time to intervene, then he used one of his special weapons and stunned my parents in their place."

Amelia then began to gesture her hands while Otto interpreted her memories from that night.

"Amelia says our parents stood frozen in their positions as Balor approached them, clapping his hands and saying, '*Impressive show you two, very impressive.*'"

Evie listened intently as Otto continued to interpret Amelia's gestures and told her that Balor then spoke and said, "*I really could've used the two of you, but it looks to me that I will have to kill you instead—unless…*"

Otto paused as Amelia continued to wave her hands in the air as Otto returned to interpreting for Evie. "Balor then took a long pause, staring directly into our father's face before he punched him in the stomach, which dropped our father to the ground. Balor then took one knee so he was almost level with our father and said, '*You tell me where the protectors are and where your son is.*'"

Otto rubbed his head and then went on, "Our father, with his head still on the ground, slowly turned his head upwards, looked Balor in the face, defiantly smiled, and then spit in Balor's face saying, '*NEVER, you filthy pig.*'"

Otto took a deep breath and continued to speak for Amelia, but Evie could see the pain in both of their eyes as he continued. "Balor then took a long rod that was at his side and beat our father's head into the ground until he was dead."

Evie gasped as Otto made a quick choking noise, which Evie assumed was because he was having to relive this pain. Otto then started again. "When Balor was done, he took the blood-soaked rod and placed it under our mother's chin as he gave her a vicious smile and asked her, '*How about you? Will you tell me?*'"

Otto and Amelia both now had tears welling up in their eyes, but before Evie could tell them to stop, Otto continued, "Our mother, even in her frozen state, was visibly trembling as Balor then knocked her to the ground, lowered himself to her level, and said, '*Talk, woman.*'"

Amelia gestured more as Otto translated for her again. "The stun from Balor's weapon was apparently wearing off because our mother was able to bring herself to her knees and come face-to-face with Balor.

Once she was staring directly into his eyes, she lunged forward and grasped Balor's neck between her hands as hot tears poured out her eyes and she screamed, '*I'd rather die.*'"

Amelia continued to gesture as Otto talked. "Balor released himself from our mother's grasp, stood up, and kicked her back down to the ground and told her, '*As you wish!*'"

This time, Evie saw that Otto and Amelia now actually had tears running down their cheeks, as well as herself, but Otto held up his hand, shook his head, and said, "Balor then took another weapon from his jacket and fired, turning our mother into a plume of dust and smoke. He wiped the dust from his jacket and told the Nox guard to raid the house for any information. A few minutes later, one of the guards found Amelia, who was already profusely bleeding from her mouth. The guard threw her at Balor's feet along with some small piece of bloody meat when the guard said, '*We found her hiding in the house. She must've seen everything because she cut out her tongue.*'"

Otto's chin sank to his chest as though he was too weary to keep his head up any longer, and Evie wanted them to stop, but she knew they both needed to finish their story, if only to let her know just how awful their world and galaxy had become. Otto then lifted his head and continued, "Balor looked down at Amelia, who not only had streaming blood coming down her chin but tears falling from her eyes. He lowered himself to the ground again as Amelia scampered across the dirt backwards in an attempt to escape him. Balor laughed at this and grabbed her leg, pulling her back towards him and said, '*You are a brave girl, stupid too.*'"

Otto continued his interpretation and said, "Balor looked over at Amelia again and then said to her, '*I think I have a way I might be able to get the information I want from you.*'"

Otto took another deep breath and finished, "Balor looked at Amelia one last time, stood up, and told his Nox guard, '*Take her back to the camp, and be sure to bring her to my personal work space. I'm not done with her yet.*'"

Amelia began to cry uncontrollably after she finished her story and fell into Otto's arms. Otto consoled her as he told Evie that Amelia was tortured with a machine that was known as the extraction machine. Its purpose was, and still is, to erase all dreams, memories, and thoughts from a person. Otto then said, "The machine is just another way Camulos has found to destroy us."

Evie stared in horror at the two of them, thinking about how much they had been through, when she asked, "But why did she cut out her tongue?"

Otto took a deep breath again and wiped some tears from Amelia's cheeks and then his own cheeks and explained, "The soldiers who invaded were directly under Balor's command. Everyone knows that if you were caught by Balor, he would torture you until you spoke up. Amelia, only being a small child at the time, knew she couldn't talk without a tongue, so she cut it out."

Evie gasped again as Otto then explained further, "I heard of Amelia's capture and told Callais I needed to leave to save her. Callais not only said that I could go but joined me before Balor could successfully continue his torture techniques on her." Otto then looked intently at Evie and stated, "The last time I saw Callais so weak was when he defeated a whole base of Camulos's soldiers to help me save Amelia along with several others Balor held captive."

Otto paused once more before he said, "This is one of the reasons why Callais is the man most hunted by the Camulus Pack and one reason he is a hero among the resistance."

Evie then asked, "What would Amelia have known Balor wanted from her at such a young age?"

"She was protecting me," Otto replied with remorse in his voice.

Evie looked at Amelia and thought how brave she was to take drastic measures to save her brother. Evie sat there for a while longer and contemplated Amelia having to watch her parents die. Although Evie's parents died when she was young, she didn't have to see it nor did she go through any of the hard decisions Amelia had to make. Evie looked over at Amelia with admiration as she placed her hand on Amelia's and said, "You're so brave. I'm honored to be at your side."

Amelia smiled at Evie and after a minute of silence, even though Newton had explained a little bit to her about protectors, she was still unclear about everything and asked Otto about them. Otto took a deep breath and said, "Callais is a lower keeper who was chosen for his bravery, commitment to The Keeper's Order and sacred text, and his compassion for others. He was handpicked by the head keeper, Magnus, for this job."

Otto rubbed his head again and then said, "The protectors were trained by Callais with the gift of travel between worlds. Thus, their special gift was to manipulate space to move rapidly between the planets in the Devas system. The protectors were also given special tools to help aid them in protecting the Devas system. These tools were ships that could help them travel between worlds on the star dust trails in the Devas galaxy as well as metallic Devas staffs that were cast with spells of protection from the sacred texts."

Evie was very interested now and was listening intently as Otto continued to explain, "There were a hundred ships, and each ship was made of the finest metals from the Sirios planet. The metals were cast with spells to make them lighter than air yet almost indestructible. The metals were specially crafted so they could be manipulated by the space around them. This gave the ships the ability to match any environment, like a natural camouflage that kept them nearly invisible. The sails on the ships were made from a plant found here on Antillis called Desmodias, finely crafted into fabric that could withstand even the harshest of climates, so the sails would never break."

Evie gasped. "I think I've been on one of those ships."

Otto gave her a curious look and shook his head. "I don't think so, Evie. As far as we know, they were all destroyed."

Evie thought about protesting and saying that she really was on a ship like that, but thought it would be better not to argue. Otto then said, "There were also metallic staffs made of the finest metals found on Sirios and had similar properties to the ships.

The staffs had protection spells that could be used to shield anyone around them within a fifty-mile radius. Each staff also had a feather of a special bird found on Alpharman, the spirit world, embedded into them. The feather came from a bird sacred to Alpharman called Andeais. This feather helped the staff levitate objects for temporary periods of time."

He then paused and took a deep breath, "My parents found one of these staffs to fight off Balor, but it wasn't enough." Otto then added, "All the protectors were trained here on Antillis, and although we are few in number, we have great spirit and bravery, like Callais."

Evie was overwhelmed by all this information and realized that Otto had told her she was on Antillis. Evie then asked, "How many planets are there in the Devas galaxy?"

"There are seven sibling planets in each galaxy across the universe." Otto rubbed his hands over his forehead and Evie realized he was wearing out when he said, "However, we lost one of our own, Terran, when Camulos invaded."

Evie sat for a while longer thinking about everything she had learned on her bizarre journey so far. She wanted to ask more questions and get more answers, but her head was beginning to hurt and she knew Otto was getting exhausted from explaining. So, she just looked back at Amelia, smiled, and figured she would organize her thoughts and ask more questions later. Amelia returned a big smile, wrapped her arms around Evie's shoulders, gave her a tight squeeze, and pulled back looking at Evie. Evie realized that if she was going to have anyone on her side during this journey, Amelia was definitely someone she wanted. Just as Evie was about to talk again, Emmeline rushed into the room. "Come quick, Callais is awake!"

Chapter 29
AMELIA'S DREAMS

◆•————————•————————•◆

Otto, Amelia, and Evie jumped from the table and rushed out the door, following Emmeline across the bridge back to Regina's dwelling. Once they reached Regina's and entered the room, Callais was still on the table, Regina softly talking to him. Callais seemed to respond when he saw the others enter the room. Evie saw that he was responsive and bounded across the room to his side. As soon as Callais saw her, he gave a weak smile and said, "I am so glad you are safe, Evie. How did you know to come here?"

Evie placed her hand on Callais's and told him Amelia found them and brought them to Otto.

Callais gave another weak smile and whispered, "I knew you would get better at this."

Evie smiled back at him and thought about telling him it wasn't really she who did this, it was just luck. Callais then closed his eyes, and Regina gently placed her hand on Evie's shoulder. "He still needs plenty of rest and I need to do some more work on him."

Evie stepped back, nodded at Regina, and rejoined the other three across the room. Otto looked at Amelia and said, "Emmeline and I have to go to the council and tell them what has happened. Why don't you show Evie around since you're not on watch today, and I'll send for you if we need you."

Amelia nodded, grabbed Evie's hand, and guided her out the door as she heard Otto and Regina speak softly. As they were ready to cross the bridge, Emmeline shouted out to the two girls, "Wait!"

Both Evie and Amelia stopped and waited for Emmeline to catch up with them as Emmeline said to both the girls, "Remember what I said, Evie. Be careful who you trust," She then turned her head to

Amelia and added, "Watch out for her please, and be careful."

With that, Emmeline turned back around and joined Otto, who was walking out of Regina's dwelling. Otto and Emmeline headed back up the root steps while Amelia grabbed Evie's hand again and they headed back over the bridge. Evie thought at first that Amelia was going to take them back to their dwelling, but they passed the home and continued downwards on some more root steps. Evie looked back up at one point and realized just how big this cave really was; it seemed to go on for miles. Then, they came to another bridge and crossed it, ending up in another cave opening when Amelia made a circle with her hands and a small orb appeared. Evie smiled and said, "You'll have to teach me how to do that!"

Amelia smiled back and proceeded to go into the cave opening. They weren't in the cave pathway for very long when they came to a larger cavern inside the cave. The cavern was beautiful. There was a small lake in the middle filled by a waterfall pouring out of the cavern wall on the far side, creating a mist where the waterfall hit the lake. There were many flowers and plants growing on all sides, and several roots also growing, covered in hanging moss of a variety of colors. The walls of the cavern seemed to shimmer and, high above, there were many orbs just floating about, so the top of the cave looked like a starry night. Amelia made her way to the side of the lake where there was a small patch of soft moss covering the ground as she sat down and motioned for Evie to join her.

Evie sat beside Amelia as she looked over the lake. Evie joined her gaze and saw that the water seemed to be glowing but, with a closer look, noticed a school of colorful fish swimming about that seemed to be the source of the glow. Just as Evie leaned over a bit to get a closer look at the fish, Amelia tapped her shoulder and Evie looked up. Amelia was pointing to the far side of the lake. Across the lake, small animals came bouncing out of a hole and then made their way to the water's edge to drink. Evie didn't recognize the animals, but they looked similar to rabbits. The girls sat in silence for a while, enjoying the view when

Evie said, "I understand why you like to come here. It's very peaceful and beautiful."

Amelia then reached for Evie's hand again and stood up, pulling Evie to her feet as Amelia dragged her towards the waterfall. When they reached the waterfall, Amelia disappeared behind it when her hand stuck out and motioned for Evie to follow. Evie slowly followed in; the rocks were wet and she didn't want to fall. As she carefully took another step behind the falls, she reached Amelia standing in an opening. Evie turned to look at the water cascading down and thought once again how beautiful it was. Amelia made a circle movement with her hands and a small orb appeared as the girls kept walking through the cave for a while when Evie spotted a light at the very end of it. The girls reached the opening and were standing on a ledge, overlooking a large valley of trees. To the side of the ledge was a small dirt trail leading downwards into the trees. Amelia began to walk down the trail as Evie followed again.

Along the trail, there were a few areas where water was streaming down the side of the rocks, making the path muddy in some areas. At one point, Evie touched the side of the walls where the water was coming out and, to her surprise, it was hot. She figured that there must be a hot spring somewhere around as she remembered a trip David and Rudy took her on to the hot springs. They kept walking until they reached the bottom of the trail, where there was a small steaming pool that smelled of sulfur. Amelia made her way around the hot spring, climbing over roots and pushing branches away. Evie followed, although not as gracefully as Amelia; a few branches hit her face and she almost tripped a few times over large roots.

At the far side of the pool, Amelia made her way into the thick trees with Evie in tow when she ducked into a hole in a large tree. Evie followed her in and found herself in a small room that was filled with paper, charcoal, some coloring utensils, as well as items like dolls and pillows. Evie realized Amelia had taken her to her secret hiding spot, a place that was only Amelia's in this world. Amelia gleefully pulled out a stack of drawings and showed them to Evie.

There were several drawings of animals and plants and a few drawings of Otto and herself with two other people, which Evie assumed were their parents. Evie admired the drawings and realized that Amelia was really good. All of her drawings were incredibly detailed. Evie looked at Amelia and said, "These are amazing!"

Amelia smiled the biggest smile Evie had ever seen. Evie then turned to the next drawing and saw it was a drawing of herself. Evie was shocked and thought, *We just met, so how would Amelia know what I looked like*, so she asked, "Is this me?"

Amelia nodded. Evie then asked, "How did you know what I looked like if we just met?"

Amelia placed her hands together like she was praying when she moved her hands to the side of her head, resting her head on her hands as she closed her eyes and made snorting noises. Evie looked at Amelia and realized that Amelia was gesturing sleep, no, she was gesturing dreams. Evie, even more stunned, asked, "You dreamt of me?"

Amelia nodded, this time with much more excitement as she began to gesture her hands around.

At first, Evie couldn't make out what Amelia was saying and asked her to slow down. Amelia waved her hand high above her head, pointing to her eyes and then at her hand flying high above her head. Evie sat and looked at her while she repeated the hand gestures over again. After a few more movements, it clicked: the hand above Amelia's head was Evie floating above the trees and Amelia spotting her. Evie said this out loud as Amelia nodded and then did the dream gesture again. "You dreamt I was coming and that's how you knew to find me!" Evie exclaimed.

Amelia clapped her hands together in joy, leaned forward, and embraced Evie. Amelia pulled back and got another stack of drawings as Evie flipped through them and recognized several drawings with not just her, but also Marina, Ellis, Callais, and even Bella. There were many drawings of things that had already happened, as well as several drawings with Evie in them that hadn't happened yet. Evie pondered for a while when she asked, "Can you see what it is going to happen before it happens?"

Amelia smiled and then shrugged as she raised her hand flat in front of her, moving it side to side.

Evie understood she was trying to say "maybe." Evie looked at Amelia and said, "That's amazing!"

Just as Evie was ready to look back at the drawing, a bird flew outside the tree opening and made a loud cawing noise. Amelia looked at Evie and sighed as she made her way out of the tree. Evie saw Amelia wave her hand in the air at the big black bird as if to shoo it away, and the girls made their way back to Otto and Amelia's dwelling.

* * *

"Took you long enough," Otto said in a scolding tone to the girls once he saw them. He then said, "Evie, I need you to come with me."

Amelia looked at Otto with pleading eyes and Otto scrunched his nose up and said, "Okay. You can come too."

Amelia clapped her hands as she and Evie followed Otto out the dwelling and towards Regina's. Instead of going into Regina's dwelling, they made their way up the steps where Emmeline and Otto had gone after leaving the girls to explore. They finally came to a large opening Evie had noticed on their way down the previous day. Inside the large room were several people surrounding a massive table, busily talking. They all stopped once they saw the newcomers. Evie took a step back, as if to hide behind Otto, when Emmeline reached for her hand. Evie felt Amelia give her a slight shove on the back. She reluctantly took Emmeline's hand as she made her way farther into the room, feeling the deep stares burning into her from all the people watching. Evie hung her head down, afraid to make eye contact, as Emmeline brought her to the table when Otto broke the silence. "Callais has given me permission to speak on his behalf until he is feeling better."

The crowd nodded in agreement as Evie slowly lifted her head to look around. There had to be about twenty people in the room, all varied in age, gender, and color. Evie noticed a few people had purple skin and some with a greenish complexion. Evie looked down at the table in front of her and saw that there were several maps laid across it with small statues scattered on different places across the maps. It looked like a war map she had seen in an Indiana Jones movie that showed the location of the allies and enemies. Otto then said, "Evie, I would like you to meet the resistance council. Council members, this is Evie, Magnus's descendant."

Several gasps, a blur of whispers, and darting stares circled the room. Otto banged his hand on the table as if to command silence and attention and said, "Callais and Evie were on a mission, and when returning to Canopiuis, they were attacked by one of the Camulus Pack destroyer ships. Callais was able to demolish the ship, but he's very weak."

The room fell silent. People were staring at Evie, some of them still whispering in each other's ears. Otto began again, "Callais believes that someone knew he was returning to Canopiuis and that's why they were attacked. He also believes that Camulos's forces were strictly after him and weren't aware that Evie was with him or who Evie is at this point. However, he also believes it's unsafe for him to return to Canopiuis and reunite Evie with the friends she left behind."

The crowd began to murmur again as Otto spoke even louder, "There are several things and people on Canopiuis that must be reunited with Evie. It's of the utmost importance that we find a way to retrieve these items and people and bring them here so we can help Evie."

The crowd then began to roar and shout.

"What about the attack we have planned?"

"We need to find the horn!"

"What about the plan to release Balor's prisoners?"

This went on for a few minutes until Otto beat his hand down on the table again with so much vigor that it shook the table. The room fell silent again and Otto said, "Has Callais ever led us down the wrong path?"

People around the room shook their heads. Otto then said, "Callais says that helping Evie might be our best chance in defeating Camulos once and for all. I know many of you have worries and there are a few plans laid out that we have worked endlessly on, but we need to set that aside for now, follow Callais's lead, and help this young girl…so that maybe, just maybe, she might be able to help us."

The room was silent for a while when someone asked, "How do you plan to help us, Evie?"

All eyes once again fell on Evie, but instead of menacing stares, she saw hope. Otto invited her to speak to the crowd and said to Evie, "Go on, girl. Tell them what you know. Maybe we can find an answer."

Her soft tone betrayed her, and her voice shook with fear as she tried to talk. Amelia nudged her arm, making a hand gesture from her throat as if to speak louder. Evie cleared her throat and began speaking louder, sounding more confident. She told the council the same story she had told Otto. The crowd listened intently while Emmeline studied people's reactions. Once she finished, the room remained silent. Then, a woman with greenish skin said, "I think it is best for the council to think about this. We can reconvene tomorrow to share our thoughts and hopefully come up with a plan."

The council seemed to be in agreement as a few members left, while a few others stayed in the room and entered deep discussions. Otto turned towards Amelia, Evie, and Emmeline and asked, "Should we go check on Callais and then head back home?"

The three of them nodded and headed back towards Regina's. Once in Regina's dwelling, Evie was hoping to see Callais up, but he was still on the table as Regina was rubbing ointment on him and chanting. The four of them watched Regina for a few minutes when she stopped, turned around, and said, "He can talk for a minute, but make it quick. He still needs his rest."

Otto and Evie made their way over to the table as Amelia and Emmeline stayed back. Callais saw Otto and asked, "Hey there, boy, how did it go?"

Otto gave him a worried look but then said, "We'll reconvene tomorrow, but I think it went well, thanks to Evie."

Otto then leaned his head closer to Callais when Callais mumbled something, but Evie couldn't hear, so she also leaned in closer as Callais looked up at her. "Evie, I know this is a huge burden, but we need you more than you know," Callais took a deep breath and added, "You are doing good, girl."

With that, Callais closed his eyes again and Regina politely pushed the guests out the door as they went back home to eat and rest. Evie climbed in the bottom bed, while Amelia ran from the bedroom door and jumped onto the top bed, hitting her stomach against the rail and kicking her legs up to get the rest of her body on the bed. Evie giggled as Amelia's head appeared over the side, smiling and waving at Evie, before she disappeared back over the top.

Chapter 30
CONTACT

After Evie fell asleep, she heard Bella barking, so she began looking for her. Lying down in front of the fireplace at Clara's house was Bella, who perked her head up and looked around as she heard Evie call her name. While Evie could see her faithful companion, Bella seemed to have a hard time locating her and Evie wondered why. Evie thought, *In the past, Bella always ended up where I was, why didn't she end up on Antillis with me?* Evie then decided that Bella didn't follow her this time because she and Callais were heading back to Kali and that Antillis was a complete accident. Evie then called out Bella's name again and Bella seemed to follow the sound of

Evie's voice, jumping up and making a circle. Evie was happy to see that Bella was safe, so Evie reassured her she would be back soon. Bella wagged her tail, which Evie assumed meant that Bella understood, so Evie decided to go back to sleep, this time trying not to dream. However, the thought of David and Ruby popped in her head as she laid back down, and as Evie drifted off to sleep, she found that she was hovering over a bed where David and Ruby were sound asleep.

Evie figured they might be able to hear her like Bella, so she spoke out loud saying she was okay and would see them soon. As soon as Evie finished talking, she saw Ruby sit up in bed, scan the room, and call out Evie's name. Evie then watched as Ruby shook David's arms and said something to him Evie couldn't make out. She then saw David sit up, reach over, and hug Ruby as Ruby began to sob. Evie realized she had been away from them for longer than she thought. She saw how much they missed her and she began to cry too. As she continued to cry and try to talk to David and Ruby, she felt someone shaking her shoulder.

Evie woke up to see Amelia gazing down at her as Evie wiped tears from her eyes and reached out for Amelia. The two girls embraced each other while Evie continued to cry even harder. Then, Evie pulled herself back and confessed to Amelia that she missed her parents and wished she could let them know she was okay. Amelia rubbed her back and then jumped up and gestured for Evie to follow her, which she did, and soon found herself back in front of Regina's dwelling. Amelia went to enter Regina's when Evie grabbed her arm and said, "Oh no, Regina is probably sleeping. We don't want to wake her."

Amelia smiled and invited Evie to enter. To Evie's surprise, Regina was still awake, sitting at the table across from Callais. Regina looked up at the girls and watched Amelia fanatically gesturing her hands and arms. Regina properly interpreted Amelia's gestures. "So, you want to send a message to your parents to let them know you are okay?"

Evie nodded as Regina invited her to sit next to her. She then placed her hands on either side of Evie's head and closed her eyes. After a few minutes, Regina opened her eyes and said, "Evie, I am sorry to say this, but I believe your parents are dead."

Evie looked at Regina horrified but soon let out a big sigh of relief and explained to Regina that her real parents were dead, not Ruby and David, her adoptive parents. Amelia and Regina both looked at Evie with some sadness in their eyes as Regina placed her hands back on Evie's head, but before she closed her eyes, Regina said, "If these are not your real parents, then they do not share Magnus's blood with you. This means I may not be able to reach them completely through the dream state at this point and may have to find another way to contact them."

Evie nodded when Regina closed her eyes, and after a few more minutes, Regina opened her eyes and said, "Well, they are on Terran. Unfortunately, I have never made contact with Terran because we believed it to be lost, but I can give it a try."

Regina paused and then asked, "Do you know if they have a watcher glass?"

Evie looked at Regina confused. "I don't know what that is."

Regina shrugged her shoulders and then placed her hands back on Evie's head and closed her eyes again. A few minutes later, Regina opened her eyes and asked, "What is a voicemail?"

Evie laughed and explained that people use a telephone to communicate over long distances where she is from and, when you can't reach someone, you leave a message on it. Regina looked confused for a minute and then said, "Well, I think I have found their voicemail. When I say go, say what you need to say."

Evie then closed her eyes and, a few seconds later, she heard Regina's signal. Evie heard the answering machine beeping noise and said, "David, Ruby, it's me Evie. I'm okay. I'm sorry I didn't call sooner. I promise I'm fine and I'll be home soon. I love you both so very much and miss you tons. See you soon, bye."

Regina moved her hands away from Evie's head as Evie wiped tears from her eyes. Regina reassured her that she would help Evie again if she needed to talk to them and told her she would work on how to contact David and Ruby in the dream state so they wouldn't have to leave messages. She then brushed away a tear from Evie's cheek and said, "Go get some rest now, girls. I have a feeling we have a long day ahead of us."

Evie thanked Regina and followed Amelia back to their dwelling. Before Amelia got back into her bed, Evie grabbed her and hugged her tight while thanking her. The girls held each other before going to bed. As they closed their eyes to fall asleep, both felt incredibly thankful to have found one another.

Chapter 31
RUBY'S DISCOVERY

———●———

Ruby couldn't get back to sleep. She was convinced that she heard Evie in her dream and Evie was trying to say something to her but she couldn't hear her completely. Ruby shook her head and realized that she was wrong to have ever questioned Evie about her dreams having real meaning because she was positive that Evie was trying to reach her in the dream. Ruby woke David and told him of Evie's dream visit and that she was worried, but he reassured her that Evie was okay. He then grabbed the phone and pointed. "Look, there's a message."

David played the message, and sure enough Evie had left one just a few minutes before they checked.

Ruby realized the ringer wasn't off and thought it was weird they didn't hear it ring but assumed that maybe Evie was using her dream powers to reach them. Ruby shook her head again at this crazy thought but then shrugged her shoulders and thought, *not any crazier than what we have discovered about The Keeper's Order the last few days.*

Ruby lay in bed thinking of what they had talked about the night before, and what David, Steven, Nadia, and Aman had discovered, shocking Ruby to her core. They had found another woman who was part of the Order, and funnily enough, this new woman was back in the States. The woman told them she would meet with them but had asked David about the rings. David, nor anyone else, had mentioned the rings yet to her, but she seemed to know that was one of the things they were seeking. The woman wanted to meet with them and go over what they had learned so far and help them restore The Keeper's Order. She told them that she was in Washington state, so David, Ruby, and the others made plans to leave soon. The woman didn't say much on the phone to them, but she did say that the rings were the key to finding the lost city of Atlantis.

Ruby almost lost it when David told her this at dinner and Ruby thought he was joking. Ruby then looked around at the others and realized they were all dead serious. Ruby couldn't believe it. Somehow, this mission to restore a secret order to save Evie now was a search for a mythical lost city.

Ruby sat thinking about this crazy idea and this crazy mission and pushed it out of her head. She was just excited to go back to the United States and even more excited because she had convinced David to stop in Colorado for a couple days so she could check on the rest of her family. Ruby snuggled back up under her blanket as she continued to think about Evie, her family, and their crazy adventure so far.

* * *

David, Steven, and Ruby landed in Colorado and made their way home. Nadia and Amam were to rendezvous with them in Washington in two days, to meet up with the mystery woman.

When they got home, their whole family was waiting for them, a barbeque on the back patio already in action. They spent the rest of the day telling everyone about their adventure and what they knew of Evie's journey. They did keep a few things private and left out a few crazy details about their mission, but either way, their family was glad to see them and interested in their stories. David and Ruby's daughters put up a small protest when they realized David and Ruby were going to leave again soon, but they finally relented when they realized that the goal was to help Evie.

David, Ruby, and Steven said their goodbyes the following day. Beth also indicated to Steven that she wanted to help, so she decided she was going to Washington with them; after all, she was part of The Keeper's Order too. Before they left, Ruby went into Evie's room to grab some fresh clothes for her. She wasn't sure when she would see Evie again, but she packed a few things anyway. Before Ruby left Evie's room, she saw the photo of Evie's parents and decided to grab it. She thought, *Maybe someone will recognize who they are if I bring the photo.*

As she grabbed the picture, she knocked a small box on the ground and two shiny objects rolled out. Ruby bent down to pick up the box and the golden objects. When she reached down and grabbed the first item, she realized it was a ring. She quickly grabbed the second one and realized it was also a ring. Ruby stood frozen for a minute and said under her breath, "No way…This can't be."

She quickly examined the rings and realized that maybe it was true. Maybe these were the rings they had been searching for—the ones that Amam, Nadia, and this mystery woman had told them about. She gently put the rings back in the box and put the picture frame and ring box in the bag. She then saw the small glass jewelry box on the bed stand and decided to pack that just in case. As she made her way down the stairs, she thought about telling David about the rings, but something inside her said she needed to keep this to herself just for now. She hated secrets and never hid anything from David, but again she just felt that this was her secret to keep for a little while longer.

Ruby joined David, Steven, and Beth waiting for her at the bottom of the stairs, and once again, they were off on their next great adventure.

Chapter 32
THE COUNCIL

Evie woke up that morning to voices coming from the kitchen. She got up and saw that Amelia had laid some fresh clothes on the end of the bed, and Evie realized she had been wearing the same thing forever now. She put on the fresh clothes and made her way to the kitchen. Otto, Emmeline, and Amelia were all sitting at the table. Evie smiled, sat down, and began eating while Emmeline and Otto were arguing playfully about a friend, Evie guessed. As she ate, she looked around the table and for the first time really analyzed each of them. Otto looked like he was probably no more than thirty years old. He had dirty blond hair that he had braided down both sides of his ears with curls sticking out. He also had fair skin, green eyes, and broad shoulders with large muscles that Evie could see under his shirt. He had a towering build and actually was extremely attractive. Emmeline had dark raven hair that was wavy and cropped below her shoulders. She had hazel eyes and her skin tone was much darker than Otto's. She was a bit taller than Evie and slim. As she stared closer at Emmeline, she also thought she kind of looked like Regina, except Regina was taller and had some gray streaks in her hair. Amelia, of course, looked similar to her brother with blond hair, a little lighter than Otto's, which was long, straight, and always tied back. She had the same green eyes and fair skin as Otto, but she also had a few freckles across her shoulders like Evie did. Amelia was fairly slim and about Evie's height, and Evie assumed that Amelia was most likely a couple years younger than herself. As they finished their meals, Otto said to Emmeline, "Guess we should head back to your mother's house and check on Callais before we go to the council meeting."

Evie was right. Emmeline was Regina's daughter. She then followed the other three out the door and back to Regina's. Once there, Evie was ecstatic to see Callais sitting up in a chair, enjoying a meal. Regina smiled as the four of them got closer. Otto then boomed, "It's good to see you up, old man!"

Callais chuckled. "It is good to see you, too, boy."

Evie could tell the two of them had a very close friendship and quite possibly, since Otto and Amelia lost their parents, Callais had become a father figure to them. Amelia followed Otto over and gave Callais a tender hug, followed by Emmeline. Evie made her way over but didn't feel familiar enough with Callais to hug him; however, Callais gently pulled Evie to him and wrapped his arm around her waist. Evie smiled and felt like she had a second, no, third family, as she once again realized how much she missed Marina, Ellis, Bella, and Aphrodite. Callais released his grip from Evie's waist and said, while looking at Regina, "I think I will go to the council meeting today with the others."

Regina shot him a glance and was ready to make a fuss when Callais added, "Do not worry about me. I am fine. I have felt much worse than this before."

Regina looked at Callais with concern and then nodded in agreement as she brought him some Virdis and made sure he finished it. Callais was still too weak to walk, so Otto bent over, picked him up, and cradled him in his arms as if he were holding a baby.

Once in the council room, Evie noticed there weren't as many people as before but figured they were early and the others would be there soon. Emmeline then pulled a chair from the far corner up to the table as Otto gently placed Callais in it. Eventually, some more people began to enter the room as they made small talk with each other. Otto disappeared behind a doorway in the back of the room and came out carrying a stack of chairs, placing them around the table. A few other men followed Otto's example and began helping with the seating arrangements. Evie felt relieved, since the last time they were in the room everyone was standing and it felt hostile. Maybe if everyone was sitting, the room wouldn't feel as tense as it did before. Slowly, more people joined, including Regina, and soon the table was surrounded by the council members. Evie took a seat on the left side of Callais as Otto took the seat on the right side while the rest all found their seats. Evie assumed Callais would be the one who started the council meetings after greeting and making small talk with other council members. However, in his weakened state, he allowed Otto to take his place again. Once all were seated and quiet, Otto looked around the room to ensure everyone was there before he started. "As you can see, Callais felt well enough to come here today."

The council all nodded and some tipped their heads towards Callais in a show of respect as Callais nodded back to the room. Otto continued to fill in the new members on the current situation and then asked them if anyone had any suggestions. The room filled with a dull chatter as the council members were bouncing ideas off each other when Callais cleared his throat and the room fell silent. After a brief period of silence, Callais said, "I know many of you are concerned that some of the plans we have made for an invasion on the far side of Antillis to regain control of this planet have to cease for a period of time," Callais took a long pause as he looked around the room. "We still have scouts looking for the lost horn, which we believe to be on this planet. However, we have been searching for years to no avail."

Callais took another long pause and went on, "I believe with Evie's help, we may be able to find the horn and have a better chance of invading Camulos's base at a later time."

The council began to murmur again when Otto stood up and stated, "I know that many of you have doubts that Evie is the savior we have been waiting for, but Callais believes she's the one and that is good enough for me, so it should be good enough for you."

The council fell silent as Callais placed his hand on Otto's arm. Otto returned to his seat and Callais continued, "It is true. I am sure many of you have doubts, but we have tried everything we can and, although we have accomplished a lot, it has not been enough and I am afraid if we do not put our trust in

Evie, we will continue to fight a never-ending war that we have already been fighting for over a thousand years, and worse, Camulos may actually win."

The council was silent. Then, a young man, probably as old as Otto, stood up and asked, "What can we do to help you, Evie?"

Evie stood up, feeling supported by her team, and admitted, "I'm not sure what to do yet to help you defeat Camulos, but I do know that I need some of my things and some of the people I left behind to help me...help us."

The council remained silent as Regina said, "Unfortunately, I am too important to Mari to join Evie, but I would if I could. You all know that it is too risky to send Callais, even if he was not in his current state. I have learned that Evie can travel the star trails with very little help, which is how she got here. Is there anyone willing to go with Evie back to Canopiuis to retrieve the items and people she needs?"

Everyone began looking around when the green woman with a large black bird on her shoulder that

Evie had seen at the last meeting said, "Canopiuis is too dangerous for any of us. Most of us here are targets of the Camulus Pack, and Canopiuis itself is crawling with Camulos's forces. It is almost impossible for anyone to enter or escape."

The room was silent again when Otto plainly said, "Evie was able to go there unnoticed twice."

Otto obviously left out the part where Evie's ship was shot down as she, Clara, and Newton made their escape. The room was filled with a few quiet whispers when Amelia began gesturing her hands, which Evie interpreted as volunteering to go with her. Otto quickly intervened. "No, Amelia, you can't go. It's too dangerous and you are too young."

Amelia shot Otto a dirty look when Emmeline stood up and said, "I'll go. Amelia is old enough to go too. For father's sake, she has survived more than most of us here. It's time she actually joins us instead of being stuck in Regina's house, learning to be a healer, which she's clearly not."

Otto's face turned dark red as he angrily said, "And risk losing the both of you? NO! Absolutely NOT!"

Emmeline and Amelia stood tall and straight, clearly not giving up. Otto glared at them but finally caved. "Fine, if you two are so adamant about going, then I'm going too."

"Me too." The young man across the table said.

Regina sat back down, smiled, and looked at Callais, who said, "Okay then. Otto and Amelia Vegas, Emmeline Freyas, and Atlas Vili will join Evie."

Callais turned his head to Evie and whispered, "You think you can handle taking all of them with you?"

Evie felt nervous and was about to back out when Callais added, "Do not worry, you are much stronger than you think. If you get lost, Regina and I will find you, I promise."

With that, Evie looked up at her small group and thought to herself how brave they all were to join her on such a dangerous journey. Evie then stood up and addressed the room, saying, "I promise to bring everyone back safely, and on my return, I hope that I can bring you what you need to defeat Camulos!"

After she spoke, the room filled with quiet chatter again as she overheard a very old woman say loud enough for Evie to hear, "She definitely has Magnus's confidence."

As the members left, Regina gently directed Evie's new traveling companions and Callais back to her dwelling. While Callais explained their traveling plans, Regina began to pack a bag. Otto was the only other person who had previous star trail traveling experience, but it had been a long time since his last trip, so he benefitted from Callais's explanation. Once Callais was done, he turned to Evie and asked her if she still had the chain. Before Evie could speak, Amelia pulled the chain out of her pocket with a big smile. Callais looked at Evie with a slight warning look as Evie hung her head, but he didn't lecture her and proceeded to have the group sit down as he took the chain from Amelia and said, "You will have four people with you this time, so the traveling may be a little slower at first. Take your time and be sure to keep your eyes open for any danger."

Callais then handed the chain to Evie. Evie took Otto's hand to the left and then she extended the hand with the chain to Amelia. She grabbed the chain as the others locked hands and closed their eyes. Evie then quickly glanced at Callais. He nodded so she closed her eyes, and soon she felt herself drift into fog and found herself floating in the star trails once again.

Chapter 33
BACK TO KALI

Evie realized Callais was right. It was much slower to travel the stars with more people in tow. She looked at her traveling companions and all of them had looks on their faces that ranged from awe to fear. Otto seemed to be the most confident. Otto then asked her, "Do you know where we're going?"

Evie realized that holding the chain definitely allowed her to hear others in the vacuum of space, and then she also realized that she didn't know where Canopiuis was and felt a little nervous. She then remembered that the last time she traveled, she thought of Declan and that brought her there. Evie decided to think of Declan again, but she couldn't bring herself to picture his face, so instead she thought of Bella.

It wasn't long after she had pictured Bella in her mind that Evie and the others found themselves floating in the direction of a white planet that Evie recognized as Canopiuis. She motioned to Otto that this was the place and they slowly made their way over to the planet. Once again, Evie found herself floating down to the small river between the broken and half-fallen buildings as the five of them gently landed on the ground. Evie was ready to walk along the river's edge again when a small boat emerged from the water. Evie was a little baffled but then heard a familiar voice behind her say, "I knew you would be back soon."

She turned her head to see Newton standing there with his toothless grin. She ran over to him and gave him a giant hug. Newton then asked, "You brought friends?"

Evie smiled and introduced everyone to Newton. He smiled and said, "Well, get in. Everyone will be so happy you are back."

The group piled into the small boat and they took off down the river. As they reached the tunnel, Newton explained to the others, who seemed a little nervous, that they were entering an underground city called Kali and that it was the only safe place on Canopiuis. As they traveled into the city, they all looked at its occupants. At one point, there was a child playing along the river's edge with a missing limb and Amelia started crying. Otto reached over and cradled her head in his big arms. He kissed the top of her head and gently whispered something in her ear. Evie wondered just how much Amelia had actually gone through and how many of her friends she had watched be tortured.

After a few more minutes, they finally reached the dock and made their way through the town square and back up the cobblestone path to Clara's house. As soon as they entered the house, Evie was bombarded by Bella and Aphrodite, followed by Apollo, Delila, Darwin, and soon Collin. Evie took a moment to revel in the joy of seeing all her friends again as Declan entered the entryway, pulled Evie to her feet, and embraced her in a big hug. Evie felt her cheeks turn red as she felt Declan's grip loosen and she pulled herself back and looked at his face. He gave her a wink and said, "It's good to see you!"

Declan headed back towards the room with the fireplace as Evie heard a loud boom and watched as Ellis came running down the stairs, missing several steps and almost falling. When he reached Evie, he grabbed her up in the biggest bear hug of all time and said, "Oh my god girl. I'm so glad yer back!" squeezing her even tighter. "I was so worried about yeh. I knew I should've gone with yeh guys."

He pulled her away from his broad chest, looked at her in the face, and she saw tears welling up in his eyes as he pulled her back in and continued his giant hug. Evie then heard Marina's voice behind her. "I am so glad you are back, girl."

Evie ran over to Marina and embraced her. Marina started crying too.

After Evie, Ellis, and Marina collected themselves and after introductions had been made, everyone found a place to sit. All the dogs but Bella and Delila ran into the adjacent room and started roughhousing. Bella crawled up in Evie's lap but not before giving Evie a quick kiss on the nose while Delila made her way over to Clara's side. Evie guessed that Delila was Clara's while Darwin was Newton's dog. Clara then turned to Evie and asked, "Where is Callais?"

Evie began to tell everyone in the room what had happened and how she ended up on Antillis, where Amelia and Otto found her. She explained that Callais was badly injured but was feeling better and Regina was taking good care of him. Clara nodded her head and then seemed to go into deep thought when Ellis asked, "Okay girl, what'd yeh think we do next?"

Evie explained why she came back, showing she still had the chain, thanks to Amelia, and that she had left the parchment papers as well as the other scrolls and maps back on Antillis. Evie chose not to mention the book about Clara again. Otto then pitched in and told the others about the resistance they had back on Antillis and that once they all got back there, they could finally come up with a plan that might be feasible to defeat Camulus Pack on Antillis. Otto then added with confidence, "Once Antillis is safe, we can start saving the rest of the Devas galaxy."

Ellis then exclaimed, "Well, what the hell are we waitin' for. Let's get goin'!"

Marina, who had been silent until then, gently said, "I know I always say this, but I think it is best if we get some food and rest before we start again." Ellis then responded with his usual grunt of disappointment.

After everyone finished eating food Declan had brought out from the kitchen and made small talk, they finally decided to get some rest. Evie realized she hadn't slept there yet and was about to ask where to go when Declan appeared behind her and said, "We don't have enough rooms, but you girls can share the room across from Marina."

Declan took the girls up the stairs to a large room and just as Evie was about to go in the bedroom, Bella came bolting past the girls and Declan and jumped happily on one of the beds in the room, followed by Apollo. Evie looked down the hall to see Aphrodite following Ellis into his room and Collin escorting Otto and Atlas across the room from Ellis. There were only two beds in the girls' room, but there was also a giant couch in front of a fireplace that Amelia ran over to and jumped on. Evie made her way to the bed Bella and Apollo were on, and Emmeline took the remaining bed. Before Declan left the room, he turned back around and said, "Oh yeah, there's a bathroom behind that door and I believe there are plenty of my mother's old clothes in the closet. Feel free to freshen up."

Evie smiled and thanked him as she felt her cheeks get flushed. She then crawled into bed and fell asleep with no dreams. She felt happy and peaceful to be in a home with so many people she loved and cared about. She thought to herself how much her family had grown and how, some day, she would love to introduce everyone to David and Ruby.

* * *

Evie woke the next morning to see Amelia and Emmeline raiding Clara's closet. They would hold up a piece of clothing to their body and fling it to the ground, shaking their heads in disapproval, and then would grab another item of clothing. Bella and Apollo were sitting in front of the fireplace, watching them. One of the things Amelia threw landed on Apollo's head. Apollo grunted and shook his head as the blouse fell off and he scrunched his nose. Bella then used her nose to place it back on his head, playing a new game. Evie laughed at the playful Bella and then made her way over to Emmeline and Amelia. Emmeline said, "Oh, good Evie, you're up. I have the perfect outfit for you."

Emmeline nodded towards Amelia as Amelia rushed over to a pile of clothing strung across an armchair. Amelia shuffled through the pile and then came running over, handing it to Evie. Evie held up a silky, deep green blouse with emerald buttons in the front and a pair of tan pants that were similar in texture and very flowy. Evie scoffed a little as Emmeline said, "Now, Evie, you're a young lady and it's time you stop wearing little girl clothes."

Evie thought about arguing with Emmeline but decided it wouldn't be worth the battle and put on the clothes. To Evie's surprise, the outfit was quite comfortable and wasn't too flashy but pretty enough that Evie did feel a little more grown up and more feminine than her usual jeans and T-shirt. Emmeline had picked out a white, silky blouse with pink buttons and was wearing a long blue skirt. Amelia was also wearing a green silk top, but it was sleeveless with no buttons and a much lighter green than Evie's. She had matched the top with dark green pants. Emmeline handed each girl a pair of slippers that stretched enough to fit each girl's feet. Evie was about to walk out the door when Emmeline said, "Wait, wait. I'm not finished. We must do something with that wild mane of yours."

Evie made her way back over to Emmeline, who sat her in a chair and began to work on her hair. Evie had such thick red curly hair, she had struggled her whole life to maintain it. After a while of tugging and pulling, Emmeline said, "There, much better."

Amelia held a mirror up to Evie's face so Evie could look at her hair. She was surprised to see what a good job Emmeline had done. Evie's hair was pinned up on either side with small curls hanging down. The part of her hair that was pinned flowed into a beautiful loose braid that fell down the center of her back. Evie was happy and looked up to see both of them smiling at her as she thanked them. The girls then headed out the room, which was still covered in Clara's clothes, and down the stairs, with Bella and Apollo right behind them.

Once the girls got downstairs to the fireplace room, everyone was already there as Declan and Collin were bringing breakfast and black tea from the kitchen. Declan herded up all the dogs and took them to the kitchen to eat while everyone sat around and made small talk as they finished their breakfast. Amelia and Evie helped Declan and Collin finish cleaning up and made their way back to the fireplace room when Evie caught Declan looking at her. She shot him a curious look as he smiled and told her she looked nice. Evie blushed a little as Amelia grinned.

Once back in the fireplace room, Clara mentioned the girls all looked nice in her clothes and she was glad they all found something that fit them.

Evie felt relieved because Clara was a hard person for her to read, and Evie was afraid Clara might be upset they were wearing her clothes. Once they were all seated again, Marina said, "So, today I think we should spend some time preparing for the journey to Antillis. I want to make sure that we have everything we need so we do not have to journey back. After talking with Otto a bit this morning, I have become aware that Canopiuis is a very dangerous place for all of us to stay, especially considering how important Evie is. I think it would be best to ensure we do not have to return unless it is absolutely necessary or until the time is right."

Everyone nodded in agreement, but Clara remained motionless. They all sat around and began conversing among themselves, making plans about what they should bring and what was necessary. Ellis, Otto, and Atlas began packing bags with several items they believed they would need to fight for Antillis. Marina and Newton collected the scrolls, maps, books, some pieces of parchment paper, and a couple other small items. Emmeline went back to the girls' room and gathered some extra clothing as she scrounged around the other rooms to find clothing for the others as well. Collin and Declan went to the kitchen to pack snacks and prepare some more green juice for everyone before their departure, while Evie and Amelia wandered around helping wherever they were needed. Evie then noticed that Clara had disappeared somewhere, but Evie just assumed Clara was collecting things she needed.

After a couple of hours, everyone gathered back in the fireplace room. Evie watched as the men made room by moving furniture around when she thought with some concern, *This is a very large group to travel with.* Then she remembered that this time she had Marina, Newton, Clara, and even Ellis to help lighten the load for her and felt a little better. The group began to sit down, but before they found their places, a thunderous roar followed by a crashing noise shook the house, and soon they could all hear screaming coming from the streets outside. The group quickly stood up as Ellis rushed to the front window and looked out. Then, more screaming and explosions began; no one had to say anything because they all instantly rushed around and started gathering everything when Newton yelled, "I do not know how, but they found us!"

In a panic, everyone grabbed what they could as Declan and Collin ushered them to the tunnel Collin had brought Evie through previously. Instead of heading straight under the tunnel again, Collin and Declan led them to a side pathway that Evie hadn't noticed the first time. They all ran under the side tunnel for about five hundred yards when it came to an end in a small clearing. Newton was the last one to enter and stood in front of the pathway they had come from, mumbling enchantments under his breath while waving his arms in the air as he turned back around and said, "That should hold them off from finding us for a while, but we do not have long."

They sat on the ground again to prepare for the trip when Evie saw that Clara wasn't with them and asked, "Where's Clara?"

Everyone looked around as Newton said, "We must go without her."

Declan went to protest, but Newton grabbed his arm and told him Clara could handle herself as they all took their spots, preparing to go. Evie remembered Marina had the fabric and said, "Marina, take out the fabric and cover us."

Marina took out the fabric and whispered for it to cover them all as the fabric cracked again with white light, changed shape, and hovered over the group before settling down and covering them all. Then, the group proceeded to hold hands, with Evie holding the chain as she closed her eyes. It wasn't long before Evie then saw the fog and the star trail, so she began to move forward. Once in the stars, she looked around and saw everyone was with her as Marina frantically shouted, "Everyone, think of Callais!"

Evie focused her attention on Callais and began to float forward. After she had a strong picture of Callais in her mind, she opened her eyes just in time to see a blinding red flash of light as a massive black ship appeared out of a cloud of dark smoke a hundred yards away from them. Evie almost screamed as the ship moved closer to them, but she held her yell in.

The others all looked at Evie for what to do, but Evie just motioned for them to all keep going. The ship stayed in front of them for a minute, but Evie could tell that the ship couldn't see them. Still, the ship was searching for something with spotlights that were mounted on the top deck. Evie was grateful she remembered the fabric because it seemed to be hiding them from the ship's search, even on the star trail. The group slowly moved forward until the ship was behind them, and soon, completely out of view. After the ship fell out of sight, Evie was able to focus on Callais again when the fabric hiding the group made another loud cracking noise, the chain warmed up in her hand, and a white light flashed around them. Soon, a small green planet came into view as everyone took a sigh of relief.

Slowly but surely, the group moved closer to the planet and were hovering over the tree line as Evie looked at Otto and asked him to lead. Otto looked at her slightly confused by this—he assumed that he was only along for the ride—but then Evie said, "We're here. I'm just not sure where to go."

Otto took Evie's hand and slowly navigated over the trees until he pointed down and they all began to move toward the trees below. The trees were so thick, there wasn't enough room for everyone to land in one spot, but they all landed close enough to each other that eventually the whole group was back together. Evie looked around and didn't see Ellis when she heard hollering a few feet away. She turned her head and looked up to find Ellis hanging from a branch, cursing and trying to wiggle himself free. Evie laughed as Ellis cursed at her and said that it wasn't funny. As Otto and Atlas tried to get him down, the branch made a sudden and loud cracking noise and broke under Ellis's weight. He came crashing to the ground below. Everyone laughed as Ellis stood up and brushed himself off, still mumbling more curses under his breath. He made his way over to the group and shot Evie a dirty look, shook his fist at her and said, "Yer lucky I like yeh girl."

Evie chuckled again under her breath as Ellis moved past her and they all followed Otto and Atlas back to the underground city of Mari.

Walking through the forest was a challenge, since there was no path and there were many branches and roots that everyone besides Otto, Atlas, Amelia, and Emmeline would trip over or get caught on. Evie thought, *Mari is a great hiding place because it is almost impossible to reach.*

Eventually, the group found themselves at the outcropping with the underground entrance below it and they made their way into the underground city. Evie looked at Ellis and Marina in front of her. They stopped often to take in and admire the sights of the massive underground city. Declan and Collin also seemed to be fairly excited by the view. Then the group made its way down the stairs as Otto and Atlas led them into the council room, which was empty at that moment. Otto told everyone to wait a minute when he left the room and soon entered with Regina and Callais, who was now walking with a cane. Otto stood behind him with his hands to Callais's back, just in case Callais was to lose his balance. Emmeline, Amelia, and Evie went over to Callais and Regina and hugged them both in a tight embrace. Atlas and Ellis then gathered some chairs from the back room and set them around the table as everyone began to take their seats. Once introductions were made, Callais asked, "Did everything go okay?"

Otto piped in and told him about their adventure. After Otto finished, Callais looked at Evie and said, "I was unaware you had the fabric."

Evie felt a little ashamed and apologized, explaining she had given it to Marina and forgot about it until they were in the underground tunnel in Kali. Callais nodded as if to forgive her. "Well, it was a good thing you did remember."

Callais then turned his head away from Evie and asked the group, "So, what do we have that we can work with?"

As the others were unpacking their bags to look over what they had, Evie remembered her bag back in Amelia's room and said, "I have to go back to Amelia's room. I left some stuff there."

Callais nodded and excused her as Evie went to go grab her bag while Amelia and Collin got up to follow her. They went back down the stairs, past

Regina's, and across the bridge. When they got to the bridge, they all heard, "Hey, wait up!"

They turned to see Declan running after them to catch up. Evie blushed a little as Amelia nudged her arm and smiled. When Declan caught up to them, they made their way to Amelia's room. Once inside, Evie found her bag on the floor at the end of the bed and grabbed it. Evie then turned to Amelia and said, "I think we should go get your drawings too. They might be useful."

Amelia shrugged and the four of them headed off in the direction of Amelia's secret cave. Just as they left the dwelling, they heard Otto holler at them and ask where they were going. Amelia made some rapid hand gestures at him as he waved his hand at them and said, "Okay, but hurry back!"

The four of them made their way across the bridge and into the cave with the lake and waterfall. Collin shouted with glee once inside and went running off in front of them, spinning around in circles while taking everything in. The other three laughed as they watched Collin play for a bit and then made their way behind the waterfall. Then off they went to Amelia's little tree hiding place. When they reached the tree house, it was too small for all of them to fit, so Declan and Evie stood outside while Amelia and Collin entered to grab her drawings. While waiting, Declan flashed Evie a smile and said, "This place sure is great."

Evie nodded in agreement as Declan walked over to a nearby tree, pulled something from the ground, and the headed back over to Evie, holding out a small white flower in his hand. As Evie reached out to grab it, he moved closer to her body and stood in front of her as he gently put the flower in her hair and took a step back, staring at her. "Now your outfit is complete."

He then flashed his beautiful smile as Evie blushed and thanked him just as Collin and Amelia exited the tree hole. Evie was a bit relieved they came out when they did because she didn't know what else to say to Declan. Amelia waved the drawings in front of Evie's face and the foursome made their way back towards the council room.

Chapter 34

THE BEGINNING OF THE NEW RESISTANCE

◆•————————————•————————————•◆

W hen the foursome entered the council room, everyone was already in deep discussion and going over all the items they brought. There were a few other council members who had joined, including the green woman whose name was Simone Scorpius, another man named Lincoln Hektoris, and the old woman, named Josephine Januis, who had made the comment about Evie's confidence at the last council meeting. Simone also had a black bird, named Indy, on her shoulder—the same bird that Evie now remember had cawed at Amelia and Evie to return the last time they were at

Amelia's secret tree. After a while, Callais cleared his throat and the room slowly fell silent. Once everyone was silent, Callais said, "I believe we have all we need. So now we need to focus on two things." He took a short pause and continued, "The first step will be to create a force responsible for finding the horn, which we believe Magnus has hidden here on Antillis; the second step will be to reach out to the resistance on other planets and bring as many as we can here and begin our fight."

The crowd murmured in agreement as Callais finally turned to Evie. "We will need your help in deciphering many of the scrolls, maps, and pieces of parchment we cannot decipher ourselves. We will need you here."

Callais turned back to the group and asked who would be willing to help Evie. Regina, Emmeline, Amelia, and Marina all raised their hands. Callais then turned to Otto. "Otto, I would like you to take my place and be in charge of finding others in the resistance and training resistance members."

Otto sat up, beaming with pride as Callais asked who would join Otto. Ellis and Atlas raised their hands. Callais then said, "I will need a team myself that would be willing to help me as well as extend help to Evie's and Otto's teams. Although I have been responsible for training the protectors, I would like to train watchers as well as have a team to help me collect and analyze what we find and when Evie or the others get stuck."

Lincoln, Newton, Simone, and Josephine all raised their arms. Callais then turned to Declan, who hadn't raised his hand yet and gave him a concerned look. Declan shuffled his feet and said, "I'm not sure where I belong."

Callais sat thinking for a minute before saying, "I think I will have you join me and train you as both a watcher and protector. When you are ready, I believe you will be helpful in aiding Otto's team."

Declan smiled and agreed. Evie felt relieved because that meant Declan would be staying with her for a while. Callais then looked at Collin and said, "I will have you help me out, too."

Collin smiled as everyone began collecting stuff from the table, when a blur of fur came running into the room. Evie laughed as she saw all the dogs in the council room, followed by a young boy who was out of breath saying, "I'm sorry it took so long. They were all playing in the forest and refused to come in."

Callais smiled as Bella leaped onto Evie's lap, knocking over the book Evie had taken from the guarded aisle about Clara. She picked up the book, glimpsed at Declan, and asked, "What about Clara?"

Newton and Callais exchanged worried glances and looked at Declan, who lowered his head. Evie couldn't tell if he was upset or not. Regina noticed the glances Newton and Callais had given each other and asked Declan, Collin, and Emmeline if they would help her with something. Declan was leaving the room to follow the others when he paused at the entryway and asked, "Is my mother a spy?"

The room fell into an awkward silence when Newton walked over and placed his hand on Declan's shoulder. "I am not sure, boy, but we have reason to believe she is."

Declan, with his head still hung low, wiped his eyes with his sleeve, pulled himself together, and stood tall. "Well, I'm here for you guys and the fight against Camulos. That's all that matters now."

He looked around the room and, by the looks on everyone's faces, he could tell they were grateful. Regina then decided that it wasn't necessary to leave the room and had them rejoin the conversation. Evie and the others sat in silence for a minute longer when Evie looked at Newton and said, "I wasn't sure about telling anybody, but I found a book on Terran with Clara's name on it. I wasn't sure if it is the same Clara and I haven't read it," she handed the book to Newton and finished, "I think you should have this."

Newton took the book and nodded as he walked back to his seat, looked at the book again, and then sat it down. Callais then looked at Marina and asked, "You said that Evie's parents, David and Ruby, are back on Terran, helping you gather more information about Magnus and The Keeper's Order. Is that correct?"

"Yes," Marina answered. "I believe that restoring Magnus's order and finding the knowledge that has been lost will be useful for us."

Callais nodded and said, "I will be sure to find a way for us to keep in contact with David and Ruby as we move forward."

Callais then turned to Regina and asked, "Maybe we can use the watcher glass to communicate with them?"

Regina looked at Callais and said, "I am unsure if they have a watcher glass. When I helped Evie reach them earlier, she did not know what I spoke of; however, I may be able to figure out how to better navigate the dream state to communicate with them since I was able to reach them with Evie last time. Maybe with some more practice, I will able to make permanent contact."

Evie then asked, "What's watcher glass?"

Regina explained that there are looking glasses that were placed across the Devas galaxy to connect with others while not in dream states. She then said, "Like your voicemails on Terran."

"That's really cool," Evie said, laughing at the comparison.

Regina and Callais smiled when Callais finally said, "I think that is all for today. We will all meet soon."

Everyone slowly left the room, leaving Callais, Evie, and Newton alone. Evie looked at both men and realized they needed to talk in private, so Evie got up to leave just as Callais reached for her arm and boldly stated, "Evie, you are now a keeper of the great Devas system. Our past and your past is now all of our future...this is just the beginning."

Glossary

ANIMALS

Fenriris Dogs/Companions (assigned to keepers)

Aphrodite: Magnus's and then Ellis's dog, an English mastiff, female.

Apollo: Callais's dog, a pit bull, male.

Bella: Evie's dog, a medium-sized black dog with tints of brown and white, similar to a mix of a Jack Russell terrier and a boxer, female.

Darwin: Newton's dog, a golden retriever, male.

Delila: Clara's dog, a golden retriever, female.

BIRDS

Indy: Simone's black bird, female.

Andeais: Rare bird on Alpharman that helps with staff's levitation power.

CHARACTERS

Abrax Aswad: Magnus's manservant and friend when Marina was a child.

Amam Kalb: Egyptian man, part of The Keeper's Order on Earth. Helps David, Ruby, and Steven restore order.

Amelia Vegas: Evie's friend, close in age. Otto's younger sister. Originally from planet Sirios in Devas galaxy and is now on Antillis. She is mute because she cut out her own tongue to protect her brother Otto.

Atlas Vili: Otto's friend and right-hand man, trained by Callais to be a protector. Part of the new resistance. Located currently on planet Antillis.

Balor Kronius: Camulos's right-hand man (Death Keeper), comes from Camulus galaxy.

Barbara: Woman in charge of residential children's home.

Beth Anderson: Evie's social worker and Steven's girlfriend. Part of The Keeper's Order.

Callais Baldais: The lower keeper in charge of the protectors and their training, chosen for his bravery, commitment to The Keeper's Order and sacred text, and his compassion for others. He was handpicked by the head keeper, Magnus, for this job. Comes from Devas galaxy and lives on Antillis.

Camulos: From Camulus galaxy. God of war, darkness, and destruction. Keeper/Ruler of the Camulus Force.

Clara Bellatrias: Declan's mother, head keeper who survived. Lives on the planet Canopiuis in the hidden city of Kali.

Collin MacDunleavy: Evie's biological father, killed in accident.

Collin Junaius: Lost boy found in Canopiuis in hidden city of Kali, six years old. Has no left hand, presents scar from left eye down to left shoulder. One of Evie's friends.

David Sr Jones: Evie's adoptive father.

David Jr Jones: David and Ruby's son.

Declan Bellatrias: Clara's son and Evie's friend. From Devas galaxy from the planet Canopiuis and found in the hidden city of Kali.

Dermot Kelley: Head of The Keeper's Order on Earth, now deceased.

Desi Jones: David and Ruby's daughter.

Ellis Ó Murchadha (Murphy): One of Magnus's heirs, found on Terran by Marina, inherits dog from Magnus.

Emmeline Freyas: Otto's girlfriend and Regina's daughter. One of Evie's friends. Is currently on the planet Antillis in the Devas galaxy. Trained as healer.

Evangelina MacDunleavy: Also called Evie, Magnus's true of heart heir.

father: Original creator of the universe along with the mother.

James Ó Cuinn: Marina's older brother and twin to Joseph.

Jenny Jones: David and Ruby's daughter.

Joe Jones: David and Ruby's son.

Joseph Ó Cuinn: Marina's older brother and twin to James.

Josephine Januis: Old woman on Antillis, part of resistance council.

Jessie Garcia: Evie's friend at the residential home.

Lauren: Evie's roommate at the residential home.

Leslie Jones: David and Ruby's adoptive daughter.

Lincoln Hektoris: Keeper on Antillis, part of resistance council.

Magnus (Deae) Ó Cuinn: The most powerful head keeper of Devas galaxy and of all galaxies.

Maria Borbón MacDunleavy: Evie's biological mother, killed in accident.

Marina Ó Cuinn: Evie's lost ancestor and Magnus's daughter, finder of Evie. Lives on Terran.

Michael Jones: David and Ruby's son.

mother: Original creator of the universe along with the father.

Mr. Heath: Evie's teacher.

Ms. Bell: Evie's teacher.

Nadia Lebedev: Russian woman part of Keeper's order and helps David, Ruby, and Steven's search.

Newton Evander: Head keeper who survived. Located on the planet Canopiuis in hidden city of Kali.

Nox Guard: Balor and Camulos's private guard, created by Balor.

Otto Vegas: Amelia's older brother and one of Evie's friends in the resistance. Trained to be a protector by

Callais. Originally from Sirios but is now on Antillis in the Devas galaxy.

Regina Freyas: Emmeline's mother and healer on the planet Antillis.

Ruby Jones: Evie's adoptive mother.

Seraphina Ó Cuinn: Magnus's first wife on Terran, Marina's mother.

Simone Scorpuis: Keeper on Antillis and part of Antillis Council.

Steven Jones: David and Ruby's son, part of The Keeper's Order.

CITIES

Donegal: Located on Terran, in the country of Ireland, where Marina's home is located.

Kali: Hidden underground city in Canopiuis.

Mari: Hidden underground city in mountainside on Antillis.

GALAXIES/PLANET

Alpharman: Planet in Devas galaxy and is the land of spirits, main element here is spirit. The planet in

Devas system where souls store their memory and spirits. Hardest planet for Camulos to control. Also, where the rare bird, Andeais, is located, helping with staff's levitation power.

Antillis: Central planet in the Devas galaxy. Main elements are flora and fauna because mostly inhabited by plants and animals. Mari is the lost city in the forest of survivors. Many of the watchers, protectors, and keepers reside here because the forest covered by the fourth day protection spell is vast and easy to hide in. The resistance is strong, so there are many Camulus factions stationed here as well on the unprotected side of the planet.

Camulus galaxy: The galaxy where Camulos and Balor are from.

Devas galaxy: The last galaxy that wanted peace and attempted to separate from the war and darkness but was invaded by the Camulus Pack. Farthest galaxy from the rest of the other galaxies.

Canopiuis: Capital planet in the Devas galaxy. Capital city is Candor, where the keeper temple was located before the invasion. The hidden underground city of

Kali is also here. The main element is air because the whole planet is highly populated with large cities. Because it is the capital planet of the Devas system, the Camulus Force is strong here.

Sirios: Planet in the Devas galaxy. The main element is metal. It is thought to be a lost mountain city where survivors live. Hostile desert lands.

Terran: Planet originally in the Devas galaxy that was cast out after the ceremony break. Now located in a far distant galaxy and cannot be found. The main element is earth. This is where Magnus escapes to and where he creates his own bloodline and Evie is found.

SACRED RELICS

The Chain of Reality: Made up of star dust from the Devas pack galaxy system. The star dust chain would leave trails of light between each of the seven siblings. Could be used to travel among the siblings in the Devas pack, enhanced with water from Alderbard to highlight powers of the spells and star trails. The spells cast on the chain were to ensure that it could only be used for good as well as protection for anyone who held it.

The Fabric of Space and Time: The fabric can change shape so that it could be small enough to fit in the hands of the smallest being or become large enough to cover an entire planetary system. The fabric was made from the element in the Devas galaxy called light matter, and light matter could only be used for good and had the extra benefit of controlling time. The fabric was also infused with Desmodias, a plant on Antillis, so that it was almost indestructible. The spells cast on the fabric ensure that it was completely indestructible.

The Horn of Infinity: Made of a sacred crystal matter connected to the very first planet the mother and father created. The horn is clear but has a shimmering glow of light that illuminates it from within. It is thought to be the first seeds of the mother and father's love.

Watcher's Glass: Help watchers see through time and through others' visions. Also helps keep contact with others who hold a watcher's glass.

Keepers, Watchers, and Protectors

head keepers: Are found in each galaxy with one head keeper per planet in each system. They are born with their powers.

head watchers: Do not have full power of keeper but the head watchers had training and apprenticeship with a head keeper for ten years. The training focused on how to manipulate the elements and time. The head watchers also had the special assignment of keeping an eye out for any approach of the darkness and the war before the separation and after the separation. So, the head watchers had the special gift of sight beyond the Devas pack, as well as sight through time. They only have powers for half of their life span.

lower keepers: Also found in each galaxy and vary in number according to need. Some may have an original bloodline and may be born with innate power, but often they are trained by a head keeper to have powers.

lower watchers: Exactly like head watchers but only trained for five years and only have powers of a quarter of their life span.

protectors: Trained by Callais in the Devas system and found on the central planet of Antillis. The protectors were given the gift of travel among worlds. Their special gift was to manipulate space to move rapidly among the planets in the Devas system. The protectors were also given special tools to help aid them in protecting the Devas system. These tools were ships that could help them travel among worlds on the star dust trails in the Devas galaxy, as well as metallic staffs that were cast with spells of protection from the sacred texts.

The Keeper's Order: The order Magnus created on Terran to help restore and keep lost knowledge.

Plants

Desmodias: Plant found on the planet Antillis in Devas galaxy. Used to make sails. It has rare properties that allow it to withstand any environment. It also helps with spells.

SHIPS AND STAFFS

Black Ships: Used by Camulus Forces to navigate and control the Devas galaxy.

Devas ships: Used for protection by the protectors of the Devas galaxy. There were a hundred ships, each made of the finest metals from the Sirios planet, including Skyclad. The metals were cast with spells to make them lighter than air yet almost indestructible. The metals were specially crafted into the ships so they could be manipulated by the space around them. This gave the ships the ability to match any environment they were in, making them naturally camouflaged so they could be close to invisible. The sails on the ships were made from a plant found on Antillis, called Desmodias, finely crafted into fabric that could withstand even the harshest of climates so the sails would never break.

Devas staffs: Given to the protectors in the Devas galaxy, the metallic staffs made of the finest metals found on Sirios had similar properties to the ships. The staffs had protection spells that could be used to shield anyone around them within a fifty-mile radius. Each staff also had a feather of a special bird found on Alpharman, the spirit world, embedded into them. The feather comes from a bird sacred to Alpharman called Andeais. This feather helped the staff to levitate objects for temporary periods of time.

9 781735 593210